This Can't Be Love

by

Debra St. John

This Can't Be Love

Cover Art by *Angela Anderson*

The Wild Rose Press
PO Box 708
Adams Basin, NY 14410-0706
Visit us at www.thewildrosepress.com

Publishing History
First Champagne Rose Edition, 2010
Print ISBN 1-60154-856-7

Published in the United States of America

**Zach's gaze dropped to her lips.
"Do you kiss and tell?"**

Jessica's heart kicked into a fast rhythm and she caught her breath. "I..."

"Shhhh." He leaned closer. "I won't tell if you won't," he whispered before his mouth claimed hers.

His lips stroked over hers, not aggressively, but softly, tenderly. He didn't touch her anywhere else, but brushed her mouth with gentle intent.

Her first instinct was to pull back, but something stirred deep inside her. A feeling she'd nearly forgotten. Whispery shivers danced along her nerve endings and fluttered in her stomach. Without meaning to she opened to him.

The kiss deepened. Their breath mingled. Her palm slid up his chest, feeling the play of muscle beneath his shirt. She fisted the flannel of his open collar in her hand.

His knuckles grazed the sides of her face.

Her body tingled with awareness. Scattered thoughts flitted through her mind, but she couldn't hold onto any of them. Not while Zach kissed her. Not when his mouth fitted so perfectly against hers. Not when the pulse racing at the base of his throat matched the cadence of her heartbeat.

She couldn't remember the last time she'd felt like this. Had felt anything.

Should she be feeling this way about Zach?

Almost as if sensing her conflicting emotions, he softened the kiss, tenderly brushing his mouth over hers one last time.

She waged a silent war within, trying to calm her racing heart.

Dedication

As always, for my wonderful husband, John.
My life is full of romance because of you.
To my fabulous family and friends, your support
and encouragement mean the world to me.
And to Bob and Barb, thanks for letting me
'borrow' your cabin; it was the perfect place
for Zach and Jessica to fall in love.

Dear Reader,

For those of you who have read *This Time for Always*, my debut novel, you'll recognize this story's hero: Zach. Zach was the guy who was always there for Sharlie, and eventually Logan too, as Sharlie and Logan fell in love all over again. Zach's such a great guy, I knew he deserved his own story and his own true love, although Jessica, scarred by past relationships, is reluctant to admit her feelings for him at first. *This Can't Be Love* also gave me the opportunity to let readers peek a little bit into what happened with Sharlie and Logan beyond their happily ever after.

The setting for *This Can't Be Love* is based on a special place my husband and I visit each year with friends. In the story, Zach and Jessica enjoy some of our favorite things to do there: ATVing, cooling off down at the swimming hole, and for me, driving a John Deere tractor. I hope you enjoy the setting and their story!

Happy Reading!

All the best,

Debra
www.debrastjohnromance.com

Chapter One

There was a naked man in her grandfather's bathtub.

At least she assumed he was naked. She didn't plan on getting any closer to verify the fact.

Jessica Hart stood in the doorway and worried her bottom lip with her teeth. The man had one well-defined arm slung lazily over the side of the claw-foot tub, fingers trailing on the floor. His head tilted back against the edge, eyes closed. Dark, damp hair curled over his forehead. A day's worth of stubble shadowed his strong jaw. Her gaze drifted lower to his chest, visible above the water in the tub.

It definitely wasn't Pops.

So who the hell was he?

She shifted her weight from one foot to the other. The last thing she'd expected when she walked into the bathroom was to find a strange man in the tub. She'd come to the creek looking for some peace and quiet. After the events of the past year she needed it. Desperately. The cabin at the creek had seemed like the perfect retreat. Spending time with Pops would help her gain some perspective and feel human again.

So where was her grandfather? The door to the cabin had been open, which wasn't unusual, but Pops was nowhere around. She'd checked his favorite places before heading upstairs. A nice long soak in his antique tub would be the perfect way to while away the time until he returned.

Unfortunately the tub was already occupied.

Well, that wouldn't do.

She cleared her throat.

The man opened his eyes and turned toward her. His irises were a rich brown, reminding her of hot, strong coffee with just a touch of cream. His gaze swept over her before returning to her own. He raised an eyebrow. "Yes?" He seemed completely unfazed to see her standing there.

Jessica placed her hands on her hips. "Who the hell are you?"

"Zach Rawlings." He inclined his head. "And you are?"

"Jessica."

"Ah, Ben's granddaughter."

"You know me?"

"He talks about you all the time."

"Oh." She paused. "What are you doing here?"

His mouth quirked up at the corners. "Taking a bath."

"That's not what I mean," she snapped. "What are you doing in my grandfather's house?"

"I'm house-sitting while he's gone."

"He's gone?" A note of dismay crept into her voice. Pops couldn't be gone. She needed him. "When will he be back?"

"About a month or so."

"A month? Where is he?"

"In Ireland."

"Ireland?" she echoed in disbelief. "What's he doing there?"

Zach straightened in the tub. Water sloshed over the side and splashed onto the wooden planked floor. "He said he wanted to see the places where his ancestors lived." He studied her. "You didn't know?"

Jessica looked away from his probing gaze. "No."

Zach shifted again, drawing her attention to the wide span of his shoulders. His naked shoulders.

She tore her gaze from him and focused on the plants set on the window ledge. "Look, can we have this conversation someplace else?" She risked another glance at him.

"Sure." He braced his arms on the side of the tub and levered himself up.

"What are you doing?" Panic laced her voice.

"If you want to talk someplace else I need to get out of the tub." His tone was conversational, but his eyes sparkled with mirth.

"Uh," she huffed. She turned on her heel. "I'll be downstairs."

His laughter followed her down the hall.

She retrieved her bags from the car. On the way back in, she stopped and surveyed the façade of the cabin.

Cabin wasn't really the right word for the three-story wooden house Pops had built, but everyone had always called it that. The spacious house nestled in a wooded corner of the four-hundred-acre property. The thick forest of trees provided complete privacy. A large deck off the back overlooked a steep drop.

Jessica shook her head and smiled. Still no railing. Pops had been promising for years to get the protective barrier put up around the deck.

She set her bags down and strolled around to the other side of the house. Planters and hanging pots overflowed with impatiens, which looked healthy and well-cared for. How long had Pops been gone? She couldn't quite imagine the rugged man upstairs in the tub caring for flowers.

Outside the back door, she stopped. A recycling bin sat next to the door, and it too overflowed. But not with flowers.

Beer cans and wine bottles filled the blue, plastic tub.

Aside from an occasional glass of wine at a holiday meal, Pops didn't drink. All of this must belong to Zach Rawlings. Was it a month's worth? A week's worth? A night's worth?

Jessica's heart hammered against her ribs, and she had to remind herself to breathe. She drew in a deep gulp of air, then released it, one heartbeat at a time.

It didn't matter. The man wouldn't be staying, so whatever nasty habits he had were of no concern. She was here now. His services as a house-sitter were no longer needed. She'd watch over things until Pops returned.

She pushed open the door and walked into the kitchen. The aromatic smell of garlic lingered in the air. A half-empty glass of wine sat on the counter. She grimaced.

Zach strolled down the stairs as she walked into the family room. He smiled at her. "Hi, again."

He was taller than she'd imagined, standing a good six inches above her own five-foot-seven frame. He'd put on jeans and a black T-shirt, which hid but couldn't dispel the image of his bare chest.

She shook her head to clear it. "Hello," she replied coolly.

"We didn't formally meet upstairs." He held out his hand. "Zach Rawlings."

Jessica hesitated before she slid her hand into his. His grasp was warm and firm. "Jessica Hart."

"Pleased to meet you, ma'am."

His husky drawl washed over her, as warm as his handshake. She yanked her hand away and shoved both into the back pockets of her jeans.

"So, what brings you here? Ben said you don't visit often."

Jessica wasn't going to discuss her life with this man. She ignored his question and asked one of her own. "How do you know my grandfather?"

"I met him up at The Corral."

"The Corral?"

"The bar where I work."

"You work at a bar?" Her stomach lurched.

4

"Yeah." Zach looked at her with an odd expression. "I'm one of the bouncers."

"Oh." She withdrew her gaze from his.

"Can I get you something? Are you hungry? I just finished dinner, but I can put something together."

Zach playing the host in Pops' absence grated on her nerves, but she smiled politely. "No, thanks. I'm fine."

"How about something to drink? A glass of wine or—"

"No."

His eyebrows rose at her vehement tone.

"I don't drink." Why was she explaining herself to this stranger?

"Ever?"

She shook her head, not about to go into detail. "How did you come to be the house-sitter?" she asked to change the subject.

"Your grandfather's been thinking about taking this trip for a long time."

She nodded. "He always talked about tracing his roots some day." She was glad he had finally found the opportunity to do it. If only the timing had been better. If only she'd known before she'd come.

"Anyway, the thought of leaving this place unattended for such a long time didn't sit well with him. So when he finally decided to go ahead and make the trip, I volunteered to watch over things while he was gone."

"Don't you have your own place?" It seemed odd a grown man would put his own life on hold to watch someone else's property for a long period of time. Did Zach have a wife? A family?

Zach grinned and spread his arms out. "This is way better than my apartment."

"Yeah, I love it here." She looked around the family room. How long had it been since she'd come

5

for a visit? It unsettled her, made her uneasy, to come back now and feel so out of place, while a stranger had been entrusted to care for things. She folded her arms across her chest and turned back to Zach.

"How long have you known my grandfather?"

"A few years now, I'd say." He paused and looked at her. "I'm sure you were surprised to get here and find me instead of Ben, but we talked about this for a long time, and he showed me how to take care of everything around here before he left." He held up his hands and smiled. "I swear, I don't have your grandfather locked up in a back room somewhere."

Without really meaning to, Jessica smiled back. Zach told the truth. She could tell. And if her grandfather trusted him to take care of his precious mountain retreat, he couldn't be all bad. But that didn't mean she'd let him stay. She'd come for peace and quiet and solitude. She could handle things around there until Pops returned.

"Did he go alone?"

Zach threw another odd glance her way. "No, your parents are with him." He paused. "Don't you talk to them much?"

She looked away. "I've been a little out of touch."

"That's too bad."

She put her hands on her hips. "Hey, don't judge me. You don't even know me."

"Whoa, easy there," Zach said in a soothing voice. "I'm not judging you. Okay?" he asked when she didn't respond.

"Okay."

He glanced at his watch and then out the window by the door. "I need to check the bluebird boxes out in the field before it gets dark, so I'm going to head out there. I'll be back in a bit, if you need anything."

If she needed anything? Who did this guy think he was? She knew the cabin like the back of her hand. She bit back a retort and retrieved her bags from the porch where she'd left them. No sense getting into an argument. Zach wouldn't be sticking around long enough to finish it.

The rumble of an ATV starting up in the barn reached her. The noise faded as Zach headed down the path toward the creek.

Inside, she tossed her bags on the bed in the loft on the third floor. Ever since she'd been a kid the loft had been her special hideaway. After a nostalgic look around, she headed back down to the first floor for a shower.

****

Zach gunned the all-terrain vehicle and splashed across the creek. He gripped the handlebars as the vehicle bounced jerkily across the rocks. Once up the slight incline, he turned right into the field. He circled the perimeter, stopping at each little wooden box placed every hundred feet or so to check the contents. Most had eggs nestled in the straw covering the bottoms. He smiled in satisfaction.

He sped to the corner of the field where he made a sharp right to head down the narrow, gravel path through the woods. He passed the cemetery on his right, then rode into the adjoining field. He opened the ATV up as he raced across the wide-open expanse. The wind tore through his hair, and he lifted his face to the rushing breeze.

He motored to the top of the glade, then sat, letting the engine idle, thinking about Jessica Hart.

Jessica who didn't drink. Ever.

Jessica who didn't know her grandfather was in Ireland with the rest of her family.

Jessica who had found him in the bathtub.

He grinned. How long had she stood and

watched him? She sure had been annoyed to find him there.

As soon as he'd opened his eyes, he'd known who she was, even before he'd asked. He'd recognized the wild, tumbling red-gold hair from the various pictures spread throughout the cabin. Although the pictures didn't do her justice. In person she was far more striking.

What was she doing here?

He'd had the impression she didn't come around a lot. From what he'd heard, she had some fancy life out on the West Coast.

She probably wouldn't stay long.

Which was too bad. He would have liked a chance to get to know her better. She intrigued him. He couldn't really say why. Shadows of something lurked in her beautiful green eyes. What had put them there?

He shrugged the thought away. She wouldn't be there long enough for him to find out.

At any rate, they could peacefully co-exist for a couple of days until she took off again. The cabin had plenty of room.

Speaking of, he'd better check to see if his house guest needed anything. He revved the throttle, executed a tight circle, and headed back the way he'd come.

Back at the barn, he drove the ATV in, coasting to a stop next to the green tractor parked to one side. Which reminded him, he needed to mow the side field tomorrow.

Whistling his favorite Conway Twitty tune, he locked up for the night, then headed into the cabin.

"Jessica?"

The sound of running water told him she was in the shower.

He grabbed a beer from the fridge and headed out onto the deck. Sitting in one chair, he propped his feet on another and took a long sip.

What a gorgeous night. The sun dipped below the horizon, bathing everything in a warm, orange glow. Soon the heavens would be arrayed in a spectacular display of stars. He loved it out here. What a fabulous stroke of luck to have met Ben O'Connor at The Corral.

The cabin was a far cry from his apartment in town. Another stroke of luck had turned up a friend of a friend looking for a temporary place to stay, and he'd been able to sublet his apartment while he house-sat.

Nope, life didn't get much better than this. In fact, times like this reminded him why he lived the life he did. Working nights at The Corral had enabled him to take advantage of the opportunity when Ben had approached him about taking care of his place. No one would ever catch him in a nine-to-five job. Mostly because nine-to-five jobs never were just that. They were more like eight-to-six, or seven. Sometimes longer.

He ought to know. His parents were career eight-to-seveners. They worked all the time. And what did they have to show for it? Sure Zach and his siblings had never wanted for anything while they were growing up. They'd had a nice house, food on the table, clothes to wear.

But people who worked a lot less than his parents had those things, too. And his parents never had time for fun. Or for their family. Zach and his brother and sister were the products of daycare, babysitters, and the proverbial latchkey.

All things considered, he and his siblings had turned out okay. And his parents enjoyed what they did. But they were always busy. Zach had no desire to follow in their footsteps. He couldn't remember the last time he'd seen his dad sit out on the back porch, prop his feet up, and relax with a beer.

"Zach?" Jessica called from inside the house, interrupting his musings.

"Out here."

"Oh, there you are." She walked onto the deck and frowned at the beer bottle in his hand.

"All settled? Did you find everything okay?"

"Of course. Why wouldn't I?"

Zach shrugged. "I don't know. Maybe some things are different since you were here last."

"Right." Her tone was crisp.

"Pull up a chair. It's a gorgeous night."

She tossed him a strange look, but complied.

As she bent to reposition the chair, her shirt rode up, and he glimpsed a tattoo adorning her lower back. In the dim twilight, he couldn't quite make out what it was.

Interesting. Jessica Hart became more intriguing by the minute.

She sat down and studied him.

"How long has Pops been gone?" she asked finally.

"Pops?"

"Yep, I've called him that since I was a little girl."

"Cute. Anyway," Zach said, getting around her answering her question. "He left the day before yesterday."

"Oh." A wistful, almost sad note crept into her voice. "I guess I just missed him."

"He didn't know you were coming?"

She looked away, not meeting his gaze. "No."

"Well, I'm sure he'll be sorry he missed you, too. I'll tell him you stopped by."

"Stopped by?"

"Sure." He took a sip of beer. "Isn't that what you usually do, stop by for a little while, then head off again?"

"How do you know what I do?" An edge of anger

10

tinged the words.

"I'm sorry," he apologized. "Truce?" he asked when she continued to glare at him.

She nodded, but it seemed forced.

He searched for a safer topic. "So how long are you going to stay?"

"How long am I—" She stopped. "Look, let's get one thing straight. This is my grandfather's place, and it was nice of you to offer to watch it while he's gone, but I'm here now, and I'm planning on staying for a while. We don't need your help anymore, but since it's late, you can stay the night. In the morning you can be on your way. I'm sure Pops will settle up with you, whatever he owes you, when he returns."

Zach stared in bemusement at the woman sitting next to him. Slowly he shook his head. He sipped his beer again.

"Honey, I'm not going anywhere."

Chapter Two

Jessica's mouth dropped open. "What? But...but you can't stay here."

Zach looked at her, an expression of utter calm on his face as he took another sip of beer. "Of course I can."

She rose, hands on hips, and glared down at him. "No, you cannot."

"Why not? There's plenty of room."

"That's not the point," she snapped. "*I'm* here now." She pointed a finger at her chest.

"You can have your grandfather's bedroom. I'll move my stuff into the loft. We won't get in each other's way."

She wanted to stomp her foot, but refrained. Barely. The man was enough to try the patience of a saint. "I always stay in the loft."

"Fine, then I'll stay in the big room."

"No. Arghhh." She threaded her fingers through the hair at her temples and clutched her head. "You're deliberately misunderstanding what I'm saying."

"Am I?"

She glowered. How could he know how to push all of her buttons? They'd met less than an hour ago.

"What I mean," she said slowly and deliberately, "is I'm here now to take care of things until Pops returns."

He raised an eyebrow. "Really?"

She put her hands on her hips. "Really. Are you implying that I can't take care of this place?"

"No, ma'am." He paused. "But can I ask you a

question?"

She eyed him warily. "Sure."

"Are you going to brush hog the side field tomorrow?"

She refused to admit she had no idea what he meant. She raised her chin a notch. "Yes."

Zach laughed. "Sorry, honey, I don't believe you. And besides, I don't have anywhere else to go."

"Stop calling me 'honey.' And what do you mean you don't have anyplace to go?" She bit back a sigh. "What about your apartment?"

"I sublet it to someone else for the time I'll be here."

"Why would you do that?" Exasperation laced her voice.

"I didn't need two places...so it made sense," he said with infuriating calm.

"I'm sure you can stay with a friend."

"Look, Jessica." He emphasized her name with a slight smile. "I'm staying here." He held up a hand to stop her protest. "There are things around here you can't do."

"Like what?"

"Like brush hogging the side field for one." He grinned.

She forced a smile in return. "It was," she struggled to find a kind word, "nice of you to offer to help Pops out, but really, I don't want to keep you from something else you need to be doing."

He sipped his beer again. "There isn't anything else I need to be doing."

"What about your job?"

"My job?"

She waved a hand. "Yeah, a job. Like what do you do to make money?"

"I told you. I work at The Corral."

Jessica gaped. "That's all you do? You don't have a real job?"

"It is a real job." Zach's voice took on an edge.

"Great. Another one," she muttered under her breath. Were all men irresponsible slackers, or just the ones who showed up in her life?

"What?"

She shook her head. "Nothing. Look, we need to figure this out. We both can't stay here."

"At the risk of repeating myself, why not?"

"Because you don't belong here," she blurted.

"With all due respect, ma'am, yes, I do." Zach rose to stand in front of her.

Jessica took a step backward.

"Your grandfather hired me to do a job." He emphasized the word 'job.' "And I intend to do it. Speaking of which..." Zach yawned and stretched his arms over his head. The bottom of his T-shirt rode up, revealing a thin trail of dark hair that disappeared into the waistband of his jeans.

She looked away from the intimate sight.

"I have a lot I need to do tomorrow, so I'm going to hit the hay. We can figure out how this is going to work in the morning. Good night, Jessica."

He strolled around the side of the house. His beer bottle clinked as it landed in the recycling bin, then the back door closed with a soft slam.

She sank into the chair he'd vacated and put her head in her hands. What an impossible man. She needed to get rid of him before she shot him.

****

Jessica awoke the next morning to a bird chirping outside her window. A glance at the clock on the nightstand revealed it was early. Too early to be up on a day she didn't need to go anywhere or do anything.

She burrowed her head back into the pillow, but to no avail. The birds continued to chatter, and far below, in the distance, the soft rushing of the creek filtered through the screen.

14

She turned on her back and stared up at the ceiling. The familiar pattern of cracks in the plaster and the aged wooden beams soaring overhead made her smile. A sense of comfort and well-being settled over her.

The smell of frying bacon and the soft clatter of pots from the kitchen turned the smile into a frown.

Zach.

Once she got rid of him, things would be darn near perfect. More perfect than they'd been in a long, long time.

Her stomach rumbled, prompting her to swing her legs over the side of the bed. She rummaged in her bag for shorts and a top—she'd unpack and get settled in later—then she brushed her teeth in the bathroom. She didn't bother with makeup. Who was she trying to impress?

At the top of the stairs, she hesitated. Her teeth gnawed her bottom lip.

She needed to figure out what to do about Zach. The idea of him living there with her until Pops returned was absurd. Zach would need to find someplace else to go if his apartment was unavailable. Would he be offended if she suggested a motel? Probably, but there had to be some alternative.

He turned from the stove and smiled at her over his shoulder when she walked into the kitchen. "Good morning."

"Morning," she mumbled.

"You hungry?"

As if on cue, her stomach growled again.

"The bacon's done and the eggs are almost ready," Zach said, turning back to the pan in front of him.

"No, thanks. I usually don't eat a big breakfast."

"Are you sure? I made extra."

She grabbed her can of protein powder and a

glass from the cabinet next to the fridge. "I'll just have my protein drink." She measured out a scoop of the powder, filled the glass with milk, and stirred the thick contents with a spoon. She took a large gulp.

"Suit yourself." His cheerful voice grated on her nerves.

She sat down at the table while he finished preparing his breakfast. His movements were smooth and easy as he slid the eggs from the pan onto a plate, then added three strips of bacon.

She ignored how good everything looked and smelled and resolutely drank her lumpy drink.

He sat down across from her. As he sipped his orange juice, he studied her over the rim of the glass.

She squirmed.

"You're up early," he commented after swallowing a bite of egg.

"Birds," Jessica explained.

"Ah, yes. Life in the country. Isn't it great?" Zach took a bite of bacon. It crunched between his teeth. He swallowed.

Her stomach rumbled.

He grinned and jerked his head toward the stove. "Really, there's plenty left. Help yourself."

"No, thanks," she said through gritted teeth. "This is fine." Why was she being so stubborn? The oniony smell of the eggs made her mouth water. It wouldn't kill her to eat the breakfast Zach had prepared.

"Must be quite a change from big-city life."

"What?"

"Coming back here after living away for so long." Zach waved his fork in the air. "Must be strange."

"It's a little different."

"So, where's home?"

"Home?" The word sounded odd. It certainly didn't describe the small, cramped apartment she'd lived in with Philip. Or the tiny loft she'd shared with a friend after calling it quits with Philip.

Zach swallowed another mouthful. "Where do you live?"

Nowhere anymore. She didn't voice the words out loud. "I'd been living in Seattle."

Giving in to the hunger still gnawing at her, and hoping to avoid anymore questions, she got a plate from the cabinet and filled it with the fluffy, scrambled eggs.

"That's my girl."

She glared at him as she set the plate on the table with a thunk. "I'm not your girl."

"Sorry, just an expression." He paused. "You planning on going back to Seattle?"

She bit back a sigh. The man never gave up. "No, I don't think so."

He looked at her as if trying to guess what she wasn't saying.

She lowered her eyes to the eggs on her plate. "So, are you from around here?" she asked, more to prevent him from asking more questions than from a real desire to know.

"Yep. My mom and dad still live in town. What about you?"

She swallowed the forkful of egg she'd put in her mouth. After savoring the taste of fresh herbs, she replied, "My parents live a couple hours north of here."

"Do you—" The ring of a phone cut him off. "Excuse me," Zach said. He flexed his hips upward and plucked a cell phone from his back pocket. He flipped it open and held it against his ear. "Hello?"

Not wanting to eavesdrop, Jessica busied herself clearing silverware and glasses from the table. Zach walked into the adjoining family room, so she loaded their breakfast remains into the dishwasher. She added the pan from the stove.

He strode back into the room. "That can't go in there."

She looked up. "What?"

"That pan can't go in the dishwasher. It needs to be washed by hand."

She stared at the item in question. "Oh."

Zach's fingers brushed hers as he took it. She yanked her hand away.

"It has a special kind of non-stick material," he explained. "It'll get ruined."

"Oh," she said again. Zach puzzled her. A man who knew about pots and pans, watered flowers, and took baths in antique tubs.

Maybe he was gay.

That would be a shame. Not that he interested her or anything. Far from it. But of its own accord, her gaze slid over him. A play of muscle strained his T-shirt as he turned.

No, flowers and bathtubs aside, he was far too rugged and masculine to be gay. But he *was* different from any man she'd ever known.

Her glance fell on the empty wine bottle on the counter. Well, in some regards he was the same as the men she'd known. One man in particular.

She shook the thought off. She'd come here to forget, not dwell on the past.

"I'll finish up here." Zach ran water in the sink. He glanced over his shoulder. "What are your plans for the day?"

"My plans for the day?"

"Yeah, what are you going to do?"

"I want you to tell me what needs to be done around here."

Zach rinsed the pan, then shut the water off. He turned, then leaned his hips against the counter and crossed one bare foot over the other. "Oh, yeah. Why's that?"

"So, when you leave," she said pointedly, "I'll

know what needs to be done."

"I thought we settled this last night. I'm not going anywhere."

"And I thought I made myself perfectly clear." She straightened to her full height. "We don't need your services anymore. So, like I said, if you tell me what needs to be done, I'll take care of it."

His gaze roved from the top of her head to the tips of her toes. "Really?" His mouth twitched as if trying to hide a smile.

"Really."

"Fine. Today the side field needs to be brush hogged, the thistles need to be cut down in the upper field, the ATV tanks need to be filled, and the garden needs to be weeded." He folded his arms across his chest, a smug look on his face.

She bit her lip.

She was pretty confident about filling the gas tanks on the ATVs. And she could probably handle weeding the garden. But that's all she was sure about. She didn't know a thistle from an eggplant, and as for brush hogging, she had no idea. Since Pops didn't own any animals, she was pretty sure it didn't have anything to do with actual hogs, but beyond that, she didn't have a clue as to what Zach meant.

Damn.

She'd have to Google it.

She glanced at Zach. He still wore that infuriating expression. Worst of all, he was right. She had no idea how to do the things he'd said.

Double damn.

She put her hands on her hips and jutted out her chin. "That doesn't sound too bad." She'd figure it out. She had to. Zach couldn't stay.

And she'd cut off her right arm before she asked for his help before he left.

He had the audacity to laugh. "Okay, then, have

it your way. Since you won't be needing me, I'll be down at the creek."

He strode from the room, whistling.

She shot a dirty look at his retreating back, then headed upstairs to the loft. She retrieved her laptop from her bag, then chewed her lip while she waited for it to power up.

Did Pops even have access to the Internet here? She hoped so, she had a lot of work to catch up on. Working from home, or wherever she happened to be at the moment, certainly had its advantages, but she wouldn't get very far with no on-line access.

Once the screen glowed to life, she clicked on the icon and sighed in relief when it connected to the Internet immediately.

She typed in "brush hogging," then hit the enter key.

A picture of a farm implement popped up. She read the caption beneath. "A brush hog is a heavily built rotary mower. Typically these mowers attach to the back of a farm tractor using the three-point hitch and are driven via the Power Take Off."

Mowing. That's all it was.

She harrumphed and shot a glare toward the stairs. Zach had probably used the fancy name on purpose just to confuse her.

Well, knowing what it was solved part of the problem. Next step would be to figure out how to actually get it done. Best place to start would be the barn. She could gas up the ATVs and check out Pops' tractor and the mowing machine.

She shut down the computer, promising herself she'd spend a good hour or two catching up on work later.

Out in the barn, she eyed the massive, green tractor parked on one side. Ignoring it for the moment, she turned her attention to the ATVs. An open space near the wide front door indicated Zach had taken one of them down to the creek. A row of red gas cans lined the far wall.

She grabbed one. The liquid inside sloshed around and the plastic container banged against her knee.

"Ouch," she grunted. The can was heavier than she'd expected.

She wrangled it over to one of the ATVs, then set it down. Hands on her hips, she surveyed the vehicle. There had to be a visible gas cap somewhere.

She bit her lip.

This was supposed to be the easiest of all her tasks. Her gaze settled on the tractor again. If she couldn't figure out how to put gas in an ATV, she didn't hold much hope of climbing aboard that and mowing anything.

With a sigh, she headed back into the cabin to use her computer. She found a diagram of an ATV, located the gas cap—Now why hadn't she seen it there?—and powered down the laptop before remembering she'd also wanted to look up how to start the tractor.

She grabbed the computer. Might as well take it with her. She had the feeling she'd be needing it a lot more before the day was done.

Back in the barn, she unscrewed the gas cap on one of the ATVs, then hefted the can, compensating for its weight this time. A splatter of gasoline peppered the vehicle before she got the nozzle into the hole, but soon a steady stream flowed from the container into the tank.

How much needed to go in? Would it take the whole can?

Almost as if in answer to her unspoken thoughts, the strong smelling liquid overflowed from the opening.

"Ooops." She yanked the can upright. She

twisted the cap back on the hole, then searched for some rags to clean up the spill.

When she finished, she spread them out carefully outside the barn. With a grimace she turned back to the remaining vehicles. One down. Three to go.

She sighed and grabbed another gas can.

The other ATVs were parked close together toward the back of the barn. She clambered over one, lugging the can behind her, then kneeled on the seat. With no little amount of effort, she managed to fill all of the vehicles.

An ATV revved in the distance. The rumble grew louder as the vehicle approached. Zach drove into sight as she scrambled to the ground. He stopped and flashed a smile. "Hi. How's it going?"

She wiped the back of her hand over her forehead. Her gaze slid over him. His T-shirt stuck to his back in damp patches, and his shorts were wet.

She corralled the uncharitable thoughts that sprang to mind. She'd insisted on doing the chores. Of course he could have spent his time packing instead of frolicking in the creek.

She put her hands on her hips. "It's going fine."

"Super." He swung off of the ATV. "You hungry?"

As if on cue, her stomach growled. She prayed he hadn't heard. "No, I'm good. I want to get started on that weeding."

"Jess, you need to eat."

She ignored the way her shortened name sounded in his soft drawl, and the flutter it caused in her stomach, and shook her head.

"C'mon," he coaxed. "It's leftover fried chicken. And homemade potato salad."

Her mouth watered. She gave in. After all, she did need to eat. "Okay."

"That's my—" he cut himself off.

As they headed toward the house, he nodded at the ATVs in the barn. "It's easier to gas them up if you pull them out first."

She glared.

Inside she washed up while he put lunch together. After grabbing a glass of lemonade, she dropped into a chair at the table. She hid a yawn and propped her head on her hand.

The bowl of potato salad he placed on the table looked delectable, as did the plate of cold fried chicken that followed.

She dug in. The creamy potato concoction slid down her throat, the combination of mayonnaise, egg, and another ingredient she couldn't identify lingered in her mouth. Next she turned her attention to the chicken. Even straight from the fridge, the skin was crisp, the meat inside tender and juicy. The food reviving her tired body, she took another mouthful of potato salad. Zach had said it was homemade. Who cooked for him? A girlfriend?

For a moment, putting the words *girlfriend* and *Zach* together in the same sentence made her feel odd. Almost disappointed. Which was ridiculous.

She peeked up at him from under her lashes. Of course he would have a girlfriend. And why should it matter if he did?

He caught her staring.

A blush crept into her cheeks. She looked down at her plate. "Uh, so who made all of this?" Unable to reign in her curiosity, the question slipped out. She bit her lip. Would he discern its hidden meaning?

"I did."

"You did?" She couldn't quite hide her surprise.

"Yep." He paused. "Is there something wrong?"

"No, no, it's delicious." She took another bite of chicken while she contemplated the new information. Did he cook often or was this a one-time thing? He'd made breakfast, too, although that didn't prove anything. Almost everyone could make scrambled eggs.

They ate in silence after that.

"So, how did it go this morning?" Zach shoved his empty plate away and leaned back in his chair.

"Fine." In an instant, she was defensive. "Why?"

"Just making conversation. Any trouble with the tractor while you were brush hogging?" The words were too innocent.

She gritted her teeth. "I haven't gotten to *mowing*"—she emphasized the word—"the field yet, but I'm sure it won't be a problem."

He ducked his head, but not fast enough to hide his smile. "Sure." He swallowed. "Look, if you need he—"

She cut him off. "I'm good." She didn't want his help with anything. "I think I'll do the field tomorrow. This afternoon I'm going to weed the garden while you pack," she added.

He crossed his arms over his chest and studied her.

She squirmed.

"Look, Jessica, do you really think this is the best way to go about this? There's a lot to do around here. Are you sure you want to tackle all of it? At least let me help you. Ben hired me to take care of this place while he was gone."

"That was before he knew I'd be here."

Zach shook his head. "I don't think he'd expect you to do everything even if he had known."

"I can manage." She raised her chin.

He sighed. "Okay, have it your way." His chair scraped across the floor as he stood. He strode from the room, but returned shortly with several sheets of paper.

He tossed them down in front of her. "Here."

She picked up the pages. "What's this?"

"The list of things that need to be done while Ben's gone." He folded his arms across his chest and looked down at her.

She scanned the papers. They were filled front and back with her grandfather's familiar handwriting. Strange words and phrases jumped out at her. She didn't understand half of what they meant. She swallowed, then bit her lip.

How would she ever get all of this done and keep up with her job?

She met Zach's gaze. It held a touch of tolerant amusement.

She sat up straighter. She'd find a way. She had to.

Zach couldn't stay.

She waved the papers. "This doesn't look so bad."

He threw back his head and laughed. "Jess, you are one stubborn lady, I'll give you that. All right, I have to work tonight, but tomorrow I'll start figuring out what to do about my apartment. I'll be out of here in a couple of days."

"You could start figuring it out this afternoon."

He chuckled as he grabbed their lunch dishes from the table. "I could." He walked over to the sink and turned on the water. "But I'm not going to," he said over his shoulder.

She fought the childish urge to stick out her tongue at him. And he thought *she* was stubborn.

Chapter Three

After lunch Jessica headed back to the barn. Once again she eyed the tractor warily. A flat piece of equipment in the same bright shade of green sat behind it. The thing balanced precariously on one wheel. Was it the brush hogger? Was the damn thing even attached to the tractor?

Well, she'd tackle that project in the morning, with a little more help from the trusty Internet.

Turning from the tractor, she surveyed the walls of the barn, where various garden tools hung. She grabbed a hoe and a rake, then rummaged through a drawer until she found a pair of cloth gloves.

She chewed her lip and contemplated the row of ATVs. Taking one down to the garden would make the trip faster, but she hesitated, unsure. For one, how would she hold onto her tools and steer the thing? And two, to be honest, she wasn't quite sure she even remembered how to drive one.

One more thing to add to her Internet list.

Halfway down the path, an ATV rumbled up behind her. Zach drew up alongside. "Want a ride?"

She kept walking. "No thank you."

"Suit yourself." He revved the engine and disappeared down the trail.

The hot sun beat down on her head as she trudged along. She shifted her tools to one hand and wiped the other across her forehead. A hat would have been a good idea. Too late now. She wasn't about to go all the way back to the barn.

When she walked into the field, her mouth dropped open. Endless rows of vegetables stretched before her. Garden hardly seemed the proper word to describe it. It looked more like an entire farm field. A farm field big enough to feed a small country in Africa.

She took a tentative step forward. Tall stalks of corn were easily recognizable, as were the tomato plants. But as for the rest, could she tell a weed from a cucumber vine? Did Pops even grow cucumbers?

She sighed, tugged on her gloves, and dropped to her knees in the dirt close to the tomato plants. Might as well start with something familiar.

An hour later she stretched. Her back ached and her shirt stuck to her skin. She swallowed to ease the dryness in her throat. She'd forgotten a water bottle.

With a determined effort, she ignored her discomfort and turned back to her task.

Another hour passed before the telltale rumble of an ATV distracted her. She gritted her teeth and kept her attention on her work as Zach eased the vehicle to a stop about a yard from her.

"How's it going?"

"Fine." Her voice was a dry croak.

He frowned and swung off his ATV. "Are you okay?"

She swallowed. "Sure."

He looked at the ground around her. "Where's your water?"

She refused to meet his gaze. "I'm fine."

"All right, enough of this." Before she guessed his intent, he leaned down, grasped her arms, and hauled her to her feet.

"What do you think you're doing?" she demanded. She yanked away from him. Swayed. Her head spun from the combination of the hot sun and her sudden change of position.

He steadied her. "Jess?" Concern roughened his voice.

She took a deep breath, then shrugged away from him again. "I'm okay. It's really hot out here today."

"Yes, it is," he agreed. He grabbed a water bottle from the ATV and then held it out. "Here, drink this."

She looked at it.

"I don't have cooties," he said with a smile. His expression changed, grew serious. "You need water. You're overheated." He laid the back of his hand across her forehead.

She jerked away from his touch and took the water bottle. She raised it to her lips. The cool liquid slid down her parched throat. She guzzled it greedily.

"Whoa," he cautioned. "Take it easy. You'll make yourself sick."

She glared at him, but took his advice, sipping more slowly.

"Better?" he asked after she'd drained the contents.

She nodded. "Thank you."

"You're welcome."

"Well, I guess I should get back to work."

Zach shook his head. "I don't think so. You're done for the day."

Jessica put her hands on her hips and glowered at him. Okay, so she'd been stupid not to remember water, and he'd shared his, but who did he think he was? No one told her what to do.

She opened her mouth, but he spoke before she could.

"Really. It's too hot out here to keep working today. You've done enough. The rest can wait until tomorrow."

She wanted to argue. To say she hadn't done nearly enough. But the lure of resting her aching muscles inside the air-conditioned comfort of the cabin was too tempting to ignore.

And he was right about the heat. Especially since she wasn't prepared.

Unexpected tears pricked her eyes. Suddenly, taking care of the property until Pops returned home seemed like an insurmountable task. How would she manage?

Her gaze slid over Zach. His hair was as damp as hers and like hers, his shirt stuck to his skin in wet patches. But he'd been playing in the creek all day. She'd been working. And not accomplishing much. She hadn't finished even half the tasks that needed to be done. The weeding would take at least a couple more hours, and she still didn't know what to do with the tractor and the mower. Let alone the fact she hadn't even thought about the thistles.

She'd bet good money Zach would have been able to accomplish everything and still had time for a swim.

"Jessica?" He looked and sounded worried.

She snapped out of her thoughts. "What?"

"C'mon, let's get back to the cabin. I'll give you a ride."

She shook her head. "I need to carry the tools back up."

"I'll take care of them." He picked them up, then slid the handles into a cut off section of PVC pipe attached to the back of his ATV.

"Oh." How foolish. Of course there would be an easier way of getting them to the garden besides carrying them.

He swung his leg over the ATV and settled himself on the seat. "Get on." He looked at her over his shoulder.

She eyed the small space behind him, then shook her head. "I'll walk. I feel much better with that water in me."

"Get on or I'll put you on there myself." His voice

brooked no argument.

She hesitated.

He shifted as if to get off of the vehicle.

She hurried over. She didn't doubt his words. No way would she let him pick her up.

She swung her leg over, scooting as far back on the seat as possible to avoid touching him.

"Hold on," he said as he revved the engine.

She grabbed the bars behind her. The vehicle lurched. Instinctively her arms wrapped around his waist to get a more secure hold.

His stomach was firm beneath her hands. The muscles bunched and flexed as he steered the ATV up the path. She ducked her head to avoid the dust churned up beneath the wheels. A damp spot on his T-shirt cooled her heated cheek.

As soon as they reached the barn, she scrambled off the vehicle.

"You go ahead and shower first," he said. "I'll close up everything out here for the night."

She nodded and hurried her steps to the cabin. A shower sounded like the promise of heaven on Earth.

She stood under the cool spray, letting the water cascade down her overheated body. She lingered longer than usual, enjoying the sweet relief and letting the pulsing stream work on her sore muscles.

With a reluctant sigh, she turned the water off and stepped out of the shower. A knock on the door made her jump. She grabbed the towel and held it in front of her.

"Jessica?"

"Wh...what?" Had she locked the door?

"Are you okay in there?"

"Yeah, sure. I'm just finishing up. I'll be done in a minute."

"Okay."

She waited until his footsteps retreated before

dropping the towel and quickly donning her jeans and T-shirt. Opening the door, she peered out into the kitchen, then scurried upstairs to the loft.

After rubbing her hair dry with a towel, she sat down on the bed. What should she do now? She wasn't exactly hiding from Zach, but on the other hand she wasn't exactly eager to face him just yet.

Their short ride on the ATV together from the field to the barn played in her head. She remembered the feel of his taut stomach muscles beneath her palms. The way her legs had straddled his hips. How her chest had pressed against his back.

She shook her head to clear the disturbing memories. It had been a long time since she'd thought about someone in that way. She didn't want to think about Zach like that.

She wanted Zach to go and leave her in peace. She shouldn't have to hide up here to avoid him. *She* belonged here. He didn't.

Downstairs, she meandered into the kitchen, trying to decide if she was hungry enough for dinner or tired enough to simply fall into bed early.

"Jess?"

She turned.

Zach stood in the doorway, buttoning the cuffs of a long-sleeved shirt. Well-worn boots made him look even taller, while tight jeans encased his legs, hugging and outlining all the right masculine places.

She swallowed and shifted her gaze to his face. A straw cowboy hat sat on his head, shadowing his eyes as he stared back.

He looked as if he'd just stepped out of the screen from an old-fashioned western movie. Rugged. Handsome. Like he was ready to ride off to rescue the damsel in distress. He'd come to her rescue earlier down at the garden. But she had no interest in playing Miss Kitty to his Marshall Dillon.

Finally he cleared his throat. "I have to work tonight, but there are plenty of leftovers in the fridge for dinner. Help yourself to whatever you want."

His take-charge attitude normally would have grated on her nerves, but tonight she was too tired to care. "Okay, thanks."

He turned to go, but then stopped. "You okay?"

She nodded. "Just tired."

"Well, like I said. I'll be gone all night, so you'll have the place to yourself."

"Great," she said without much enthusiasm. Odd. All she'd wanted to do since finding him at the cabin was get rid of him. Now, for some reason the prospect of not having anyone around made her feel lonely. She wrapped her arms around her waist.

She must be more tired than she thought.

"All right, then I guess I'll see you later." He smiled.

"Sure."

After Zach had gone, she wandered around the cabin. With all the work she'd been doing—well, trying to do, she corrected with a grimace—she hadn't had time to look around since arriving. The familiar surroundings warmed her heart and soothed the ache there. The mobiles and dream catchers Pops made hung from the ceiling rafters along the sliding glass door leading out to the deck. Framed pictures stood on the end tables next to the worn, comfortable couch. Pops' rocking chair sat in front of the fireplace. His metal working tools and other craft supplies rested on the hearth within easy reach.

She fingered one of his paint brushes. Tears welled in her eyes. Why of all times had he decided to go off exploring now?

Impatiently she wiped her eyes. Hadn't she cried enough? A well-thumbed through magazine lay next to the art supplies. She glanced at the title:

32

Cooking Today.

Not something Pops would read. Zach's?

She turned away from the fireplace to look once again at the pictures scattered throughout the bookshelves and on the end tables in the room. A lifetime of memories stared back. It really had been too long since she'd visited.

One of her and Philip caught her eye. She picked it up and stared at it for long moments. Then she flipped the frame over and pried up the back with a fingernail. She slid the photo out from beneath the glass. With slow precision, she tore it into tiny pieces, then tossed them into a nearby garbage can.

Although Zach was staying there, she couldn't resist peeking into her grandfather's bedroom, right off the family room. Shorts and a T-shirt were strewn across the unmade bed. Magazines littered the bedside table. She ventured closer to peek at the titles: *Simple Tastes* and *Recipes from the Heart*. Interesting. A pair of boots lay in the middle of the floor. A black cowboy hat rested on the dresser.

The photograph tucked into the frame of the mirror caught her eye. She wandered over. Zach posed with three other people. The men in the picture wore dark suits, the lone woman wore a wedding dress. She stood between Zach and another, raven-haired man. A third man stood to Zach's right. All four people were stunningly attractive.

Was it Zach's wedding picture?

A closer inspection revealed one of the other men wore a tuxedo, not a suit. He was the groom.

She sighed as she glanced around the room again. The crisp scent of aftershave lingered. Zach certainly had made himself at home.

****

Zach stared unseeing at the bowl of peanuts on the bar in front of him. Idly, he picked one up, but tossed it down without tasting it. He couldn't stop thinking about Jessica. She was so determined to do it all herself. So adamant about not letting him help.

Her heat-flushed face popped into his mind. Trouble was, she might kill herself in the process.

Was she always so stubborn? Or did he bring out that trait in her?

"Hey, what's up?" Jake slid onto the stool next to Zach.

Zach had thought long and hard on the way to The Corral about what to say—if anything—about Jessica. He'd come to the conclusion he wasn't ready to share.

At least not yet.

"Same old, same old." He yawned.

"Busy day at the cabin?"

"Not really. Actually I spent most of the day at the swimming hole."

"Rough life."

"Tell me about it."

"Glad to hear Ben's getting his money's worth with you."

"Hey, it was hot out there today." He frowned. Guilt flooded through him as he remembered Jessica working out in the hot sun without water. She'd looked ready to pass out by the time he'd driven up. Even though she'd insisted, and he'd been trying to make a point, it went against the grain to let her work like that.

He'd felt like a total cad all day.

Seeing her distress had worsened the guilt.

Like it or not, she had to get it through her stubborn head she needed his help around there. His lips quirked as he pictured her determined face when she'd told him to go pack. He had the feeling she'd have a few suggestions as to where he could put his things.

"What's so funny?" Jake interrupted.

Zach shook his head to clear it. "Nothing. Hey,

can I ask you something?"

"Sure, shoot."

"Do you think there are certain things a man can do and certain things a woman can do?"

Jake tossed him a strange look. "Like what?"

Zach traced his finger across the pattern in the wood on the bar and avoided Jake's gaze. "I don't know. Like the things I do at the creek for Ben. Mowing the field?" His lips quirked. He'd really gotten under her skin with that one. "Or weeding the garden?"

"Well, I think there's a difference between 'can' and 'should.' *Can* a woman do that work? Sure. But *should* she do it is another thing entirely."

"What do you mean?"

"I mean, if there's a man around, *he* should have enough respect for her to be doin' that kind of work. Not lying around the swimming hole all day."

Zach's head jerked up. How had Jake guessed? Obviously Zach hadn't been subtle enough in his questions.

Might as well go all the way. "So, hypothetically speaking, if the woman is too stubborn for her own good and insists on doing the work, what should the man do?"

Jake raised an eyebrow. "Hypothetically speaking, huh?"

"Yes," Zach said firmly.

Jake shrugged. "Be the man, I guess."

"Be the man? Great, that's helpful."

"You know, sweet talk her. Turn on the charm. Make her see things your way."

Zach rolled his eyes at the thought of trying to sweet talk Jessica. She'd just as soon bite his head off than let him charm her. "Yea, right."

Silence fell.

Jake fidgeted beside him. "So, who is this hypothetical woman?"

Zach glanced over at the stairs, where the first customers were descending into the bar. He clapped Jake on the shoulder and rose. "No one you need to worry about."

Chapter Four

The next morning Jessica once again awoke to the chittering of birds outside her window. Determined to get at least a few more minutes of shut-eye before facing the day, she yanked the covers over her head.

The muscles in her arms throbbed in protest. She rolled onto her back and moaned. Her shoulders ached. Easing to a sitting position, she stretched each limb in turn. Soreness radiated from the inside out.

Upon further examination, she found a bruise on her knee, which she attributed to the gas can, and another on her shin. Where in the world had that one come from?

She sighed. Normally she wasn't such a wimp, but it had been a long time since she'd done physical labor.

Or tried to do physical labor. She hadn't been very successful. Chalk it up to another thing she was a dismal failure at.

She tucked her legs to her chest, ignoring the stiffness, and wrapped her arms around them, dropping her head to her knees.

What was she going to do?

Despite her boasts yesterday, she was very unsure about taking care of everything around the property while Pops was gone. If yesterday's attempts were any indication, things would be a wreck by the time he got home.

She had to face facts. She couldn't do it. She needed help. She needed Zach.

She imagined the smug look on his face if she asked for his help. No, there had to be some other way. Besides, she couldn't imagine the two of them trying to coexist at the cabin for the next month and a half. She'd figure something out. She had to.

With another groan, she swung her legs over the side of the bed and stood. Time to face the day. And Zach. Had he decided what to do about a place to stay?

Downstairs, he stood in his usual spot before the stove. He seemed to really enjoy cooking.

"Mornin'," he greeted her.

"Hi," she mumbled as she grabbed her protein powder.

"Eggs?"

"No thanks."

He shrugged. "Suit yourself."

"I will," she retorted. The words were harsher than she'd intended, but her muscles were screaming at her as she lowered herself onto a chair.

Zach's lips quirked as he seated himself across from her. "You usually do."

She set her glass down with a sharp thud. "What's that supposed to mean?"

"Nothing. Really," he added. "I'm just admiring your...determination."

She grunted and took another sip of her drink.

He put down his fork and looked at her.

She squirmed under his scrutiny. "What?"

"I want to talk to you about something, and I don't want you to argue with me."

She folded her arms across her chest. "We'll see."

He smiled. "Somehow I knew you were going to say that."

She ignored the little flutter in her stomach caused by his smile. "Well? What is it?"

He took a deep breath, then slowly expelled it.

38

His eyes met hers. "If you really want me to go, I will." He held up a hand when she started to say something. "But before I do, I'm going to mow the field and take care of those thistles."

She bit her lip. His offer—well, declaration—tempted her. If he took care of those things, at least she wouldn't feel so bad about not finishing up yesterday, and it would give her time to study the other things on Pops' list and figure out what to do about them.

She hesitated, still reluctant to let him help.

Why? she argued with herself. Was she really that stubborn? The man had offered to help *and* to leave when he was done. A win-win situation. But if she let him help, would she feel bad about kicking him out later?

"Deal?" Zach's gaze hadn't strayed from her.

She blew out a breath before nodding. "Deal."

He sat back in his chair, looking relieved. "Thank you." He rose from the table, gathering his breakfast dishes. "So, what are you going to do today?"

She shrugged. She'd never finished the weeding yesterday, but resuming the tiresome task held little appeal. She also had a lot of work to catch up on. At the very least, she should touch base with a couple of clients. However, her motivation was severely lacking at the moment. "I don't know."

"The ATV's are all gassed up," he smiled, "if you want to tool around."

"Yeah, maybe."

"And don't worry, I'll keep out of your hair. It'll take me most of the morning to mow the field and take care of those thistles. This afternoon I'll make some phone calls to see what I can do about getting out of here."

She nodded.

After Zach left, she headed back upstairs. She

sat on her bed, looking around.

Not up to tackling anything on Pops' chore list, but not knowing what else to do—perhaps solitude wasn't all it was cracked up to be—she changed into her swimsuit, put a T-shirt on over it, and grabbed a book from the shelf downstairs.

Eschewing the ATVs in the barn, she walked down to the swimming hole at the creek. She sat on the rocks and dangled her toes in the clear, cool water. A small fish, attracted by the glitter of her ankle bracelet, swam over to nibble on the chain. Dragonflies hovered a few inches above the water, their wings a blur of motion.

After a while she rose to stroll through the shallow water toward the walking bridge. She smiled to herself. The so-called bridge was more like a thrill-seekers challenge. Definitely not for the fainthearted.

She positioned a lawn chair in the creek above the waterfall. The soothing sound of the rushing water echoed around her. A deep, appreciative sigh whispered through her. This was why she was here.

The morning passed slowly as she tried to lose herself in the book, but found she couldn't concentrate. The events of the past year paraded through her mind in an endless line. How had something that had started out so right gone so wrong? Philip had blamed her. Was it her fault? Was there something wrong with her?

The faint rumble of an engine drew her attention from her morose thoughts. The sound grew louder and soon Zach drove into view seated on a large, green tractor. He wore a battered cowboy hat, pulled low over his eyes. He rolled the vehicle across the creek, then stopped on the other side. He shut off the engine and hopped off the big machine.

"I guess you found something to do." He nodded at the book in her hand as he made his way over the rocks toward her.

She looked down. "I guess." Her feet kicked idly at the water.

"Can't get into the story?"

"Not really."

"Did you take one of the ATVs out?"

She shook her head.

"Tell you what. Let's go for a ride."

"No thanks, I—"

"Come on. You said you haven't been here in a while. I bet there are some things you haven't seen around here, or haven't seen in a long time. Take a tour to reacquaint yourself with this place." He held out his hand.

Jessica eyed him. She couldn't make out his expression beneath the shadow from the brim of his hat. Slowly she put her hand in his and let him help her up. She withdrew from his grasp as soon as she'd scrambled to her feet.

"I need to put the tractor away in the barn, so I'll meet you up there. I'd offer you a ride, but she's only built for one." He patted the side of the vehicle.

"That's okay," she said. "I don't mind walking."

Zach vaulted onto the seat and turned the ignition key. He put the machine in gear, and it lurched up the gravel path.

In deference to the diesel fumes, she followed at a distance, her thoughts once again troubled. Was it a good idea to be spending time with Zach? She didn't want to encourage him. She wanted him to go.

But reacquainting herself with Pops' place after all this time sounded logical. And if she were honest with herself, she had to admit the things on Pops' list were way out of her area of expertise. She hadn't had the chance to look over the list again, but she'd bet most of it wouldn't be any clearer than yesterday.

She bit her lip. Maybe she and Zach could strike

some kind of deal. One that didn't involve them living together at the cabin.

By the time she reached the barn, Zach had already parked the tractor. Two ATVs sat out front.

"Zach?"

He poked his head out from behind a stack of wooden crates. "You ready?"

She nodded.

"Do you have a pair of sunglasses? It's been dry around here, so we'll kick up a lot of dust."

"Inside."

He rummaged in a cabinet. "There should be a couple extra in here. Ah ha." He found a pair and handed it to her, then fitted his own glasses into place.

He tossed her a can of insect repellent. "Better spray yourself down."

The spray was cool against her heated skin. The chemicals stung her freshly shaven legs.

They walked out to the ATVs. He pointed. "Any color preference?"

She chose the smaller of the two. It had been a while since she'd ridden one. "I'll take blue."

Zach hopped astride the red vehicle. "Do you need a refresher?"

She shot him a dirty look and swung her leg over the seat of the blue ATV. She bit her lip as she looked at the controls. What had that diagram looked like? "Dammit," she muttered.

Zach's lips quirked, but he didn't say anything. He got off his ATV and ambled over, his eyes unreadable behind the dark glasses. "All of your controls are on the handle bars. Start it like this." He showed her the switch.

She pressed it and the vehicle roared to life. The vibration rattled through her.

"When you want to go, press this with your thumb." He indicated the proper spot. "Brakes are on the right, like a bike." He stepped back. "Give it a try."

Gingerly she released the brake. The machine jerked, then rolled forward a couple of feet. She squeezed the lever to stop.

"There you go. Keep your legs away from this back part, it gets really hot." He swung his leg over the seat and settled onto his ATV. "You want to lead or follow?"

"Follow."

"We'll swing around by Broken Arm Bend and then—"

"Broken Arm Bend?"

He shrugged. "Yeah. About a year ago Ben invited a bunch of us to come out and go ATVing. My buddy, Tom, took a curve too fast and flipped his ATV. Fractured his wrist."

She rolled her eyes. "So, of course, Pops named the spot for him."

Zach grinned. "Of course. Anyway, we'll head out to the glen first so I can check those thistles. After that we'll just tool around, okay?"

A vague, half-forgotten image of the glen formed in her mind.

"All right, let's go." Zach roared off down the gravel path.

She followed at a slower pace, catching up to him where he'd stopped at the creek.

"Aim for the bigger rocks. This part's bumpy, so hold on tight."

She guided the lurching ATV across the rocks, a deep satisfaction filling her when she made it to the other side and drove up the bank. A wide smile broke out. She remembered this now.

Zach looked over his shoulder at her and matched her grin with his own. "That's my girl."

He sped away before she could reprimand him for the comment. She followed as he led the way down a narrow gravel path through the woods. They turned into a large open field, and she drove up alongside him, grinning as she revved her machine and raced past him.

The wind snatched at her hair, tumbling it into wild disarray. For the first time in a long time she felt free. And at peace with herself. She reached the end of the field, then turned to wait for Zach. He stopped beside her.

"It's all coming back," she said breathlessly.

"There's nothing like this in Seattle, is there?" He took off his sunglasses. His eyes twinkled at her.

Too exhilarated to take offense, she didn't reply. He could pry all he wanted. He wouldn't get anything out of her. Seattle was none of his damn business.

She looked around. The path ahead jogged her memory. She nodded toward it. "You can follow me to the glen," she sassed.

He swept his arm out. "Lead away." He slid his glasses back onto the bridge of his nose.

She gunned the engine and sped off. Taking the sharp turn, she drove into the shady coolness of the woods. The damp air settled over her. The ATV bucked under her on the uneven trail. Zach's vehicle rumbled close behind.

She ducked under a low hanging branch, then steered around another curve. Dappled sunlight filtered through the trees on either side. The light winked and flashed over her. Another turn and she drove out into the brilliant light of an open field, squinting despite the dark glasses shading her eyes.

She braked and turned as Zach rolled up beside her. "Ta da." She couldn't keep the pleasure out of her voice.

"Nicely done."

Jessica acknowledged the compliment with a nod of her head.

Zach thrust his chin toward a group of tall plants off to one side. "Those are the thistles your grandfather's worried about. If he doesn't keep up with them, they'll take over and kill all the good stuff." He dismounted from the ATV, then retrieved a pair of gloves and a cloth sack from the box strapped to the back.

"You want to head back or tool around in the field while I take care of this?"

"Or you could tool around while I take care of the thistles."

He sighed. "Haven't we been through this? You agreed to let me take care of this, remember? Besides"—he winked—"Ben is paying me very well to work here while he's gone. I don't want him to think he's not getting his money's worth."

"Fine. I'll tool around." She shook her head, half disgusted with herself. Had she made a mistake agreeing to let him help her out with some of Ben's chores? Would he read more into it than she'd intended?

Oh well. Why worry? If Zach was so adamant about doing the work, who was she to stand in his way? Besides, she'd probably find some way to screw up pulling thistles. She threw the throttle in reverse, backed around Zach's ATV, and sped forward across the field.

****

Jessica raced away. The wind ruffled the back of her shirt up, revealing the butterfly tattoo on the small of her back.

Zach grinned. One mystery solved.

Only about a hundred more to go as far as Jessica Hart was concerned.

He tore his gaze from the gentle curve of her hips astride the ATV and turned his attention to the much less interesting thistles. But his thoughts continued to spin while he methodically clipped each plant and placed it in the sack. Why had she agreed to come riding with him? The offer had been an impulse. She'd looked so sad and alone when he'd ridden over the creek on his way back to the barn. He hadn't expected her to accept.

The putter of her engine drew his attention once again. She raced the ATV around the field in a wide circle, her face raised to the sky, her vivid hair tumbled by the wind. A smile curved her lips. For the first time since she'd arrived, she looked happy.

He finished with the thistles and strode back to his ATV. He started it, then drove to where Jessica had stopped to look over the rolling landscape.

She turned toward him as he approached, a half smile on her face. "I'd forgotten how beautiful it is here."

"Absence makes the heart grow fonder?"

Her smile faded. Her lips pressed into a thin line. "What's that supposed to mean?"

"Nothing," he assured her. Was she always so touchy? "Really, I just meant that if I were you and hadn't been here for a while, I really would have missed this place."

"Oh."

He shrugged off her mood swing. "I need to head back. I have people coming over for dinner tonight, but you can stay out if you'd like."

"You have people coming over?" A note of disapproval tinged her voice.

"Yes. Is that a problem?"

She averted her eyes, not meeting his gaze. "I thought maybe you'd be ready to leave tonight." She paused. "I don't like you taking advantage of my grandfather."

Zach folded his arms across his chest. "How am I taking advantage of him?"

Jessica looked back at him. "This isn't your place, Zach. I'm sure Pops didn't plan on you having wild parties while he's gone."

"Nobody said anything about a wild party. I'm having a couple of friends over for dinner."

"Oh, like the couple of friends you had over who filled the recycling bin to overflowing with wine bottles and beer cans?"

"What?"

"I know what kind of person you are. I mean, come on, you work in a bar."

"So?" He clenched his teeth so hard his jaw ached.

"So, you're just a good old boy who likes to party."

"Is that what you think?"

Jessica nodded.

"The other day you accused me of judging you without really knowing you. Now you're doing the same. Kind of hypocritical, don't you think?"

She opened her mouth, but he cut her off. "And not that it's any of your business, but Ben knows I'll be having people over for dinner." He emphasized the last words. "In fact, he encouraged it."

He restarted the ATV and turned it away from her. "Not that you'd be interested, but I'll set a place for you at the table," he said over his shoulder before he headed off across the field.

Chapter Five

"Zach?" Her voice tentative, Jessica walked into the kitchen later that night. The mouth-watering aroma of garlic and other Italian spices filled the air. She inhaled appreciatively. Zach's cooking smelled incredible.

China and cloth napkins graced the table. In the center, candles sat, waiting to be lit. Wine glasses stood at four out of the five places. A water tumbler stood at the other.

Was that a place for her? Or had he changed his mind about having her join his guests for dinner? She wouldn't blame him.

He turned from the stove to face her, but didn't say anything. His white shirt hung untucked from his jeans, and he had a blue and white striped towel slung over one shoulder.

He looked...sexy.

She shrugged off the inappropriate thought and bit her lip. She owed him an apology for the things she'd said. She'd been feeling like a first-class jerk all afternoon. "Look, I'm sorry about earlier."

"Don't worry about it." He turned his attention back to the pot on the stove.

"No, really. I shouldn't have said those things to you." She paused. "You were right. I judged you, and it wasn't fair. But it's strange. Having you here. I didn't expect Pops to be gone when I got here. And you—"

"And I don't belong here."

She winced, then said quietly. "No, I think you do."

He turned. "What?" Surprise tinged his voice.

She'd done a lot of thinking since returning to the cabin after their ATV ride. "The things you've been doing around here"—she swept her arm out—"I don't know the first thing about handling any of them. I couldn't mow the side field or take care of thistles. Heck, I don't even know what a thistle is."

Zach grinned. "I got very specific instructions from Ben before he left."

Jessica smiled in return. "I'm sure you did." Then she got serious again. "So, do you think we can find a way to make this work?"

Zach grabbed a handful of long, thin noodles and tossed them into a pot of boiling water before replying. "You mean you want me to stay?"

She hesitated. Staying here with him still didn't seem like the best idea, but she needed him if she didn't want Pops' place to fall into disarray while he was gone. Despite yesterday's boasts, she didn't know a darn thing about what needed to be done. So she swallowed her pride and nodded. "I need your help. Would you be willing? To help me out that is."

"So, what? We'd stay here together?"

"No." She bit her lip. "I was actually thinking that I would stay here, and you could just come by during the day."

His lips quirked. "Of course you were."

"Look, I—"

He held up his hand. "I told you yesterday I'd make some phone calls. I won't go back on my word, but I'll need a little time to figure things out. Can we make it work until I do?"

She considered. Finally she nodded. How long could it take?

"Great. Thank you." He turned to the stove, scooped a spoonful of sauce from the pot, and held it out, his hand cupped beneath it. "Taste." He slid the spoon into her open mouth.

Her eyes popped wide as a delicious medley of herbs and spices exploded on her tongue. Garlic. Oregano. Basil. She swallowed. "This is fabulous."

"You sound surprised."

"No. That is, I mean, most men I know don't know how to cook."

"Is that a sexist remark?" His eyes twinkled at her.

"No, just a fact."

"I see."

"So where'd you learn to cook like this?" She waved her hand at the stove.

Zach shrugged. "Mom and Dad were at work all the time." The words sounded bitter. He slid a tray of garlic bread in the oven. "I wound up making dinner for my brother and sister a lot. After I moved out, I always lived on my own, so if I didn't cook, I didn't eat."

"No, that's not what I mean. That's making dinner. Anybody can do that. This," she gestured again, "is cooking. Like five-star chef cooking."

Zach looked pleased. "Over the years I got bored with mac and cheese and got creative."

The taste of garlic still lingered in her mouth. "I'll say. Seriously, Zach, I've never tasted anything like this."

"Thank you."

She studied him. He intrigued her. She'd never met anyone like him. How had she gone from wanting to kick him out to practically begging him to help her in less than twenty-four hours? But she needed him. She couldn't let Pops' place fall into disrepair.

She looked away when he caught her staring. She couldn't meet his gaze now that they'd agreed to stay at the cabin together. At least temporarily until he figured out his living situation. Like he'd said, they'd make it work somehow.

It wouldn't be so bad. Most of the time during the day, he'd be working around the property, and at night he'd go to his job at the bar. They wouldn't see much of each other at all.

Still, how strange to have agreed to sleep in the same house with him. The expected trepidation and nervousness hadn't come. The only emotion running through her was relief he'd agreed to take care of the place. And after all, Zach would be down here on the first floor in Pops' bedroom, and she'd be all the way upstairs in the loft. An entire floor would separate them.

Not that it would be an issue anyway.

Her gaze darted back to him as he stirred the pot on the stove. She shoved her hands in the back pockets of her jeans. "Can I help you with anything?"

"No, I'm good here." He looked at his watch. "Everyone should be here any minute now."

Her glance fell on the table once again. "Who's coming to dinner?"

"Friends of mine from The Corral." The words held the hint of a challenge.

She winced, but before she could say anything, the back door opened and a slim woman with long, blond hair walked in. "We're here. Sorry we're late, we—" She stopped when her gaze met Jessica's. "Oh, hello." She studied Jessica, keen interest in her eyes.

Zach kissed the woman on the cheek before turning to Jessica. "Jessica, this is Sharlie. Sharlie, this is Jessica, Ben's granddaughter."

Sharlie smiled. "Oh, of course. Ben talks about you all the time. It's a pleasure to meet you."

Before Jessica could respond, a tall, raven-haired man holding a baby carrier strode through the door. Something clicked and she recognized him from the picture on the mirror in the bedroom. The couple was the bride and groom.

"Hey, Zach," the man said, setting the carrier

down.

"Logan, this is Jessica. Jessica, Logan Reed, Sharlie's husband."

Logan held out his hand, and Jessica placed hers in it. "Nice to meet you, Jessica."

"You, too."

Zach peeked into the baby carrier. "How's my boy?"

"Sleeping like an angel," Sharlie said, a tender look on her face as she, too, gazed upon the infant.

"How old is he?" Jessica asked.

"Four months. We got him about two months ago."

"Got him?"

"We adopted Owen," Sharlie answered, then smiled up at Logan as he placed his arm around her.

A special look passed between the two. Not wanting to intrude on the intimate moment, Jessica looked away and caught Zach's eye. An emotion she couldn't read flickered in his gaze before he turned his attention back to the dinner preparations.

"Mooning over each other again, I see." A voice from the doorway drew everyone's attention.

"You know it." Logan laughed. "Hey, Jake, what's up?"

"Not much," the other man replied. He clapped Zach on the shoulder. "Smells good, buddy." Then he noticed Jessica. "Hello," he said, a charming smile on his face. He held out his hand. "I'm Jake."

Jessica placed her hand in his for a brief shake. "Jessica."

"She's Ben's granddaughter," Zach cut in, steering Jake away. His voice held a warning.

Suddenly Jake's face split into a wide grin and he laughed. "Oh, the hypothetical woman." He glanced at Jessica again. "Nice."

"What?" Sharlie looked puzzled.

Jessica was equally confused. She looked at

Zach. Was he blushing? What was going on?

"Uh, Jake, why don't you pour the wine?" Zach said.

While Jake took care of the wine, Zach dished up generous helpings of pasta, chicken parmesan, and garlic bread. "Okay, everyone have a seat." He held out a chair for Jessica.

She slid into it with a murmur of thanks.

When everyone sat down, Jake raised his glass. The others followed suit. "To Zach, the best damn chef I know."

"Hear, hear." They clinked glasses.

Her water tumbler looked out of place next to the delicate wine glasses. She bit her lip. Would anyone comment? She glanced around the table and then straightened her shoulders. She didn't care what these strangers thought of her. Not drinking was her business.

Jessica rolled strands of spaghetti around her fork, then slid it into her mouth. She followed it with a bite of chicken. The perfect blend of spices and cheeses tantalized her taste buds.

"Zach, you've outdone yourself again," Sharlie praised.

"Yeah, too bad the food's not this good at The Corral," Jake teased as he looked at Logan. "You wouldn't be able to keep the people away."

Jokes and laughter highlighted the meal. Zach and his friends were obviously very close, but included Jessica in the conversation and made her feel welcome.

****

After dinner, Zach stood outside with Jake.

"Where'd everybody else go?" Jake asked. He handed Zach one of the bottles of beer in his hand.

"Thanks. Jessica went to grab a sweater, and Sharlie and Logan are putting the baby to sleep."

"It takes both of them to do that?"

Zach laughed. "When it's those two it does."

"So what's the story with Jessica? She *is* the hypothetical woman, right?"

"Right," Zach admitted. "And there's no story. I told you, she's Ben's granddaughter."

"That's all?"

"That's all," Zach said firmly.

"What is she doing here? I mean, since Ben's gone."

"Besides driving me crazy?" In more ways than one. He shrugged and answered Jake's question. "She just showed up the other day. Found me in the bathtub." His lips quirked at the memory.

"Really?" Jake's voice held new interest. "Then what?" A comical leer distorted his features.

Zach punched his shoulder. "Nothing."

"Nothing?" Jake's expression changed to one of dismay, and he shook his head. "A gorgeous woman finds you in the bathtub and nothing happens? You need to get out more...experience life to the fullest. Now if it were me—"

Zach held up a hand to stop the words. "I don't want to hear it."

"Yeah, yeah," Jake complained good-naturedly. "So how long is she staying?"

Zach shrugged. "I don't know. Like I said, she showed up out of the blue, didn't know Ben wasn't here. Tried to kick me out, but I dug in my heels." He grinned.

"So, what, the two of you are just going to live here together for some undetermined length of time?"

"Sure, at least until I figure out where to stay while my apartment's being sublet."

"Don't look at me. You'd cramp my style."

Zach laughed. "I wouldn't think of it. Besides, if I drag my feet long enough, I won't have to move out."

Jake grunted and took a sip of his beer. "And you think that will work?"

"Why not?"

"Have you seen the woman?"

"Of course, but I'm not interested in her that way."

"Then maybe I should ask her out."

"No." Zach looked away from Jake's knowing expression. "I mean, that's not a good idea. Because of Ben and all."

"Right."

Before Zach could reply, Sharlie and Logan strolled out onto the deck holding hands. She raised her face to say something to him. He smiled and dropped a kiss on her lips.

Jake groaned and rolled his eyes. "Get a room, you two."

Sharlie stuck her tongue out at him.

Zach grinned.

****

After retrieving her sweater, Jessica joined Zach and his friends out on the deck. They sat and chatted. Sharlie and Logan had declined a refill on their wine, but Zach and Jake each had grabbed a beer after dinner, which they sipped leisurely.

So much for her visions of a wild party. Guilt tugged at her. She'd let past experience cloud her ability to see Zach for himself. On the other hand, he did drink a lot. Wine with every meal. A beer or two each night. How long before the social habit got out of control?

She mentally shook herself. It didn't matter. As soon as Pops got back, she'd never see Zach, or his friends, again. She and Zach had come into each other's lives purely by accident. Under ordinary circumstances, she never would have met him. Their time together would end long before his drinking turned into a real problem.

She forced away her disturbing thoughts and focused on the conversation around her. The night passed quickly, until finally Logan looked at his watch. "We should be going." He rose in a fluid motion, held out his hand, and helped Sharlie from her chair. He kept her hand in his as they said their good-byes.

The way Logan looked at his wife twisted something inside Jessica. She couldn't tell if it made her feel like she'd had the chance at something like that and lost it, or if she'd missed out entirely.

"I'll see you guys at work tomorrow," Zach said.

When everyone had gone, Jessica and Zach sat alone on the deck. The night had grown cooler, and Jessica drew the edges of her sweater together. Zach put on a flannel shirt over his T-shirt, but didn't button it.

They sat with their feet dangling over the edge, looking out at the darkness. An owl hooted. The bushes rustled nearby.

"Your friends are nice."

"Thanks."

"How long have y'all known each other?"

"Sharlie and I have been working at The Corral together for about ten years, although she doesn't come in as much now, with the new baby and all. We met Jake about seven years ago when he started working there."

"What about Logan?"

"I met him a couple of years ago."

"You're all bouncers?"

"Nope, just Jake and me. Logan and Sharlie own The Corral."

The tone of his voice niggled something in the back of her mind. "You used to have feelings for Sharlie."

Zach wouldn't meet her gaze. "What makes you say that?"

Jessica shrugged. "I can tell."

He looked over at her, but in the dim light filtering out from the cabin behind them, she couldn't read his expression. "Oh yeah?"

"Yeah." She paused. "So what happened?"

This time Zach shrugged. "Nothing, really."

She nudged him with her shoulder. "C'mon, kiss and tell."

He laughed. "There's nothing to tell."

"Ah, so no kissing."

"No kissing."

Jessica waited. After a moment her patience paid off.

"It never would have worked. I knew as soon as Logan moved back."

"Moved back?"

"They were high school sweethearts who went their separate ways. Twelve years later, he came back."

"Wow." She couldn't imagine waiting twelve years for someone.

Zach glanced at her. "Yeah, well, anyway, seeing them together makes me realize I never stood a chance. They belong together."

"Like baseball and hotdogs?" she suggested.

"Like apple pie and ice cream," he countered.

They laughed together, then fell silent. Crickets chirped in the darkness. The scent of Zach's aftershave drifted to her on the light breeze.

After a while, he turned toward her. "Do you?"

"Do I what? Like apple pie and ice cream?"

"No," he said softly. His gaze dropped to her lips. "Do you kiss and tell?"

Jessica's heart kicked into a fast rhythm and she caught her breath. "I..."

"Shhhh." He leaned closer. "I won't tell if you won't," he whispered before his mouth claimed hers.

His lips stroked over hers, not aggressively, but

softly, tenderly. He didn't touch her anywhere else, but brushed her mouth with gentle intent.

Her first instinct was to pull back, but something stirred deep inside her. A feeling she'd nearly forgotten. Whispery shivers danced along her nerve endings and fluttered in her stomach. Without meaning to, the action was purely a reflex, she opened to him.

The kiss deepened. Their breath mingled. Her palm slid up his chest, feeling the play of muscle beneath his shirt. She fisted the flannel of his open collar in her hand.

His knuckles grazed the sides of her face.

Her body tingled with awareness. Scattered thoughts flitted through her mind, but she couldn't hold onto any of them. Not while Zach kissed her. Not when his mouth fitted so perfectly against hers. Not when the pulse racing at the base of his throat matched the cadence of her heartbeat.

She couldn't remember the last time she'd felt like this. Had felt anything.

Should she be feeling this way about Zach?

Almost as if sensing her conflicting emotions, he softened the kiss, tenderly brushing his mouth over hers one last time.

She waged a silent war within, trying to calm her racing heart.

She still clutched his shirt. She relaxed her fingers one at a time, releasing the twisted fabric from her grasp. Finally she drew in a deep breath, then slowly let it out.

Her eyes found his.

Zach's gaze searched hers. He smiled. A smile as soft and tender as his kiss. He touched his finger to her lips, then rose. "Good night, Jess."

****

Zach closed his bedroom door and then collapsed on the bed. His heart raced and blood pounded in his ears.

From a simple kiss.

From a simple kiss he shouldn't have taken.

He looked around the room. Jessica's words from earlier, about taking advantage of Ben, rang in his ears. What was he thinking, kissing the man's granddaughter? He was there to take care of Ben's property. Not step out of line with Jessica.

He wasn't quite sure why he'd done it. The impulse had come on him suddenly. He hadn't consciously thought about it. Hadn't planned it.

Hadn't considered the consequences. They'd reached a fragile peace earlier after their argument in the field, with her agreeing to let him stay. Had he ruined that? Would she ask him to leave immediately?

He wouldn't blame her. Bottom line, he shouldn't have kissed her. And as hard as it might be to resist, if she let him stay, he wouldn't do it again.

He had to put the kiss out of his mind. Had to forget the feel of her lips trembling beneath his own before she'd opened to him.

He groaned, rolled over, and punched the pillow. Jake had been right. How the hell could he live here with her?

Now that he'd tasted her.

He had to find a way. She'd put her trust in him. Had agreed to let him stay until he could move back into his apartment. He wouldn't undermine that trust. He wouldn't take advantage.

No matter how difficult it was. He couldn't give in to temptation. He wouldn't kiss her again.

He stripped off his clothes and then slid beneath the sheet. Sleep wouldn't come easy that night. Visions of Jessica would haunt his dreams for sure.

****

Jessica lay awake, staring at the ceiling,

although she couldn't really see it in the darkness.

Her body hummed, her lips tingled.

She'd nearly forgotten what it was like to be kissed. She and Philip hadn't spent a lot of time kissing over the last couple of years. Not the way things had been. But even when things had been good between them, not one of their kisses had ever been like the one she'd shared with Zach.

The feelings had surprised her. Maybe she wasn't cold inside after all. Maybe it wasn't all her fault things had gone wrong.

Of course, because she'd felt something, didn't mean Zach had. He'd broken off the kiss. Hadn't tried anything else. Hadn't tried to go any further.

Not that she wanted him to. Not that she would have let him.

But still, what had he been thinking? Why had he kissed her? Why had he stopped?

What would this do to their living arrangement? Would it make it awkward again? Would it even work? Should she insist he leave in the morning?

And the most important question of all, if he stayed, would Zach kiss her again? The notion scared and excited her in turn. Would it feel the same if he kissed her again, or had tonight been a fluke? Had her response come more from surprise than passion?

What did passion feel like? She'd known. Once. Maybe. But things were different now.

Did she know how to feel? To let herself go and open up to someone again. To trust.

Was Zach someone she could trust? In some ways, the answer was an unequivocal *yes*. She trusted him to take care of Pops' property.

But was that really trust? Or just knowing he'd take care of his responsibilities.

She'd put her trust in a man once.

Trusted him with her body and her heart.

Pledged her life to him.

And where had that gotten her?

Alone, trembling from the aftershocks of a kiss from a near stranger, afraid to trust herself.

Chapter Six

Zach looked up from the table the next morning when she walked into the kitchen, but didn't quite meet her gaze. "Good morning."

He sounded odd. Or was it her imagination? Her heart thumped painfully in her chest. She should ask him to leave. After what had happened last night it wasn't a good idea for him to stay. He'd had no right to kiss her.

She tamped down the secret place hidden deep inside of her that still tingled from the memory of his kiss. The part that wanted him to kiss her again. "Good morning."

"There's French toast on the stove if you're hungry." He pointed with his fork.

"No thanks, I'll just have my—"

"Protein drink," Zach finished for her with a hint of a smile. His eyes met hers briefly before sliding away.

Jessica mixed her drink, then sat down across from him. The awkward silence thundered in her ears. She opened her mouth to say something, but changed her mind.

Zach rose from the table, taking his plate with him. "I have a lot to do today, so I need to get a move on."

She nodded, even though his back was to her as he washed his dishes.

He shut the water off, but remained still, his hands resting on the rim of the stainless steel sink. Finally he turned around.

Still he didn't meet her gaze. "Jessica, about last

night. I'm sorry."

Her stomach churned. "Sorry?" The word was a strangled whisper. Of all the things she thought he'd say in the morning, 'sorry' hadn't even crossed her mind.

An uncomfortable look crossed his face. "Yes. I'm sorry I kissed you, but don't worry, it won't happen again." He paused. "I don't want you to get the wrong idea."

"Of...of course not."

"Okay, and uh, just so you don't think I've forgotten, I'm still working on finding some place else to stay. I'm sorry it's taking so long."

She nodded.

"Well, then, I, uh, need to get some work done around here." He strode from the room.

Jessica stared after him. Her heart faltered. She took a deep breath.

She hadn't expected an apology. She hadn't known how Zach would act in the morning, but saying he was sorry?

Familiar doubts assailed her.

Of course he wouldn't want to kiss her again. Of course he didn't want her to get the wrong idea and think he could be interested in someone like her.

Someone who didn't know what it took to please a man.

Was it that apparent after one kiss?

She took a shaky sip of her drink, but it tasted like chalk. She dumped it out in the sink and stared out the window.

Staying here with Zach wasn't going to work. They couldn't live together until Pops returned. Not after last night.

Not after this morning.

He needed to stay. He could take care of the place. She should be the one to leave.

Where would she go? Her parents' house? They

were in Ireland with Pops. Their place was empty. She could find her peace and solitude there. Away from anyone else.

Away from anyone she might disappoint.

Jessica sighed. She could get away from Philip. She could get away from Zach. But could she ever get away from herself?

Not wanting to dwell on the disturbing thought, she headed upstairs to pack. If she hurried, she'd be gone before Zach returned.

Throwing her meager items into her bags didn't take long. She took a last look around the cabin. She'd come back someday soon. When Zach was no longer there.

She bit her lip. Should she leave him a note? Would he be worried?

She grabbed a pad of paper from a kitchen drawer and scribbled a few words, then set it on the table.

Outside, she tossed her bags into the back seat of her car. She'd made it past the barn and halfway down the path toward the creek, when the car shuddered and wrenched toward the left.

She stopped and got out, then groaned. A flat tire. She'd probably picked up a rock from the gravel road.

Hands on hips, she stared at the offending wheel. "Dammit." The curse echoed in the stillness, frightening a nearby bird, who took to the air with an outraged shriek.

The trunk revealed no spare. Of course not, why would there be one? That would mean something was going right in her life.

With a heartfelt sigh she retrieved her bags from the car and trudged back up the path to the cabin. Maybe she could coax a tow truck to venture out and fix the flat.

An hour later she tossed down her cell phone

and expelled a long breath. No one was available until the next morning for a non-emergency situation. One of the many disadvantages of small town life.

Zach was stuck with her for one more night.

She spent a restless day, feeling caged and trapped. Now that she'd made up her mind to leave, it galled her to be forced to stay.

Zach returned late in the afternoon.

"Jessica? Is everything okay? Why is your car on the path?"

She grimaced. "Flat tire. Sorry, was it in your way?"

"Of course not." He paused and looked at her. "Were you going somewhere?"

She hedged, suddenly not wanting him to know she planned on leaving. Not until she could actually escape. She avoided his gaze. "I was going into town to pick up a few things."

"I have to work tonight, but I'll fix it for you in the morning."

Jessica waved a hand. "No, that's okay. A tow truck will be out tomorrow to fix it."

"You don't have to pay for a tow truck, I can take care of it."

"There's no spare," she explained.

"Doesn't matter. I'd like to help you," he said quietly.

Tired of arguing, she gave in. Zach could fix the tire first thing in the morning, and she could be on her way. "Okay, that would be great." Not having to spend the money at a garage would also be helpful. She was way behind with work, and when she didn't work, she didn't get paid.

"I'm going to grab a quick bite before I get ready for work. You hungry?" he asked as he headed for the kitchen.

"No, thanks. I'll have something in a little

while."

A second later he poked his head around the door frame. "What's this?" He held her note in his hand.

She bit her lip and mentally kicked herself for forgetting to throw it away.

"Are you leaving?"

She couldn't meet his gaze.

"Jessica?"

Her eyes met his before darting away. "I thought it would be best."

"Because of last night?" He leaned against the jam.

Oh hell. She nodded.

He tilted his head back and studied the ceiling. Finally he looked at her again. Regret swam in his eyes. "I really am sorry."

She gritted her teeth. She'd scream if he said he was sorry one more time. How much more foolish could she feel?

"Please don't go. I would feel awful if you did."

"Why?"

"Why?" Zach looked taken aback by the question. "I shouldn't have kissed you."

Her heart squeezed.

"I was out of line. I'd never want you to think I was taking advantage of you." He took a step toward her.

She fought the urge to take one back.

He turned away. "Maybe I should go. I can crash at Jake's for a couple of nights."

"No."

Her denial stopped him.

"I mean, you can't." She looked anywhere but at him. "I told you yesterday, I can't take care of this place." She bit her lip to stop the tears that threatened. She couldn't do anything. "Pops needs you here. You have to stay."

"What about you?"

She shook her head. "I don't need to be here."

"But you want to be here. You came here, to this place, for a reason."

She'd come to escape. Instead she'd found Zach.

"It wouldn't feel right if I stayed and you left." He paused. "Besides, Ben wouldn't take too kindly to me chasing his granddaughter away. Look," he said when she remained silent. "I'll be gone tonight. You'll have the place to yourself. At least sleep on it. In the morning, if you still feel like you want to go, we'll figure something out."

Jessica nodded. What other choice did she have? Her car had a flat, so she wouldn't be going anywhere tonight.

"Thank you." He looked at his watch. "I really need to get going, or I'll be late for work." He strode into Pops' bedroom. At the door he turned. "And, Jessica, I promise what happened last night won't happen again."

She almost doubled over. The words hit her like a kick in the stomach.

****

"I kissed Jessica."

The Corral hadn't opened yet for the night, so Zach and Jake had the barroom to themselves.

Jake nodded. "Nice."

Zach shook his head. "Not nice."

Jake raised an eyebrow.

Zach laughed. "No, that's not what I mean. The kiss was nice. More than nice. But I shouldn't have done it."

"Why not?"

"She's Ben's granddaughter. I feel like I'm taking advantage of him. Of her."

The other man looked at him. "Did she kiss you back?"

The memory of her lips trembling, then opening

beneath his jumped into his mind. His pulse sped. Zach swallowed and nodded.

"Then you're not taking advantage of her. Did anything else happen?"

"No. I did apologize."

"You what?" Jake sounded scandalized.

"Apologized." Zach looked at the almost comical expression of disbelief on Jake's face. "Why?"

"Haven't you learned anything from watching me all these years?" Jake asked in mock dismay. "It was a mutual kiss, you both participated. You don't apologize for something like that. It'll make her feel bad."

"Why would it make her feel bad?"

"Look, if there's one thing I know a little bit about, it's women."

Zach rolled his eyes. "You think?" Jake was the resident ladies' man at the bar. He could charm the pants off, sometimes literally, any gal who walked through the doors. Saying he knew a little about women was like saying Johnny Cash knew a little about music.

Jake made a face. "Yeah. Anyway, a woman does not want to hear you're sorry you kissed her."

"But I am sorry I kissed her. She wasn't really happy to find me at Ben's place. I don't want to make matters worse by having her think I'm looking for an easy score."

The blond bouncer shook his head. "I'm telling you, women think differently than we do. She's probably thinking you didn't like kissing her. "

"What? That's the most ridiculous thing I've ever heard." Zach couldn't keep the frustration from his voice. "I was trying to reassure her. To let her know I wasn't taking advantage of her or the situation."

Jake clapped him on the back as a few customers descended into the bar. "That may have been your intention, but I'm telling you, an apology was not the way to go."

Zach didn't mention the fact he'd apologized twice. "Great, so what do I do now?"

Jake shrugged. "Are you looking to have a relationship with this girl?"

"A relationship? I've only known her for a couple of days."

"Then I wouldn't worry about it." He glanced over at the stairway. "Duty calls. I get to check IDs tonight."

Zach cursed softly as Jake walked away. He'd made a fine mess of things.

****

The next morning as Jessica threw things into her bags, her cell phone rang. She'd tossed and turned all night, thinking about Zach. Thinking about their kiss. Thinking about what he'd said. Thinking about staying at the cabin with him.

By morning she'd decided she couldn't stay.

The phone rang again. She flipped it open and held it to her ear. "Hello?"

"Jessica, sweetheart, how are you?" Her mother's scratchy voice filtered through the small receiver. Reception was sketchy at best in the mountains.

"I'm fine. I hear you're in Ireland."

"Yes, we are. We're having a great time. Your grandfather is so excited to be seeing everything here."

"I'm glad he finally got to take the trip. He's been talking about it for years."

"It's hard to hear you, Jessica, so I won't keep you. But I wanted to tell you we're flying back into California in a few weeks, so we thought about renting a car and swinging up to see you and Philip. It's been a long time." Even the poor connection couldn't hide the slight note of recrimination in her mother's voice.

Jessica chewed her lip. Damn. "Uh, Mom, I'm not in Seattle." Eventually she would need to tell her parents what had happened, but now wasn't the time.

"Oh. Where are you?"

"I'm at the cabin."

"You are?"

"I decided to come for a visit. I was surprised Pops wasn't here. I didn't know you guys were taking this trip."

"I'm sorry, sweetheart, I didn't think you'd care. You're always so busy."

The words hurt, but she couldn't deny the truth in them. She'd neglected her family.

"But, that's great you're at the cabin. Is Philip with you? How long are you planning on staying?"

She ignored the first question. "I'm not sure. I was thinking of heading up to your place for a while. We can visit there when you get back."

"No, don't be silly. Stay at the cabin. We'll be heading back there to drop Dad off anyway. That way we can all have a nice visit together. We'll be back early next month, if you're planning on staying that long. It'll save us the trip back and forth."

Jessica sighed and dumped the contents of her newly packed bag out onto the bed. "Yeah, I'll be here."

"Wonderful. Oh, hang on a sec. What?" she asked someone at her end. "Dad wants to know how the caretaker is doing. Any problems?"

Jessica grimaced. Problems had cropped up all right, but none Pops needed to worry about. "No, everything's fine here."

"Super. Well, I have to run. We'll see you and Philip when we get home."

Jessica didn't bother to correct her. "Sounds good. Bye, Mom."

"Bye, hon."

Jessica sighed and flopped onto her back on the bed. Great. Not only had she just committed herself to staying with Zach for another several weeks, but she needed to come up with a way to explain to her family what had happened between her and Philip.

She hadn't burdened them with the details of the troubled relationship. Hadn't wanted to worry them. In part she'd kept things to herself so they wouldn't know what a dismal failure she was. What would they say when they found out?

More pressing at the moment, how would Zach react when she told him she'd decided to stay? Would he regret trying to persuade her to do so?

He regretted kissing her, he'd said as much.

Well, she couldn't hide in the loft forever. Sooner or later she'd have to face the day. And Zach.

With a fortifying breath, she headed down to the kitchen, knowing she'd find him there as she did every morning.

"Hi," she ventured.

He looked up from the bowl of cereal in front of him. "Good morning."

"No fancy breakfast today?"

"I wasn't in the mood to cook."

Uh oh. Maybe he had changed his mind about wanting her to stay.

"If you want something, I can make it for you."

"No, don't be silly."

He mushed the cereal around with his spoon and didn't say anything. Jessica made her usual morning drink and sat down across from him.

"So, did you decide?" He didn't look up.

No sense beating around the bush. "I'm going to stay."

His head jerked up. "Really?"

Was that disappointment or relief in his eyes? "My mom called this morning and, when she found out I was here, she kind of convinced me to stay."

"Oh." His voice sounded odd.

"That way I can spend some time with my family when they get back. I haven't seen them in a while."

Zach rose, then dumped the uneaten cereal from his bowl into the sink. He flipped a switch. The low growl of the disposal hummed in the silence.

He turned. "I looked at your car this morning. I'll have to take the tire into town to get it fixed. Unless you need the car today, I thought I'd take care of it tonight on my way to work."

"No, that's fine. But, really, I don't want you to go to so much trouble on my account."

"It's no trouble. I'm happy to do it."

She nodded. "Thank you."

"You're welcome." He walked out of the kitchen. At the doorway, he stopped and looked back. "I'm glad you decided to stay."

****

Settling into a routine with Zach proved to be easier than Jessica had expected. She didn't see much of him. During the day he kept busy around the property. Although whether there really was that much to do or whether he was avoiding her, she couldn't begin to guess. Most nights he worked at The Corral.

One night as she worked on her computer in front of the fireplace, he padded barefoot into the room. He wore faded jeans and a T-shirt instead of his usual western attire.

She glanced up. "You're not working tonight?"

"Nope. Do you mind if I read in here while you work?"

"Of course not."

Zach picked up a cooking magazine and stretched out on the couch, his head propped up on one armrest, his feet on the other. They sat in companionable silence. Rain pattered against the windows. Jessica's fingers clicked over the keys of her laptop. From time to time the pages of Zach's magazine ruffled.

A cozy, homey feel settled over her. Every now and again she peeked over at Zach. Once he caught her looking at him and smiled. She looked away as heat stole into her cheeks.

After a while he tossed the magazine onto the coffee table. She glanced over at him. He stretched, then rose from the couch in a fluid motion. "I'm going to grab a drink. You want something?"

"A glass of water would be great."

"You got it." He ambled to the kitchen, his bare feet slapping against the wood floor.

She stared at the roll of his hips as his easy swagger carried him from the room. She blinked and shook her head to clear it.

Soon he returned with a beer in one hand and a glass of water in the other. He handed her the glass, then took a sip of beer. He leaned over the back of her chair. "What are you working on?"

She wrinkled her nose at the smell of beer on his breath. "I'm designing a website for a client."

"You know how to do that?"

She rolled her eyes. "It's what I do. It's my job."

"Looks complicated."

She laughed. "That's what everyone says. But it's actually pretty easy. You just have to know where to direct everything." She demonstrated by typing a URL into its designated space, then saving the information. Using the touch pad on her computer, she clicked on an icon. The screen faded to a new page.

"You made it do that?" Zach sounded impressed.

"Yep."

"Cool. Mind if I watch, or will that distract you?"

The interest in his voice surprised her. She

shrugged. "It won't bother me, but it's really not that exciting."

He shifted behind her, leaning farther over her chair. The crisp scent of his aftershave washed over her. It reminded her of his kiss.

She pushed the thought aside and concentrated on her work.

Half an hour later, she powered down the computer and closed the laptop. She stretched. Behind her, Zach straightened.

She looked up at him. "I told you it wasn't very exciting."

"No, that was really neat. I liked watching you work." He moved to the other rocker across from her and sat down. "So that's what you do, design websites for people?"

"Yeah, more or less. Every once in a while I do some computer graphic design work, but I enjoy doing the websites the most."

"Do you have an office?"

"Nope. I work from home." She glanced around the cabin. "Or wherever I happen to be. As long as I have Internet access, I'm good to go."

"Interesting."

She laughed. "Yeah, right."

"No, really. I'm impressed." He rose. "I'm going to turn in. Thanks for letting me watch."

"No problem."

"Good night, Jess."

****

The next day Jessica's mind kept returning to the cozy scene from the night before. It had been...nice...to sit and work with Zach in the same room. And he'd seemed genuinely interested in what she'd been doing.

Philip hadn't ever shown an interest in her work. He hadn't understood why she wanted to have a job. All he'd wanted was for her to follow him from place to place as he did his thing.

But she'd known almost from the beginning Zach was different. Her lips twitched into a rueful smile. Somewhere over the last few weeks, her attitude toward Zach had done a complete one-eighty. The feeling of contentment stayed with her throughout the day, enough to try her hand at making dinner. Zach enjoyed doing the cooking, but she wanted to do something for him for a change.

After spending most of the afternoon in the kitchen, she surveyed the meal she'd put together. Salad, garlic bread, and spaghetti with sauce from a jar. Compared to the restaurant-style cuisine Zach always prepared, hers seemed sadly uninspired. She bit her lip. Would he be disappointed?

She jumped when the door slammed softly.

"Jessica?"

"In here."

He poked his head around the kitchen doorframe. His hair was disheveled, like he'd taken off his hat and run his fingers through it. "Hey, what's up?"

"I thought I'd give you a break tonight and make dinner. I hope you don't mind."

"Of course not, that sounds great."

"It should be ready in about half an hour."

"Perfect, that gives me time to take a quick shower."

"Are you working tonight?"

"Nope, I'm off." He studied her. "I need to do a couple of things in the barn, so I won't be in your way."

His words brought a stab of disappointment. She didn't think she could take another night alone. Last night had been a welcome change. The solitude she'd craved wasn't all it was cracked up to be. "Oh, sure."

While Zach showered she set the table, then

threw together the small salad. She pulled the bread from the oven when he strode back into the room.

"Smells good."

"Thanks. It's not as fancy as the things you cook, but I thought you—" Her finger touched the side of the white-hot pan. "Ouch!"

The pan fell with a clatter on the stovetop. She stuck her stinging finger in her mouth.

In an instant Zach arrived at her side. "Let me see," he said, taking her hand in his. He examined the small red mark on her skin. He dipped his finger under the faucet and smoothed cold water over the burn. "This should help."

"Thanks."

"Better?" he asked. His gaze captured hers. He stood so close the darker flecks in his mocha-colored irises were visible.

Jessica sucked in a breath. He hadn't looked at her, really looked at her, since he'd kissed her.

The memory of that kiss gave her courage. Or made her foolish. Before she could stop them, the words slipped out. "Why don't you want to kiss me again?"

Chapter Seven

The words hung in the tension-filled air.

"Why don't I—" Zach bit the words off.

"Didn't you like it?"

"What?" The word came out strangled.

"Never mind." Jessica tried to remove her hand from his. His grasp tightened.

"What are you talking about?"

Dammit, why had she asked him that? "Nothing. I shouldn't have said anything. I—"

"Jessica."

Something in how her name sounded coming from his lips compelled her to go on. "Well, you kissed me that night, and then, well, you said you were sorry, so I thought maybe you didn't like it. That it didn't make you feel anything."

He laughed without humor, the sound strained. "Not feel anything? Jessica, I've laid awake at night remembering what you taste like, wanting to kiss you again so damn badly I ached, but telling myself I shouldn't, for your sake."

Zach wanted to kiss her again? The confession set her heart pounding. But could she believe him? She bit her lip. "Then you didn't think I'm a bad kisser?"

Zach smiled and shook his head. "Oh, my sweet Jessica, what am I going to do with you?" His head lowered and his mouth captured hers.

She closed her eyes and let herself feel. The gentle pressure of his lips against her own. The moist warmth of his breath. The beat of her pulse as it throbbed at the base of her throat and thundered in her ears. The trembling in her limbs. The hollow sensation in her stomach.

With tender, relentless intent he stroked over her lips until, as before, she opened to him. His tongue soothed the tender spot on the inside of her lip she'd bitten, then slid inside her mouth to touch hers. A jolt of awareness flared deep in her womb. Her knees wobbled.

Strong arms banded around her back. His strength flowed into her. The thin cotton of their garments couldn't contain the heat radiating from him. Warmth spread like licks of flame throughout her body.

His aftershave drove the scent of the garlic bread from her nostrils. She inhaled the sharp aroma. Her arms wound around his neck, holding him closer. A tingling began where their bodies touched, and spread, leaving desire in its wake.

How long had it been since she'd wanted someone? The half-forgotten feeling intensified as Zach slanted his mouth across hers, deepening an already passionate kiss. She moaned.

Zach gentled the kiss, then pulled his mouth away and rested his forehead against hers. His uneven breath stirred the tendrils of hair around her face. He took her hand and flattened it against his chest. His heart thundered beneath her palm. "Do you still think I don't feel anything when you kiss me?" His voice was ragged.

Jessica rocked her forehead across his, unable to form coherent words. She gulped a deep lungful of air, trying to calm her own racing heart. Her body trembled. Aftershocks from the kiss tumbled through her.

"I...I," she tried, but the words still wouldn't come.

"Shhh, honey, come here." Zach tugged her back into his arms and tucked her head beneath his chin.

He murmured soothing words as he smoothed his hands down her back in long, comforting strokes.

Gradually her heartbeat slowed. The sound of his beneath her ear steadied as well.

Her gaze rose to his. He looked down at her, his eyes dark with passion. How long had it been since someone had looked at her that way?

He started to say something.

She cut him off. "Don't even think about apologizing for kissing me again."

Zach chuckled. He dropped a quick kiss on her upturned lips. "I wouldn't think of it." Then he turned serious. "Is this going to complicate things? Make it weird for us to be here together? 'Cause, Jess, I have to tell you, after this, I'm not going to be able to stop myself from kissing you again."

****

Zach wanted to kiss her again.

Jessica's mind whirled with the revelation as she sat out on the deck after dinner. She propelled the swing with her foot. The gentle rocking motion soothed her. She'd managed to make it through the meal, although food had a hard time making it over the lump of excitement in her throat.

She'd reacted as if it had been her very first kiss. Which maybe wasn't too far from the truth. Had she ever been kissed like Zach had kissed her? A kiss that made her body hum all the way down to her toes and into the deepest depths of her soul?

Could a kiss really feel like that? Didn't the tingly shivers racing along the nerves in her body only exist in the movies or in books? They certainly hadn't existed in her life. Until now.

Was she reading too much into it? Probably.

"Hey, mind if I join you?"

Even the sound of his voice sent a small thrill through her. She scooted over to make room for him on the swing. He sat, not quite touching her, but close enough so that his heat penetrated her light T-shirt.

"I thought you had work to do."

Zach looked away. "Uh, I... No, that is, it can wait until morning."

"Have you been working so hard around here to avoid me?" she asked shrewdly.

He glanced at her, then away again. "Sort of. Don't get me wrong. There's plenty to do, but it also made it easier to stay away. I wasn't sure I could trust myself around you."

Her breath caught. "And now?"

He didn't answer right away. "I won't ever do anything you don't want me to do," he said finally.

The soft words curled into her heart.

They fell silent. A breeze rustled the leaves of the nearby trees. Below, the stream burbled. A bullfrog added his hoarse *grrmp* to the nighttime symphony.

Zach picked up the beer bottle he'd set on the deck.

"Do you have a beer every night?"

He stopped with the bottle halfway to his lips, before lowering it. "No, not every night." He paused and looked at her. "Would it bother you if I did?"

Jessica shrugged and looked away. Even after the mind-melting kiss they'd shared, she still didn't feel comfortable revealing deep, dark secrets.

He set the bottle down and then turned toward her.

Unconsciously, she tensed. Was he going to kiss her again already? Were things moving too fast? Despite her response to him earlier, she was unsure, nervous. Was he expecting more?

But he didn't touch her.

"It must have been great coming here as a kid."

She let out her breath. "I loved it. Not so much when I was a teenager."

"Really? Why?"

"I felt cooped up, like I had no place to go."

"With all this wide-open space?" Zach swept out his arm.

"Let's just say family vacations weren't really my style in high school. I wanted to be on my own. Independent."

"Teenage rebellion. We all go through it, I suppose."

"Oh, I rebelled all right. You see, Daddy missed his calling. He should have been a Southern Baptist preacher. Hell, fire, and damnation were his trademarks. Of course, the more he told me not to do something, the more I wanted to do it."

"Sounds about right."

"I took it to the extreme. I had sex with my first boyfriend when I was sixteen."

Zach whistled.

"Yeah. Mom cried the first time she saw him. Of course he had a nose ring and hair longer than hers. Looking back now I can't say I blamed her."

"Then what?"

"I moved out and followed another boyfriend to the West Coast when I turned eighteen."

"Bet that didn't go over too well."

"To say the least."

"So, how did you wind up back here?"

Jessica hesitated. She'd already revealed far more than she'd intended. But talking to Zach was easy. Natural. She shrugged, what the hell? In for a penny, in for a pound. "Then I continued to make one bad decision after another for the next ten years. That's what brought me here. I needed distance from...the latest horrible decision."

"You haven't been back in ten years?"

"Only for short visits from time to time. I never stayed too long."

"If things were so bad, why didn't you let anyone

know? Ben thought you had a great life out on the coast."

"That's what I wanted everyone to think."

"Why? Don't you think your family would have wanted to know?"

She shrugged. "I didn't want them to worry." Or know what a complete failure she was. "Besides, when things went wrong, I was too embarrassed to let anyone know. I wanted to handle it on my own. I was the tough chick, you know?"

"Ah, so that explains the tattoo." Zach's voice held a teasing note.

"Tattoo?"

"Your butterfly." His hand motioned to the small of her back.

"Oh, right." Sometimes she forgot she even had a tattoo. Other days it provided a colorful reminder of past mistakes and her reckless impulsiveness.

"Why a butterfly?"

"No special reason. I liked the way it looked."

Zach nodded. "It suits you."

"You think so?"

"Definitely."

When he didn't elaborate, she turned to him. "What about you?"

"No tattoos."

She shook her head. "That's not what I meant. Tell me something about yourself."

"Like what?"

"Anything. I really don't know anything about you."

"I grew up in town here. Never lived anywhere else."

"What is your family like? Any brothers or sisters?"

"I have one of each. Van and Ellen."

"Van? That's a unique name."

Zach smirked. "Yeah, I think my parents named

him for the place he was conceived."

"What?"

"I've never actually asked, but it's always been a hunch."

"Interesting."

"Yeah, right." Zach laughed.

"No, really. Your family sounds interesting."

"That's one way to put it."

"What are your parents like?"

"Busy." His tone was clipped. "Mom and Dad work all the time. Always have, always will. They never have any time to enjoy themselves."

"That's too bad."

"Van and Ellen are just like them." Disapproval colored his voice.

"How so?"

"Ellen's an accountant, and Van is studying to be a lawyer. Talk about high-stress, have-no-fun jobs."

"None of that for you, huh?"

"Nope. I like taking things easy and living life to the fullest. That's why I like working at The Corral. The people are great. It's an easy schedule, I have my days free most of the time. And I can do something like this on the side."

"What about the future? Are you going to work there forever? Don't you want a real job?"

Zach shrugged. "I'm happy working there now. The future will take care of itself. There's no need for me to worry about it. For now I'm going to take life one day at a time."

The familiar-sounding words settled like a heavy weight over Jessica. How many of her poor decisions had started with listening to, and agreeing with, guys who sounded just like Zach? At one time she'd wanted the same kind of carefree life he talked about.

Look where it had gotten her.

She'd learned her lessons. She had the emotional scars to prove it. If she ever got involved in a relationship again, and at this point that was a big maybe, it wouldn't be with someone like Zach.

On some level this saddened her, because although he kissed like no body's business and made her feel things she'd long forgotten how to feel, he wasn't really any better than all the others.

"Jess?" Zach's voice broke into her troubled thoughts.

"Hmn?"

"You got awfully quiet there. I thought maybe you fell asleep on me."

"No."

"Come on." He rose and held out his hand, then hauled her to her feet when she placed her hand in his. "It's getting late. We should probably turn in."

Jessica's heart stuttered, and her imagination flew into overdrive. Did he mean it to sound like they were going to turn in together? He said he wouldn't be able to stop himself from kissing her again. Would he want to take it even further?

He leaned down toward her. Her pulse rate increased. The breath stuck in her throat.

His lips grazed her forehead. "Good night, Jess." He picked up the beer bottle he'd set aside and poured the contents over the edge of the deck. "See you in the morning," he said over his shoulder before disappearing into the house.

****

Zach lay awake for a long time trying to figure out the puzzle that was Jessica Hart. For such a free-spirited person, she sure had issues with his career choice. All-in-all she was a bundle of contradictions. The uncertainty in her eyes earlier when she'd asked why he hadn't kissed her again was a direct contrast to the mind-melting kiss they'd shared. Why in the world would she think he didn't like kissing her?

Fact of the matter was, he liked kissing her too much. Which wasn't good. She was Ben's granddaughter. That, more than anything, made her off limits. And even though he'd told her he wouldn't be able to resist kissing her, that's exactly what he needed to do.

He didn't want to betray Ben's trust.

And he didn't want to add to the hurt lurking in Jessica's eyes. Despite the outward appearance of having everything together, beneath the surface he sensed a vulnerability about her. She was fragile. Hurting about something.

The butterfly suited her perfectly, even if she didn't realize it. Beautiful, yet delicate. One wrong touch and she'd fall to pieces. She'd opened up tonight and shared a part of herself with him, but he didn't want to push her too fast. Scare her away. He could sense the hurt bottled up inside of her, and he didn't want to add to it.

Ironically he'd done just that with his determination to stay away from her. To save her from his baser instincts. She'd taken his apology for kissing her that first time the wrong way.

Jake had hit the nail on the head with that one.

****

The next night, Zach sought Jake out as soon as he got to The Corral. "You should write a book."

"What?" Jake turned from the bar with a puzzled frown.

Zach sat down on a high stool next to him. "You were dead on about me apologizing to Jessica for kissing her."

Jake grinned. "I suppose it wouldn't be nice of me to say 'I told you so'?"

"Nope, not nice at all."

"So, what happened?" Jake took a bite out of the hamburger in front of him. He made a face. "The food here sucks. Want to sneak into the kitchen and make me a real burger?"

"Sure."

The two made their way upstairs and into the kitchen.

"Hey, Rico," Zach addressed a short man in a paper chef's hat. "Mind if I make Jake a burger?"

"Make yourself at home."

Zach tied on an apron over his jeans and shirt, washed his hands, and got to work. While he diced and chopped, he picked up the thread of their conversation.

"She came right out and asked me why I hadn't tried to kiss her again. Wondered if I didn't like it."

"You never listen." Jake's expression was smug. "What did you say?"

"I didn't say anything." He molded the ground beef mixture into a patty and slapped it onto the grill. "I kissed her again."

"Please tell me you didn't apologize again."

Zach grinned. "Nope, not this time."

"So, what then?"

"Nothing. We had dinner, she cooked. We sat outside for a while, and then we went to bed. Separately."

Jake's face fell.

Zach flipped the burger, then turned to Jake, waving the spatula. "She told me a little about her past, but I get the feeling there's a lot more she's not telling me."

"Everyone has a past."

"I know, but I think this is something big."

"Did you change your mind about having a relationship with her?"

Zach placed the burger on a bun and handed the plate to Jake before answering. "She's Ben's granddaughter."

Jake doused the burger with ketchup and

mustard before adding a pickle. "You've said that about a million times. What's that got to do with anything?" He took a bite. "Oh, man, now this is a burger."

Zach leaned his hips against the counter. "I feel like I'm betraying Ben every time I look at her, let alone kiss her."

Jake took another bite of burger, chewed, and swallowed. "It's not like she's sixteen. She's a grown woman. Believe me, she's not doing anything she doesn't want to be doing. She wouldn't be doing it otherwise."

"I guess." She'd seemed so vulnerable, when she'd looked up at him with those big green eyes and asked why he didn't want to kiss her again. And why would she think he didn't feel anything when he kissed her? Hell, he still felt it.

"Look." Jake downed the rest of his burger, then wiped his hands on a napkin. "If it bothers you that much, don't kiss her again."

Zach grimaced. "Easier said than done." He feared even pain of death couldn't stop him from kissing her again given the opportunity. No matter what he'd vowed.

"True enough. Once you've opened the door to the promised land, it's hard to shut it again."

Zach laughed as they walked out of the kitchen. "Seriously. Think about a book."

Chapter Eight

"You up for some fun today?"

Jessica looked up from her breakfast drink and eyed Zach warily. "What kind of fun?"

Zach grinned, causing her heart to stutter. "I thought we'd toss a couple of canoes in the back of my truck and head over to the river."

"I haven't been canoeing in ages."

"It's like riding a bike, you never really forget how to do it."

Jessica hesitated.

"Come on," Zach cajoled. "I'll give you a refresher course."

Getting out and about did sound like a good idea. As much as she'd sought the peaceful solitude of the cabin, she hadn't left it since she'd gotten there. Maybe the time had come to venture out into the real world for the day. "Okay."

"Great. We can throw some picnic things together and head out in say, an hour?"

In less time than that they were headed toward the river.

While he drove, Zach explained the procedure. They'd leave his truck in the parking lot by the launching site. Downriver, when they were done, he'd call a shuttle to come and get them to bring them back to the lot.

Once there, Zach lifted the canoes out of the bed of the truck and placed them at the water's edge.

Jessica gulped when he yanked his T-shirt over his head. She'd never seen him without a shirt on.

She'd bet good money the well-defined muscles

in his chest resulted from honest work, not a daily regimen at the gym. A light dusting of hair covered his breastbone and spread across his pecs. His stomach, firm and flat, boasted the proverbial, but subtle, six-pack. The ridge of his pelvic bone jutted above the low-riding waistband of his swim trunks.

He was sexy as hell.

"Anything you want to put in here?" He held a waterproof bag toward her.

"What?" Jessica jerked her gaze away from his naked torso. "Uh, no, I'm good."

He tossed his T-shirt into the bag, then pulled out a bottle of sunscreen. He applied the lotion to his chest and back, while Jessica checked out a canoe that didn't need to be checked out.

"Sunblock?"

"What?"

Zach waved the bottle. "Do you need sunscreen?"

"Uh, sure, thanks." She grabbed the bottle, ignoring the tiny jolt when his fingers brushed hers. She applied the lotion to her arms and face, before spreading some above the scoop neck of her tank top. She squeezed more into her hand and aimed at the awkward spot across the middle of her back below her neck.

"Do you need some help with that?"

"No."

He raised an eyebrow at her vehement tone.

"I mean, no, thanks, I'm okay." She handed him the bottle, avoiding his gaze.

"All right." After putting the lotion in the waterproof bag, he folded the top over, tied it closed, and secured it to a seat in one of the canoes. He fastened the bag containing their lunch to the other vessel. "Ready for that refresher course?"

She nodded.

"Okay, canoeing is all about balance. Sit in the middle of the seat and let the flow of the river do most of the work. Stroke a bit on each side with your paddle to stay on course. You don't want to overdo it. Use nice gentle stokes." He paused. "Any questions?"

"What if it tips over?"

He grinned. "You get wet. There hasn't been much rain lately, so the river's pretty low and should be running slowly. We should have a nice, easy ride."

He shoved one canoe into the water. "Ready?"

Jessica nodded. Zach held the small vessel steady while she climbed in, then nudged it farther out onto the river. He jumped into his own canoe and then pushed off from the shore with his paddle.

He maneuvered alongside her. "Lead or follow?"

She grabbed a paddle. "Follow."

"We'll go for an hour or so then find a sandbar and have lunch, okay?"

"Okay."

He headed down the river. She dug her paddle into the water and followed in his wake. At first she wobbled, but soon the familiar rhythm settled over her as she dipped into the water with sure, even strokes.

Zach looked over his shoulder at her. "There you go. See? Just like riding a bike."

Now that she had the rhythm down, Jessica took in more of her surroundings. Trees lined the banks of the river, providing a lush pathway as she and Zach made their way along in the gently moving current. Birds circled overhead, calling softly to one another. A slight breeze ruffled her ponytail and provided a measure of relief from the warmth of the sunshine pouring down.

Ahead of her, Zach plied his paddles, the muscles in his back bunching and flexing with the easy movement. She jerked her gaze to the trees.

"So, uh, do you do this often?"

"Not as often as I'd like. Careful," he said over his shoulder, indicating a log protruding from the water.

She steered around the obstacle, pleased when the canoe responded readily to her strokes.

"I would have thought with your carefree lifestyle, stuff like this is all you'd do." The words sounded snottier than she'd intended. What had made her say that? She didn't want to ruin their pleasurable day.

"Oh, I find lots of things to keep myself busy."

She couldn't tell by the tone of his voice if she'd offended him with her comment or not.

"Girlfriends?" Jessica bit her lip, horrified the question slipped out.

"On occasion."

"Recently?" Her mouth had a mind of its own.

"No, not recently. I date from time to time, not as much as Jake, of course. I've had a couple semi-serious relationships, but nothing ever really came of them."

She mulled this over, listening to the soft splash of their paddles as they dipped into the water.

"What about you?"

"What about me?"

"Any recent boyfriends?"

Oh crap. Why had she started this conversation? "No, not really." It wasn't exactly a lie. But then again it wasn't the whole truth. Before he could ask anymore questions, she asked one of her own. "So, Jake dates a lot?"

"Yeah, he's the resident Casanova at The Corral. All the ladies like Jake, and Jake likes all the ladies." He paused. "Why do you ask?" His tone was a little more than curious.

"Just making conversation."

"I don't think he's your type."

"What?"

"Jake. I don't think he's your type," Zach repeated.

She bit back a smile, even though his back was to her, and he couldn't see her. "Zach, I'm not interested in Jake."

"Oh," he said. "Okay."

Silence fell once again. They floated down the river for another half hour before Zach pointed ahead. "There's a small rapid ahead, so—"

"Rapid?" A hint of panic crept into her voice.

"Nothing big," Zach assured her. "There's a slight bend in the river, so steer wide as we go around the rocks. Just follow me."

"Okay." She gripped her paddle. The canoe bounced over the small waves, but maneuvering around the rocks proved easier than she'd expected.

Zach looked over his shoulder as they drifted out into the straightaway once again. "That's my girl."

Excited by her small victory over nature, Jessica didn't even reprimand him for the comment.

"You getting hungry?"

"I could eat." She also had to pee, but Zach didn't need to know that.

"There's a gravel bar a couple hundred yards up." He pointed with his paddle. "We'll beach the canoes there and have lunch."

"Sounds like a plan."

The spot Zach indicated appeared after a couple more minutes, and he applied more force to his paddles to ground the aluminum craft on the makeshift beach. Jessica paddled close so he could grab the front of her canoe and wedge it onto the shore.

He held out his hand. She grasped it, and he helped her from the canoe.

She scanned the area, finding a spot where the gravel veered away into the trees. She headed toward it.

"Where you going?"

"Uh, I just need to, um, I'll be right back."

Zach hid a smile and bent over the canoe. "Sure."

By the time she returned, he'd arranged their picnic items on a towel. She sat down next to him, folding her legs beneath her.

She averted her gaze from his sun-dappled shoulders and bit into the peanut butter and jelly sandwich he handed her. She savored the nutty taste on her tongue. "Yum. I haven't had one of these since I was ten years old."

"Ah, but you've never had one with my secret ingredient."

"What's your secret ingredient?"

"Not very familiar with the definition of secret, huh?" he teased.

"Come on, I won't tell."

"Neither will I." He considered her while he chewed a bite of his sandwich. "Tell you what. For a price, I'll let you know."

"What's the price?" Jessica asked warily, noting the twinkle in his eye.

"A kiss." His gaze dropped to her lips.

Her mouth went dry, making swallowing the bite of sticky peanut butter difficult. Kissing Zach on the deck or in the kitchen was one thing, but kissing Zach out on an open beach when he had no shirt on was another matter entirely. She bit her lip.

He raised his eyes to hers again. "Deal?"

Without really meaning to, but unable to resist the look in his eyes, she nodded. "Deal," she whispered.

Zach leaned toward her, bracing himself on the towel. His lips touched hers, then darted away, only to return and nibble once again. He teased her mouth with feather-light strokes, before deepening the kiss, parting her lips with insistent pressure from his own.

Despite the hot sunshine pouring down, fine

shivers raced along Jessica's nerves and danced in her stomach. He raised one hand to her face. His knuckles brushed her cheek. The kiss softened. He pulled back.

Slowly, her breath returned to normal. She took a deep gulp of air and let it out. "So?" she asked. Her voice only shook a little.

"So what?"

"So, what's the secret ingredient?"

Zach smiled and the twinkle returned to his eyes. "There isn't one."

Jessica's mouth dropped open. "What?"

He kissed her open mouth. "There's no secret ingredient," he whispered. His breath caressed her skin.

"Uh!" Her palm smacked against his bare skin as she shoved him away. "You."

He grinned unrepentantly.

"That's low," she said, trying to sound as fierce as possible when her heart still hadn't slowed to its normal pace.

He shrugged. His expression sobered. "Are you really mad?"

She sighed. How could she be mad when his kisses made her feel more alive than ever before in her entire life? "No."

"Good." He leaned in and kissed her again. A brief touch of his lips against hers. "You ready to hit the road? Or the river that is?"

"Sure, I'm set."

They gathered the remains of their lunch, shoving everything back into the waterproof bag. Zach fastened it to a seat in his canoe.

Jessica climbed back into her canoe. Zach did the same.

"You want to lead this time?"

She looked out over the water. "The river looks wide enough, why don't we go side by side?"

"Side by side it is."

She pushed against the gravel with her paddle, and the canoe scraped against the rocks until it floated freely on the water.

They paddled leisurely down the river. Occasionally Zach turned to comment about something on the shore, or a rock or log in the water she needed to steer around. But mostly he remained silent.

Jessica didn't mind. The silence was companionable and allowed her to enjoy the sounds of nature around her. The chittering of birds in the trees. The rushing of the river as they passed by outcroppings of rocks. Even the buzz of insects as they flew around her head.

After about an hour, Zach turned. "We're coming up to another set of rapids. Just do like you did last time. Take it wide. Use the paddle to control your direction."

"Got it."

"We'll go one at a time."

"Okay."

The choppy water of the rapids approached sooner than she'd expected. Jessica floated ahead of Zach. She dug her paddle in the water, steering through the maze of rocks dotting the river. A large rock loomed suddenly, and she stroked hard on the left to veer around it. But she over-compensated. Before she could react, the canoe tilted and spilled her into the water.

She surfaced to the sound of panic in Zach's voice. "Jessica?"

"I'm okay," she assured him, shaking water out of her eyes. She grabbed the empty canoe as it floated by. It twisted and banged against one of the rocks, wrenching her arm and jerking her around. Her back slammed into something hard, robbing her of breath. A wave crashed over her head.

She came up gasping.

"Jessica, let go of the canoe." Zach's voice held a deeper note of concern. He paddled closer.

Despite the pain radiating from her shoulder down her arm, she gripped the canoe, unwilling to let it float away. She grasped the aluminum edge tighter as the shifting current dragged her under again.

Chapter Nine

Strong arms towed her to the surface. "Damn it, Jess, let go."

"The canoe," she gasped, straining to hold on despite the opposite pull of the water.

"I don't care about the damn canoe."

"But—"

"Let go."

This time she obeyed the urgency in his voice. She released her grip. Zach held her to him and swam with a strong, one-armed stroke to the bank of the river, where his canoe was lodged against the rocks.

"I need you to climb up. Can you do that?"

Unlike the spot where they'd stopped for lunch, large rocks lined this part of the shore. They formed a steep bank.

"Yes," she said, but her voice hitched around the word, betraying her lack of confidence.

"I'll help you."

His hands spanned her waist and lifted her from the water. She scrambled up the rocks, groping for a handhold. He guided from behind until she rested on the top.

Her breath huffed out in short pants. A deeper breath sent a searing wave of pain across her back.

Zach levered himself up, the muscles in his arms bulging with the effort. He sat beside her, his chest heaving. "You scared the hell out of me."

"I scared the hell out of me, too." She tried a smile, but it turned into a wince when she raised her arm to tighten her ponytail.

"What's wrong?"

Jessica gingerly rotated her shoulder. "I must have pulled something. And my back is killing me. I banged it against a rock."

Zach leaned behind her and raised her sopping tank top. His fingers brushed against her spine. She jumped away from his light touch, the movement spreading another wave of pain.

"Sorry," he murmured. "You're going to have a bruise. It's already red. We'll have to get some ice on it as soon as we get home."

She nodded. "I'm really sorry about the canoe."

He cursed. "How many times do I have to tell you? I don't care about the canoe."

"But it's gone. And the bag with your shirt and the sunblock."

"Jessica. Look at me. I. Don't. Care. If it's a problem, I'll buy Ben a new one."

She nodded. "Thank you for saving me."

Emotion flashed in his eyes. He nodded. "We can rest here as long as you like. When you're ready, we'll double up in my canoe."

"I'll be ready in a minute."

"No rush."

After a few moments, she carefully got to her feet. Already her body was stiff and sore. "Okay, I'm set. Let's get going."

Zach rose to stand beside her. He looked down at the canoe. "This is going to be tricky. The canoe is lodged pretty well up against the rocks. I'll lower you down, and then I'll get in."

She looked at the water. It seemed really far away, more so because of the steep incline leading down to it.

"Give me your good arm." He grasped her upper arm and held on while she scooted down the bank. He squatted at the top, stretching to keep his hold until she made it into the canoe.

He followed her down. The canoe rocked as he got in behind her. Jessica grabbed the sides, her knuckles turning white.

"You good?"

"Sure."

"Let me know if you want to stop and pull over for any reason."

"I just want to get back to the truck and go home." A sudden lethargy weighed her down. All she wanted to do was crawl into bed.

"We're almost at the end. Then we have to call the shuttle to take us back to the parking lot."

The remainder of the trek down the river didn't take long, and soon they were in a van heading to where they'd left Zach's truck. The pain in her shoulder and back had turned into a constant, dull throb.

He settled her in the cab, tossed the canoe into the bed, and then poked his head in her window. "You okay?"

"I'll live," she murmured, leaning her head against the headrest and closing her eyes.

"I'll be right back."

Less than five minutes later, he spoke again. "Jess?"

She opened her eyes.

He passed her a baggie filled with ice. "You can alternate between your shoulder and your back."

"Thank you." She plopped the bag on her shoulder, closed her eyes, and fell asleep.

"Jessica." Zach's voice brought her awake.

She forced her eyes open.

"We're home."

"I don't want to budge." The ice had numbed her shoulder, but with the slightest movement the pain would return.

Zach smiled and got out of the truck. On her side, he opened the passenger door. "Come on, you'll be more comfortable in your bed."

She dragged herself down off the seat and shuffled toward the front door. He followed her up the stairs. She sank onto the bed.

"Why don't you get out of those damp clothes, I'll get you more ice."

He disappeared out the door.

She tossed her wet clothes in a pile on the floor, then pulled on an oversized T-shirt. She slid beneath the covers. Her aching body sank into the mattress.

Zach's footfalls on the stairs announced his return. "Here's your ice. Why don't you turn on your side and set it against your back?"

She rolled. Zach placed the cold compress against her spine. "I'll check on you in a little while."

"Mmhm." She closed her eyes and drifted to sleep.

****

Downstairs in the kitchen, Zach grabbed a beer from the refrigerator. He sank into a chair. He took a sip from the bottle. His hand shook.

He cursed and set the drink down.

In his mind he pictured the water closing over Jessica's head.

He rose. He'd left her less than five minutes ago, but he needed to see her again. Needed to assure himself she was really all right.

He walked into her room on silent feet. Her even breathing told him she was asleep. He stared down at her. A riot of damp auburn curls spilled across her pillow. One hand cradled her cheek.

He resisted the urge to touch her.

Careful not to wake her, he adjusted the towel-wrapped baggie resting against her back. The skin along her spine had turned a dull purple color. He replaced the ice.

She stirred.

He sat down in the nearby chair and watched

her sleep. For all his vows to the contrary, despite his best attempts, he always wound up hurting Jessica. First emotionally. Now physically.

He shuddered again as the image of her in the water formed in his mind. The bruises on her back were his fault. He put his face in his hands, guilt flooding through him at the proof of the pain he'd caused. His day of fun had turned out to be anything but. He should have been more careful.

But even before that. On the gravel bar where they'd had their picnic. He'd kissed her. Again. Despite his promise to himself not to.

Kissing Jessica wasn't good for her. Too many past hurts still shadowed her eyes. But the temptation had been too powerful. And he hadn't been strong enough to resist.

A battle raged inside him. The desire to protect and care for her warred with his desire for her. Would he be strong enough the next time? Or would he give in to the baser side of his nature?

And what would Ben say if he ever found out? How would Zach face the other man when he returned home? Look him in the eye, when he'd betrayed his trust.

Zach leaned back in the chair and sighed. He'd sure made a mess of things.

He must have dozed off, because he awakened to the sound of his name.

"Zach?"

He bolted upright. "What?"

"What are you doing in here?" The slight slur of sleep couldn't hide the wariness in her voice.

Damn. He didn't want her to be afraid. He cleared his throat. "I wanted to make sure you were all right."

"Oh."

He rose and stepped to the bed. "Do you need anything?"

She dragged the covers up to her neck. "No, I'm okay."

"More ice?"

"No, not right now."

"Well, I'll be downstairs if you need anything."

"Zach?" Her soft voice stopped him at the door. He turned.

"Thank you."

"No problem." He nodded toward the chair. "I didn't mean to frighten you."

"Y...you didn't. I was just surprised to see you there." She paused. "I meant thank you for saving me earlier."

He nodded again. "Get some rest. I'll see you in the morning."

****

Jessica awoke to the usual sound of chirping birds the next morning. She rolled onto her back.

Pain shot up her spine. She groaned. And took stock of the rest of her injuries. Her shoulder ached. Her head throbbed. She felt as if she'd been run over by Pops' tractor.

With slow, deliberate movements, she eased herself to a sitting position until she could swing her legs over the side of the bed. She got dressed and then headed downstairs.

Zach sat at the kitchen table. He looked up when she walked into the room. "You're up and about early. I thought maybe you'd sleep in."

"I couldn't sleep anymore. I need to take an aspirin or something."

"Still sore?"

"Oh yeah."

"Have a seat." Zach rose. "I'll get you something."

"No, that's okay, I can—"

He put a gentle hand on her good shoulder and urged her into a chair. "I insist."

He set a glass of water and two aspirin in front of her. She swallowed both in one gulp.

"Hungry?"

"I could eat something."

"Protein drink or something more substantial?"

She glanced over at the remains of Zach's breakfast on the counter. "What did you make for yourself?"

"Omelet."

"Sounds divine." She rotated her shoulder in an attempt to coax tightened muscles to relax. Pain radiated down her arm, but soon subsided as she continued the slow, steady movement.

"You should take it easy today." Zach placed a plate in front of her.

She looked up with a smile. "I didn't have big plans anyway. Thanks." She cut a slice of the omelet with her fork and raised it to her lips. The fluffy egg concoction melted in her mouth. The taste of tomato, sharp cheddar, and herbs burst to life on her tongue. "Oh, Zach, you've outdone yourself again."

He sat down across from her. "You flatter me."

She took another bite, chewed, and swallowed. "No, I mean it. Have you ever considered being a professional chef?"

"You mean get a real job?" He winked.

She smiled, even though something about his teasing tone made her sad. "Something like that."

"Nope. A real job would take all the fun out of life."

He spoke the words in jest, but Jessica couldn't help but be disappointed by them. He really had no long terms plans for his life.

She changed the subject. "What are you up to today?"

"I need to do some weeding in the garden, but that's about it. Why don't you hang out at the creek? The cool water will probably feel good on your shoulder and your back. Sit where the waterfall comes down and let it run over your shoulder."

"That does sound nice. Like my own personal spa."

"Without the spa price." He rose and cleared the dishes from the table. "Maybe I'll join you down there when I'm through."

"Great."

Jessica took Zach's advice and headed down to the creek. The rocks formed a natural chair at the base of the waterfall. She sat and let the cool water cascade over her shoulder. The pulsating effect soon eased the remaining ache.

After a half hour, she climbed out of the creek. She stretched out on her stomach on a towel and let the warmth of the sun dry the water from her body.

The rumble of an ATV approaching made her sit up and grab her T-shirt. She tugged it over her head as Zach rode into view. He stopped the vehicle on the rocks, then climbed off.

"How's it going? Feeling better?" He dropped down beside her.

"Almost good as new."

"That's what I like to hear." He nodded toward the water. "You going back in?"

"No, I don't think so."

His glance swept over her. She resisted the urge to tug her T-shirt further down.

He studied her. "You really did scare the hell out of me yesterday." His lips quirked in a half smile.

Hers lifted in response. "Yeah, I scared the hell out of me, too." She looked down, then met his gaze again. "I can't stop thinking about yesterday."

"I'd never let anything happen to you." He raised a hand to her face.

"I know." She blinked back tears. "That's what I can't stop thinking about." Her hand gripped his, holding it against her skin. "You're a good man,

Zach."

Something flickered in his eyes. He brought her hand to his mouth and kissed the palm.

Her mouth went dry. She licked her lips.

His eyes tracked the gesture, before he raised his gaze to hers. The mocha irises darkened, although indecision swam in the deep orbs.

She willed him to kiss her. He smiled, as if reading her thoughts, but made no move toward her. Her heart thudded. Could he hear it? Well, if he wasn't going to kiss her, she'd have to kiss him.

She took a deep breath, then slid one hand to the back of his head, threading her fingers through his hair. The other flattened against his chest. She leaned toward him. His eyes darkened further.

A millimeter at a time, she brought her mouth closer to his. At the last moment, before their lips met, she darted her gaze to his, closed her eyes, and touched her mouth to his.

Tentative at first, but then bolder when his mouth opened beneath the light pressure from hers, Jessica kissed him. Their breath mingled.

Beneath her palm, his heartbeat accelerated. A new sense of confidence flooded through her. She touched her tongue to his bottom lip.

He groaned and wrapped his arms around her. She could feel a fine quiver in his muscles, but still he didn't take control of the kiss.

Her mouth worked against his until she needed to suck in a deep breath. She opened her eyes. His heartbeat tripped beneath her hand.

In that moment looking deep into his eyes, she discovered something. She wanted to make love with Zach.

Wanted—no, needed—to know if there was more to the weak-kneed feeling of kissing him.

If she trusted him with her life, shouldn't she be able to trust him with her body?

Not here and now. But soon.

She shivered. Not out of fear. But anticipation. She wanted to know what he felt like against her. Inside her.

She wanted to know if she could make him tremble and yearn the way she did. The way she did from just his kiss.

****

A mixed buzz of fear and anticipation hummed through her. The idea, and the excited vibration, seemed as foreign as an alien abduction. Which was kind of how she felt. As though some other force, some other being, had taken over her body and her mind. How long had it been since she'd wanted someone?

More importantly, how could she make Zach want her? Men always thought about sex, right? All she had to do was get him thinking about having sex with her.

She nibbled her lip. Easier said than done. She had no idea how to seduce a man. Was that even the right word?

She wasn't sure where to begin. And even if she did, would Zach be interested in her? In that way?

What would get him in the mood? A romantic dinner? A night out? Sexy clothes? She had no idea. She'd spent a lot of time avoiding anything sexual. How strange to be thinking about it again. To be thinking about initiating it herself set her stomach to quivering.

And led her back to one of her original questions. Where to start? She glanced around the room, seeking inspiration. Her gaze landed on her laptop.

Of course. The Internet. It had everything. She powered up the computer.

Now, what to type in? *Sex? Seduction?*

Her eyes widened and her jaw dropped at the

graphic pictures materializing on the screen. Whoa. That was a little advanced for her. She quickly X'd out of the page, a blush heating her cheeks.

Her fingers drummed on the laptop as she stared into space. The Internet wasn't going to work. At least not until she figured how to narrow down, and tame, her search. So, what now?

The empty screen taunted her. Her mind was just as blank.

With a heartfelt sigh, she switched off the computer, then swung her legs off the bed. Hopefully an idea would come to her soon. Time worked against her. She didn't want to rush things, but she did have somewhat of a deadline. Everything...the seduction, the sex...had to happen before Pops returned. Or before Zach got serious about moving back into his apartment. He hadn't mentioned it lately, and neither had she. And now, she didn't want him to leave. More than ever, she needed him to stay.

Inspiration struck later that night. Once again by unspoken agreement, she and Zach retired to the family room. He stretched out on the couch, and she curled up in Pops' chair by the unlit fireplace.

She settled her laptop across her knees. At the touch of a button, the screen glowed to life. She scrolled through her files of work in progress, looking for one in particular.

Ah, there it was.

She bit her lip, then clicked on the highlighted file. Zach usually wandered over to see what she was working on, and she hoped he'd do the same tonight.

It should at least give him something to think about.

They sat for about a half hour before Zach stretched. She smiled. She knew him well already.

She refused to dwell on why that wasn't good.

"Water?" he asked as he passed by her chair.

The question was rhetorical. He asked the same one whenever they sat like this.

As always, he handed her the water before leaning over the back of her chair to peer at her screen. Almost immediately he shifted.

She hid a smile and snuck a glance up at him out of the corner of her eye. His eyes grew wide as they flicked over her work.

After a moment he cleared his throat. "Uh, Jess, what is this site supposed to be selling?"

"Sex." She hoped she sounded as matter-of-fact as she wanted to. Truth be told, her heart raced and her hands shook. She tucked them in her lap to hide the tell-tale tremors. She wasn't sure how to go about seducing a man, but getting him thinking about sex had to be a good start, right?

"Sex?"

"Well, sex toys. And lotions, creams, lingerie, books, that sort of thing."

"Oh."

"Ever use any of this stuff before?"

"What?" The word sounded strangled.

"Just curious." She tried to sound innocent. Hard to do with her stomach inside out.

She looked up at him. Was he blushing?

His mouth opened. Then closed. His gaze met hers for a brief instant before darting away. "I, uh, I think I left the barn open. I need to go check." He turned on his heel. The door closed behind him.

Jessica collapsed back in the chair. She definitely had him thinking. Now how did she get him thinking about her?

Chapter Ten

Zach sucked in a deep breath, letting the cool evening air flood his lungs. He passed by the barn, its door securely closed and locked, and headed for the creek. He sat on a rock and stared out over the moonlit water.

The rushing water cascaded over the short waterfall with a muffled, thundering echo. He concentrated on the sound, hoping it would dispel the images burning in his mind.

Images of Jessica in one of the sexy nightgowns on her screen. Images of him rubbing scented lotion across her back and down her arms and legs. Images of the two of them coming together, their bodies slick with oil.

He groaned and buried his head in his hands.

Kissing Jessica was one thing. Making love to her was another.

He hadn't thought about that. Well, he hadn't *let* himself think about that.

Bad enough he wanted to kiss her all the time. He couldn't think about much else. And he shouldn't be thinking about even that.

Trouble was, he couldn't help himself. Jessica was sweet and beautiful and intriguing. And sexy as all hell. Kissing her was like nothing he'd ever experienced before. When *she'd* kissed *him* out by the creek the other day he'd almost lost control. Every male instinct in his body had screamed at him to take it further. To lower her onto the rocks and claim her. Take her as his own.

But she wasn't his to claim. Despite how

perfectly their bodies fit together when they kissed. Despite the way his heart beat a faster rhythm whenever they were in the same room. Despite his desire for her. She wasn't his.

She was Ben's granddaughter. To be entertaining thoughts about her in any other way was a betrayal. What would Ben say if he found out what Zach had done? What he'd imagined. What he desired.

****

A couple days later Jessica sought out Zach by the barn. She figured he'd had enough time to digest the web page she'd shown him, now it was time to get down to some real action.

"Do you feel like a swim?" She hoped the question sounded as nonchalant as she wanted it to. The whole seduction thing still filled her with uncertainty, but swimming should be a good place to start. They would both be wearing less clothing than usual.

"Sounds perfect." He wiped his arm across his forehead. "It's beastly out here today."

"Great. I'll go change and meet you back here." She hurried upstairs. The suit she'd chosen revealed more of her body than it hid. She hadn't worn anything nearly so daring in front of Zach. The black tank scooped low in the back, revealing her tattoo. The legs were cut high on her thighs, making her legs look longer.

She gnawed her lip. An awful lot of skin showed.

Then she straightened her shoulders and shook off her unease. If she wanted to entice Zach, she'd need to open up and feel more comfortable in her own skin.

She had to get over her fear.

She slipped flip flops on her feet. A sheer cover-up completed her outfit.

With a fortifying breath she headed down.

Zach had pulled two ATVs out of the barn. He sat astride his favorite red one.

"I'm all set," she announced to draw his attention.

He looked up. Sunglasses shaded his eyes, so she couldn't be sure, but had his gaze slid down her body before returning to her face?

Her heart pounded as she climbed aboard her vehicle. Had he noticed her suit?

At the creek Jessica climbed from the ATV. When she had Zach's attention, she let the cover-up slide from her shoulders to pool at her feet.

She cast a furtive glance over her shoulder. He'd paused in the act of stripping off his shirt.

With a noticeable shake of his head, he tossed the shirt on the rocks, discarded his sunglasses, and walked to the water's edge. He stared out over the rushing creek, but didn't jump in.

She took a moment to admire the sunlight playing over his shoulders before joining him. She placed her hand on his arm.

He jerked away. "Sorry," he mumbled. "You startled me."

"You going in?"

He glanced down at her. "Yeah." He made a clean dive.

They swam for a while, then spread towels out on the rocks.

"Zach?"

He turned toward her and raised an eyebrow. "What's up?"

"Can you, I mean would you, help me with this lotion? I don't want to burn, and I can't reach my back."

He swallowed. "You want me to put lotion on your back?" His voice sounded huskier than usual.

She held out the bottle. "If you don't mind?"

He hesitated before grabbing it from her. "Uh,

sure."

She rolled over onto her stomach and held her hair out of the way. In a moment his fingers brushed her back. The lotion cooled her sun-warmed flesh, but the pressure of his hands as he rubbed the thick liquid into her skin created a new rush of heat. Heat that had nothing to do with the sun.

Could he feel it too?

His fingers feathered over the small of her back, where her tattoo was visible in the low scoop of her suit.

His hands stilled. He cleared his throat. "Uh, you're all set."

She rolled over, then propped herself on her elbows and stared up at him. "Thanks."

"No problem." His voice sounded strained.

She wished his sunglasses weren't hiding his expression.

"Do you need me to put lotion on you?"

"No." His voice held a slight hint of panic. "I mean, thanks, but I think I'll go back in."

"You just got out."

He tossed his sunglasses on the towel, then stood. His glance slid down her body. For a brief moment his eyes met hers before darting away. "It's hotter than I thought out here." He turned and dove into the water.

****

A few days later Zach found Jessica in the family room. She was curled up on the couch reading a book.

"I'm going to do some laundry. Anything you need thrown in?"

Jessica shook her head. "No. Thanks. Oh, but I think I have some things in the dryer." She sat up.

"Sit," he said. "I'll take it out."

"Thanks."

In the laundry room, Zach tossed his clothes in

the machine, added the detergent, and started the cycle. Whistling, he snagged the basket from the floor, then reached into the dryer to grab Jessica's things. Soft satin slid through his hands. He looked down. The whistle froze in his throat.

A silky thong dangled from his fingers. He swallowed.

A peek at the remainder of the items in the dryer revealed a jumble of panties and bras. He closed his eyes and groaned. Behind his closed lids, a vision of Jessica in the skimpy garments played in his mind. His heart tripped faster.

He ground his teeth together as his eyes popped open. With a determined shake of his head, he forced the image away. Doing his best to ignore the erotic feel of satin and lace slipping through his fingers, he transferred the rest of her things from the dyer to the basket, then closed the door with a little more force than necessary. The resulting bang echoed in the tiny room.

He strode into the kitchen. Jessica had her back to him, fiddling with something on the counter. His gaze drifted over the curve of her hips. What was she wearing beneath her jeans?

He blinked and swallowed. "Here's your laundry. I'll put it on the steps for you."

She turned, an ice cream cone in her hand. "Thanks."

Her gaze slid to the dripping confection she held. "Oops." Her tongue darted out to lick the ice cream dribbling down the side of the cone onto her fingers before disappearing back between her lips. "Mnnn." She closed her eyes on a blissful sigh.

Zach nearly dropped the laundry basket. His eyes were riveted on her as she repeated the action. What would her tongue feel like on him? His breathing grew shallow.

She caught his stare. "You want some ice

cream?" She waved the cone.

"No." His voice cracked.

A bemused expression settled over her face. "Are you okay? You sound funny."

"Fine." He pivoted and headed for the door. He needed to get the hell out of there.

"Zach?"

He turned halfway back toward her. "Yeah?"

"My laundry?" She gestured toward the basket in his arms.

"Oh. Right. Sorry." He set it on the stairs, then almost ran out the door.

****

That night at The Corral, he and Jake sat in their usual spots at the bar before opening.

"So how's it going with Jessica?" Jake asked. "How's that whole living-in-the-same-house thing working out?"

Silky lingerie popped into Zach's mind. "Not good."

Jake shot him an *I-told-you-so* look.

"Everything she does turns me on. The other day she innocently asked me to put sunscreen on her back, and it almost killed me. And then today, the laundry. And the ice cream. Oh, the ice cream." He bit back a moan at the memory.

"Ice cream?" Jake sounded puzzled.

"Never mind," Zach muttered. His head dropped into his hands. "I'm going insane."

"Then do something about it." Jake's voice was matter of fact.

"I can't." Zach huffed out a breath. "She's Ben's granddaughter."

Jake cast him a wry look. "You're really hung up on that, aren't you? Personally, I don't see what the big deal is. You're both adults. Consenting adults. Just let it happen. If she's sending you all these signals, obviously she wants to."

Zach shook his head. "She's not sending signals. Problem is, I take one look at her, and all my common sense flies out the window. I can't think straight."

Jake laughed. "You've got it bad, man. Tell you what, the girl I'm going out with tomorrow has a sister. I could hook you up."

"No thanks." The refusal came quickly to his lips. Although making love to Jessica was out of the question, being with someone else held little appeal.

Jake shrugged. "Your loss." He paused. "So, what are you going to do?"

Zach grimaced. "Get used to taking cold showers."

Jake threw back his head and laughed. "Nice." He clapped Zach on the shoulder. "You're a stronger man than I am." He sauntered away as customers descended into the bar.

****

Jessica couldn't tell if her plan was working or not. She had the feeling she'd gotten Zach thinking, but she wasn't sure. Several times she'd caught him staring at her, but he looked away as soon as their eyes met. What did that mean?

Were her little attempts at seduction having any effect at all? He'd seemed unsettled after retrieving her bras and panties from the dryer, and she hadn't even planned that one. He still kissed her from time to time, but that seemed different too. Almost as if he were reluctant or holding something back. Or maybe he'd lost interest? Had there really been any interest in the first place?

A familiar feeling of inadequacy settled over her as the thoughts spun in her head. She pushed her food around on her plate with her fork, not much interested in eating.

"Jess?"

She glanced up at Zach. "Hmn?"

"You're not eating much. Are you feeling okay?"

Insecure. Unsure. Incompetent. But she couldn't say any of those things out loud. "I'm fine. Just tired I guess."

"Why don't you—" Zach's phone rang, cutting him off. He fished it out of his pocket. "Hello? Hey, Logan, what's up?" He paused. "Yeah, I could be up for a card game. Hang on a sec." He held the phone away from his mouth and turned to Jessica. "Would you mind if the guys come over to play cards here tonight?"

She shrugged. "Why would I mind? Sounds like fun."

"You sure?"

"Of course."

"Jess, you're the best." He winked at her before speaking back into the phone. "I'm in." He listened. "Oh, okay." Another pause. "Hey, Sharlie, what's going on?" His eyes flicked to Jessica. "Uh, sure, she's right here." He held out the phone. "Sharlie wants to talk to you."

She took the phone. "Hello?"

"Hi, Jessica. Since the guys are doing their guy thing tonight, I was wondering if you wanted to catch a movie. Something girlie to counteract all of the testosterone flying around at your place."

Jessica hesitated. She wasn't really in the mood to go out. But then again, hanging around while the guys played poker wasn't appealing either. And maybe some time away from Zach would be good. "Sure, a movie would be nice. Do you have anything particular in mind?"

"Actually, I don't know what's playing these days. Let's just head out and figure it out as we go."

"Works for me."

"Great. We'll be over around seven, I guess. I'll leave Owen with the guys, so we can head out on our own."

"See you tonight." She disconnected the phone and handed it back to Zach.

"You going to hang with Sharlie?"

"Yeah, we're going to catch a movie." She looked at him. "You don't mind, do you?"

He shot her a puzzled frown as he rose to gather the dishes from the table. "Why would I mind?" He repeated her words from earlier.

"I don't know. Aren't you afraid she'll tell me some of your deep, dark secrets?"

Zach grinned at her teasing tone. He grabbed her wrist and drew her from her chair. His arms banded around her. Coupled with her earlier morose thoughts, the action surprised her. "I don't have any secrets." He kissed her softly. "And if I did, I'd share them all with you anyway."

Jessica's heart beat faster at the intimate tone of his words. How had the conversation taken such a serious turn? Before she could say anything, his mouth covered hers again, and all coherency fled at the intense pressure of his lips on hers.

He kissed her slowly, leisurely.

When he pulled away, his eyes were shadowed with regret. He tugged her close, tucking her head beneath his chin. The unsteady beat of his heart sounded beneath her ear.

"I could do this all night, but I need to get ready. The guys will be here in an hour or so." His chest rose beneath her cheek as he sighed.

Suddenly a movie with Sharlie held less appeal than before. She'd been waiting for a response like this from Zach. Should she take it further, right now? How? What should she do?

She'd never been so unsure about what to do with a man before. It shouldn't be this difficult. Shouldn't require so much thought.

Before her thoughts could unscramble into anything coherent, Zach sighed. "The dishes are calling."

Jessica tamped down her disappointment. "I'll take care of those. You get ready for your friends."

In less than an hour, Sharlie and Logan, toting Owen's carrier, arrived. Jake followed a couple of minutes later, carrying a case of beer. Jessica frowned. Wasn't that a bit much for three guys playing poker?

"Can we put Owen to sleep in the bedroom?" Sharlie asked.

"Sure."

Sharlie and Logan settled the baby, then walked back out into the family room.

"Have fun," Logan said. He leaned down and kissed his wife. Their eyes held for a moment.

Jessica looked away. Her glance caught Zach's. His darkened.

She blushed and lowered her eyes. Would he kiss her again in front of everyone else? She bit her lip.

"All right, ladies. We've got some serious poker to get to, and you wouldn't want to be late for your movie." Jake's voice drew her attention.

"Okay, Jake, we can take a hint." Sharlie laughed. "C'mon Jessica, we don't want to delay their poker game anymore than necessary."

They chatted on the way to the theater. Jessica enjoyed being with Sharlie. It had been a long time since she'd indulged in girl talk.

"So, is Zach a good kisser?"

"What?" Jessica fumbled with the popcorn bag as she took it off the counter. She blushed and didn't meet Sharlie's gaze.

Sharlie laughed. "Don't tell me there hasn't been any kissing?"

Jessica shook her head. "You're bad."

"Nope, just nosey." She chewed and swallowed a mouthful of popcorn. "So?"

"So?"

"Is he?"

Jessica found a seat in the semi-darkness of the theater before giving in and responding. "Fabulous." The word was woefully inadequate.

Beside her, Sharlie nodded, a smug expression on her face. "I thought he might be."

Jessica turned. "So you two really never?"

"Nope. He's one of my best friends. I never felt that way about Zach. For me, it was always Logan. Even while he was gone." Her voice took on a melancholy note.

"You guys were apart for a long time."

"Zach told you the story, huh?"

"Just a little bit."

"So, what's going on with you and Zach?"

Before Jessica could reply, the lights dimmed. The screen lit up with coming attractions.

She breathed a silent sigh of relief. How would she have answered Sharlie's question? What would the other woman say if Jessica told her she wanted to use Zach for sex?

And would she be lying? Was that all there was to it?

It had to be. She wasn't interested in a relationship. Not now. Not with someone like Zach. Someone with no goals and future plans.

Thankfully, Sharlie didn't mention the topic again after the movie.

When they arrived back at the cabin, the guys were still playing poker. Empty beer bottles were scattered across the table. Zach and Jake each held one in their hands.

Jessica frowned.

Sharlie wrapped her arms around Logan's neck. She kissed his cheek. "Haven't you guys had enough poker for one night?"

"You can never have enough poker," Jake said.

"You can say that again." Zach raised his beer bottle in a toast.

A shiver of unease snaked down Jessica's spine. She smoothed her clammy hands down the front of her jeans.

"Did you ladies have a good time?" Logan asked.

"You bet," Sharlie said.

"Uh, yeah, sure," Jessica mumbled. She looked away when Zach smiled at her. His eyes looked a little too bright.

"What did you gals end up seeing?" Jake asked. He tossed his cards down on the table. "I fold."

"Chick flick," Sharlie replied.

"What movie did you see, Jess?" Zach asked. He took another sip of beer. "I'm in." He slid a poker chip to the center of the table.

"Are you drunk?" Her abrupt words hung in the sudden silence. Those gathered around the table looked first at her, then at Zach.

He tossed his cards down. "No."

"Yes, you are." Tears threatened, but she fought them back. She wouldn't cry.

Zach stood. "I'm not drunk." His voice was hard, but she could tell by his mannerisms he lied. He'd had too much to drink.

"It's obvious you've been drinking."

"I've had a few beers. What's the big deal?"

She couldn't bear to look at him anymore. After all they'd shared over the last couple of weeks, she thought she could trust him. Depend on him. Thought he was different. She'd been wrong.

She shuddered. Had she really considered being intimate with him? Making herself vulnerable again?

She turned to go.

"Jess, wait." He reached for her arm.

"Get your hands off of me." She backed away from him. "Don't touch me." Her voice trembled.

"What—" Zach began. He took a step toward her, but Jake laid a hand on his arm.

"Let her be," Jake said softly.

"Just leave me alone." Jessica fled from the room.

Upstairs in the loft, she threw her bags on the bed. She tossed things from the dresser into them. Her throat was thick and tight with unshed tears, but she refused to give in to them.

She zipped the bags, heedless of the clothes sticking out, and slung them over her shoulder.

Someone knocked at the door.

"Go away," she said over the loud thumping of her heart.

"Jessica? It's Sharlie. Are you okay?"

"Fine," she lied.

"Can I come in?"

Jessica hesitated, but opened the door. She stepped aside to allow Sharlie to enter. The other woman's gaze touched on the bags before coming back to meet hers.

"Are you going somewhere?"

"I can't stay here. Not with him like that."

Sharlie nodded. She sat down on the edge of the bed. "Do you want to talk about it?"

"No." How could she explain? Especially to Sharlie. She was one of Zach's closest friends.

"You know," Sharlie said gently. "Zach's not drunk."

"What?"

"I mean, yes, he's had a few drinks, but he's not out of control."

Jessica lowered her eyes.

"Look, you don't need to tell me anything, but I think you should talk to Zach."

"No." Jessica's head snapped up.

"It doesn't have to be tonight. In fact, you don't even need to be around him tonight. He can go to

Jake's. You don't need to go anywhere."

Jessica chewed her lip, then nodded. "Okay." She didn't have anywhere to go at the moment. She'd figure it out in the morning.

She couldn't talk to Zach. She'd be long gone before he returned. But Sharlie didn't need to know that. "Thank you."

Sharlie rose and hugged her. "Everything will be okay."

Jessica managed a smile, albeit a false one. She doubted it. In her experience, when things like this happened, they were never okay.

At the door, Sharlie turned. "Zach would never hurt you," she said quietly before closing the door behind her with a soft click.

Jessica sank onto the bed.

****

Zach looked up when Sharlie walked down the stairs. He rose. "I need to talk to her."

Sharlie shook her head. "Not tonight. Give her some time." She paused. Logan put his arm around her shoulders. "I think you should stay at Jake's tonight."

"What?" A lump of dread settled in Zach's stomach. "Did she say that?"

"No, it was my idea. She needs some space. You can talk to her in the morning. When she's calmer."

He dropped back down in the chair and cradled his head in his hands. "She's really that upset?"

"Yeah."

He looked up again. "I'm not drunk, Sharlie."

"I know." Her voice soothed. "I have the feeling this isn't really about you. But, like I said, you can talk to her in the morning."

"What if she leaves?" The words sent a stabbing pain through his heart. The sensation surprised him. When had he gotten so emotionally involved?

Sharlie didn't reply. It made him feel worse.

122

He sighed and levered himself out of the chair. He threw some clothes in a duffle bag, then slung it over his shoulder. He looked at Jake. "I guess I'm your roommate for the night."

"Yeah, I guess so."

"Should I leave her a note?"

Sharlie shook her head. "She knows where you'll be."

"Right."

She laid a hand on his arm. "It's going to be all right. I'm sure you two will work this out."

Zach glanced at Logan and then at Jake. "I guess we should go."

Logan picked up Owen's carrier. He clapped Zach on the shoulder with the other hand. "Things'll look different in the morning."

"I sure hope so." Even to his own ears, the words sounded bleak.

He took one last look up the stairs before following Logan and Sharlie out the door.

Chapter Eleven

Jessica looked up from the breakfast she wasn't eating when Zach walked in the back door the next day.

Their eyes met and held. He looked tired and wary.

"I wasn't sure you'd still be here when I got back." Zach set his duffel bag down.

"I wasn't sure either." She looked down at the table, then back up. "I guess we should talk."

"Yes."

She rose and dumped the contents of her glass in the sink. "Have you eaten?"

He nodded. "At Jake's."

She shoved her hands in the back pockets of her jeans. "Where, uh, where do you want to go?"

"Go?"

"To talk."

"Oh, how about out on the deck?"

"Sure." She followed him outside.

He sat in one of the lounge chairs. She took the swing, tucking her feet beneath her.

His gaze captured hers, but he didn't say anything.

She looked away.

"I—" She cleared her throat. "I guess you're wondering about last night."

"You could say that."

She exhaled, her breath ruffling the curls falling over her forehead. Where should she start? She hadn't really talked about this with anyone.

She bit her lip and looked out over the trees in

the distance. "You see, I just got out of...this relationship. And my...the guy drank. A lot. When we first met it wasn't so bad, you know? But after a while he couldn't go a day without having something to drink. And soon he was drinking all the time. I asked him to stop. I told him I'd help him. He needed to get help. But he didn't want to hear any of it." Her gaze met Zach's for a brief instant before sliding away.

"When other people drink, it just reminds me of how bad things got. It scares me. He, uh, he was mean when he was drunk."

"Did he hurt you?" Zach's voice held an edge.

She shivered and hugged herself. "No, not in the way you're thinking. But he...he said things."

"Said things?"

"Told me it was my fault the relationship wasn't working. Said I didn't understand him. Didn't support him."

"He hurt you."

She glanced over at him. The look in his eyes matched the dangerous tone of his voice.

"Not physically," she whispered.

"Son of a bitch," Zach muttered beneath his breath.

"So," she blew out a shaky breath, "I came here to get away. To escape from everything. From him. When I found you here, I couldn't believe it. All I wanted was to be alone."

"Jess, I didn't know." Pain laced his voice.

She looked up. "Of course you didn't. But over the last couple of weeks, I discovered I liked having you around. I enjoyed being with you. I trusted you."

"And now?" His voice held a cautious note.

"When I came home last night and saw you'd been drinking, it freaked me out. I got scared."

"I'd never hurt you." The soft words whispered over her.

"I know."

Zach walked over and hunkered down in front of the swing. "Look at me," he prompted when she wouldn't meet his eyes.

Her gaze rose to his. The dark orbs swam with compassion. And regret.

"Do you still trust me?"

She nodded.

"Because if you didn't, I don't think I'd be able to stand it, knowing I'd broken that trust. That I'd hurt you again."

She laid her palm against his face. His unshaven jaw scratched her skin. "I trust you."

He closed his eyes and released a breath. When he opened them, their expression turned hard. "You'd better hope he never comes around here. I might kill him."

****

The ax bit into the wood with a satisfying thunk. Zach yanked the handle, and the metal blade broke free. He swung again.

Sweat trickled down his forehead and rolled down his back between his shoulder blades.

The stump cleaved in two. The separated halves fell on either side of the block. He picked up another piece of wood.

He grunted as the steel embedded itself once again. He'd been working at the chopping block for over an hour.

Trying to forget.

So far, it hadn't worked. Jessica's story played itself over and over in his mind. He wanted it to be her ex's head receiving the brunt of the ax. Of course, he deserved no better. He'd hurt her, too.

Pain lanced through him.

Would he have done things differently had he known? Would he have kissed her that first time? Knowing how hurt she was. Knowing how vulnerable she was.

"Damn it to hell." The words accompanied the crack of the log as it split. The sounds echoed in the still air.

He rested his forearms on the upturned handle of the ax and gazed at the distant mountains. Ben would be home in a week or so. Having to face Ben made Zach feel sick inside. He'd betrayed the other man's trust by kissing his granddaughter.

One good thing about Ben coming home. Zach would go back to his own apartment and try to forget all about Jessica. About how he'd hurt her. Despite his vows not to, he had.

He wiped his arm across his forehead and picked up another piece of wood. Forgetting would be easier said than done.

The look on her face when she'd walked in last night played in his head. The expression of betrayal. But other images played in his mind as well. Things he felt like a cad for thinking about right now. The first time he'd kissed her. When she'd asked him why he hadn't kissed her again. When she'd kissed him.

One thing for sure, he wouldn't be kissing her anymore. He'd promised himself the same thing before. But this time he needed to mean it. She deserved better than him. And God knows he didn't want to add to her hurt.

Not to mention kissing her only made him want to do more things with her. Things he had no right to be thinking about. Especially now. He'd betrayed her trust once. He wouldn't do it again.

****

"So how did things go with Jessica this morning?" Jake asked. As usual, they had the barroom to themselves before it opened for the night.

Zach shook his head. "I'm not sure."

"She's still upset, huh?"

127

"No, it's not that." He paused. How much could he reveal to Jake without betraying Jessica's confidence? "She told me a little about her ex-boyfriend." His gut clenched just thinking about it. "Apparently this guy was quite a piece of work."

"Men can be assholes," Jake agreed. "So, what does that have to do with the two of you?"

"Let's just say there are some things I would have done differently if I'd known what she'd been through." Or things he wouldn't have done at all. "She's still hurting."

"Just give her some time." Jake clapped him on the shoulder. "You're good for her."

Zach snorted. Good at causing her more pain. "Why do you say that?"

"Because you're not an asshole."

Zach didn't reply. At the moment, he didn't agree.

****

Jessica tossed her T-shirts and jeans into the washer. She added the detergent, closed the lid, and twisted the knob to start the cycle.

She stared at the rumbling machine. She couldn't help the smile that quirked her lips as she remembered the last time she'd done laundry, and Zach had found her panties in the dryer. She hadn't even planned that one, but it had gotten under his skin.

It seemed like a lifetime ago she'd come up with the idea to seduce him. Things were different since the poker game the other night and their discussion the following morning. Had she done the right thing in telling Zach everything? Would she have been better off just leaving?

Too late now.

To be honest, it had been nice to tell someone. To share the burden in a small way.

And she hadn't lied. She trusted Zach. More

than that, she still wanted Zach. The question remained, did he want her?

Their time alone together was running out. Pops would be home soon. Before he returned, she had to know the truth. Could Zach please her? More importantly, could she please him?

He wasn't the kind of guy she wanted to settle down with. He had no goals. He was over thirty and still worked as a bouncer at a bar. The next time she let herself get involved in a relationship, it would be with someone who had a secure future. Someone who wasn't at loose ends not knowing what they wanted to do with their life, if anything.

On some level it disappointed her Zach held such little stock in the future. But in the long run, what did it matter? She had no inclination to date him. She had no interest in dating anyone right now. She only wanted to know if the yearning ache caused by Zach's kisses went further.

And there was only one way to find out.

She'd have to get serious about the whole seduction thing. Her subtle attempts hadn't worked. She needed to pull out all the stops.

Trouble was she had no idea what to do next.

She hadn't tried a candlelit dinner. Would that work? Romantic music? Sexy clothes? Come right out and say, *"Zach, I want to have sex with you."*?

It had been so long since she'd been interested in being intimate with a man. What if she didn't know how?

Of course, that was the root of the entire problem.

So, what should she do?

Maybe one of those women's magazines would help. One of them had to have a 'how to' column for these kinds of things. For that she needed to head into town.

She hadn't seen much of Zach since they'd

talked. He'd been at work last night, and this morning he'd said he had things to do and wouldn't be back to the house until late afternoon. Which could be true. Or he could be avoiding her. What if she'd freaked him out with her story?

What if? Of course she'd freaked him out. Who wouldn't be after hearing it?

Well, he'd just have to get unfreaked out.

Jessica scribbled a quick note and placed it on the kitchen table. She grabbed her purse and headed out the door. Her hand shook. It took three tries to get the key into the ignition.

Once in town she wandered into the small department store. Her gaze fell upon the cosmetic counter. She hadn't worn makeup since she'd been at the cabin. Maybe it was time for a little spruce up. And it had been forever since she'd had her hair cut.

A plan firmly in mind, she headed off on her quest.

Several hours later she walked back into the cabin. She tossed a stack of magazines onto the kitchen table. The note she'd left for Zach still lay there. He hadn't returned while she'd been gone. Yep, he was definitely avoiding her.

With a sigh she opened one of the magazines. Her finger traced down the table of contents. *How to be Sexy for Your Man*: the words jumped out at her.

"That should do the trick," she muttered. She flipped to the correct page, then scanned the article. Half of it had her rolling her eyes. The other half had some merit. She gathered her things, grabbed a pair of scissors from the drawer, and headed up to the loft.

She found a T-shirt and a pair of jeans in a drawer. She held the shirt in one hand, the scissors in another. She gnawed her lip, contemplating what she was about to do.

"Oh, what the hell?" She cut several inches off

the hem of the shirt. Then she cut the legs off of the jeans, turning them into shorts. Very short shorts.

She slipped out of her clothes and into the newly created ones. In the bathroom, she looked at herself critically in the mirror. Her hair frizzed and waved around her face. Dark makeup highlighted her eyes, and a bronze blush graced her cheeks. Her lips shimmered with coral lipstick. Overall the effect was way more dramatic than her usual, natural look.

She stepped back to get a look at her outfit. A blush suffused her face at the amount of flesh visible. The cut-off jeans made her legs look impossibly long, and the T-shirt exposed the flat plane of her abdomen. She twisted around and glanced over her shoulder. The low-slung jeans revealed the colorful butterfly in the small of her back.

She pulled a deep gulp of air into her lungs. Was she really going to do this? Could she go downstairs looking like she did? How would Zach react?

If this didn't do the trick, nothing would. Was she ready? Her hand trembled as she tucked her hair behind her ear.

She steeled herself. She needed to do this. She had to know. And she trusted Zach.

Downstairs, he still hadn't returned, so she opened the refrigerator, searching the contents for something she could put together for dinner. Everything looked way too exotic for her limited expertise.

She checked the freezer. Frozen pizza it was. Not very romantic, but at least Zach wouldn't need to cook.

She preheated the oven, then set the table with paper plates and napkins. With nothing else to occupy her mind, she paced the kitchen.

The oven dinged. She jumped.

After sliding the pizza in, she set the timer, then

resumed her walk back and forth in front of the cabinets. She chewed her lip.

When would Zach return?

The timer read five minutes when the back door opened. Jessica took a deep breath and turned toward Zach.

"Sorry I'm late, I—" He froze as he looked up. His gaze swept down her body before returning to her face. He swallowed. And averted his eyes.

Her heart plummeted. "I, uh, I put a pizza in. I wasn't sure when you'd be coming back."

"Great. I need to hop in the shower before we eat." He didn't look at her as he walked toward the family room.

"Zach?"

He turned, but kept his eyes locked on hers. A muscle jumped in his jaw.

"Um, what do you want to drink?"

"Soda's fine." He hurried from the room.

Jessica sank onto a chair, her trembling legs unwilling to hold her anymore. He'd hardly looked at her.

Where had she gone wrong?

****

In the bathroom, Zach leaned his hands on the counter and took a deep gulp of air into his lungs. He willed his heartbeat to slow to a normal rhythm.

In the mirror, his eyes looked wild, unfocused. He closed them. Mile long legs and a bare midriff appeared behind the closed lids.

He swore as he yanked his shirt over his head, then tossed it to the floor. His jeans followed.

In the time he'd known Jessica he'd never seen her look like that. What the hell? Had all of her clothes shrunk in the wash?

He turned the shower knob to cold. The icy spray cascaded down his over-heated body. A heat that had nothing to do with the strenuous work he'd done outside.

Was she purposely trying to drive him insane?

No, of course not.

But damn, with her looking like that, he'd have an awfully hard time keeping his resolution not to kiss her again. Let along resist doing all the erotic, delicious things that had popped into his head the moment he'd seen her.

He finished in the shower, dried himself haphazardly with a towel, and pulled a clean T-shirt over his head. Thanks to the cold water, he was able to zip his jeans.

Back in the kitchen, Jessica regarded him, an unreadable expression in her eyes. Even her face looked different for some reason tonight. His gaze lingered for a brief moment. She wore makeup. A lot of it.

"Pizza's done."

"Great, I'm starved." With a determined effort he kept his eyes focused on his plate. "Thanks for making dinner tonight." He bit into the gooey slice of pizza. The hot sauce burned the roof of his mouth. The pain brought a welcome distraction.

She slid into the chair across from him. "I didn't do much."

He swallowed.

She put her elbow on the table and cupped her chin in her hand. "So, are you working tonight?"

"No, but, uh, I have some things I need to do out in the barn I didn't get to today."

"Oh." Her face fell. Her teeth bit into her lower lip. "I could help you."

"No." The word slipped out harsher than he intended. "I mean, that's okay, it's really messy out there. I wouldn't want you to—"

She cut him off. "No problem, I understand." She leaned back in her chair and picked at her pizza.

Her dejected expression sent a tiny stab to his

heart. He'd hurt her again. "Jessica?"

She didn't look up. "What?"

"I'm sorry. I didn't mean to sound so rude."

She waved a hand. "You don't need to apologize. It's my fault. I shouldn't have expected you to want me"—her voice broke—"to help you."

Zach gazed at her in horror. Was she crying? He'd made her cry? "Jess, I—"

"You know, I'm not really hungry." She stood so quickly her chair unbalanced and crashed to the floor. "I...I'll be upstairs." She turned and ran from the room.

Chapter Twelve

Upstairs in the bathroom, Jessica scrubbed at her face. The offending makeup tinted the sink peach and black before swirling down the drain.

"Jess?" Zach's voice interrupted her regimen.

She grabbed a towel and pressed it to her dripping face. "What?" She looked over at him. He leaned against the jam, a puzzled frown on his face.

"Did I miss something downstairs?"

She fought the urge to scream. Oh, he'd missed something all right. Or maybe she had. This whole seduction scene wasn't her. She should have known better.

"No, I..."

"You what?"

"Look, can we just drop this please?" She didn't want to rehash the whole humiliating scene.

"I'd love to. If I knew what we were dropping."

"I don't want to talk about it."

He took a step into the bathroom. "I thought we'd decided you could trust me. Why won't you talk to me?"

Jessica gritted her teeth and raised her eyes to the ceiling. "I do trust you. That's why I was trying to seduce you."

Zach froze. "What?" Shock echoed in his voice.

"Why do you think I was dressed this way?" Her hand swept over her skimpy attire. "I got my hair done and did my makeup, and you couldn't have cared less." Her voice cracked.

"You were trying to seduce me?"

"Yes." She lowered her eyes to hide her shame.

"For a while now. Why do you think I kept asking you to put lotion on me or help me with my zippers and things?"

She risked a glance at him.

He stared at her, a dumbfounded expression on his face. "You mean you were doing all those things on purpose?" His voice sounded rough. Gritty.

She put her hands on her hips and rolled her eyes. For the moment, frustration overrode her earlier embarrassment. "Duh."

"I don't understand. I've been trying like hell to keep my hands off you, and you've been driving me insane on purpose?"

His words caused a little hitch in her heart. She'd been driving him insane? "Why have you been trying to stay away?"

"For one, after what you told me the other day, I didn't want to hurt you again. And two, you're Ben's granddaughter."

"So?"

"So? It wouldn't be right."

"Look, I don't care if I'm the pope's granddaughter."

"Uh, Jess, isn't that impossible?"

"That's not the point," she snapped. "Why does it matter whose granddaughter I am? I'm a big girl, Zach."

"Oh, I know it." His gaze searched hers. "Every time I look at you, I'm reminded how grown up you are."

"But, tonight, I wanted to—I tried to...and you didn't..." She looked away.

He stepped closer and raised his hands to her face. He forced her eyes to meet his. "Jess, what's going on? Why were you doing all this?"

"Because I need to know."

"Know what?"

She shook her head despite his grip on her face.

She closed her eyes, unable to bear the look in his anymore. "Please, it doesn't matter. Can we just forget about this?"

"I don't think so." He paused. "You looked beautiful tonight."

She snorted.

"You did. You just didn't look like you."

Her eyes opened. "What?"

He shrugged. "All of this," he gestured toward her, "was great. But it wasn't you. You're so much," he paused as if struggling to find the right word, "more than this. Your makeup made you look like a vamp, a vixen. I'm not saying it wasn't hot. Hell, I almost swallowed my tongue when I walked into the kitchen."

"Really?" She bit her lip.

His mouth quirked up in a smile, and his thumb smeared over her bottom lip. "Do you have any idea how sexy you look when you bite your lip? It drives me crazy."

Her breath caught. "But you don't want me."

"Then why do I go to bed hard every night and wake up the same way?"

The blunt statement robbed her of breath. She swallowed. Twice. "Then why won't you—"

"Because I'm trying to be a good guy here. I'm trying not to take advantage of you. To hurt you anymore."

"You won't."

"And besides, you can't force these things. You have to just let them happen. In their own good time."

"But if you're being so damn good all the time, how is that going to be possible?"

Zach chuckled and tucked her against his chest. "Oh, Jess. What am I going to do with you?"

"I have a suggestion," she mumbled against his shirt.

"Obviously." His tone was wry. He held her away from him to look into her eyes. "You don't need any of that makeup stuff. You're beautiful just the way you are." He kissed each of her eyelids, now devoid of gooey shadow and thick mascara.

"Really?" She cringed at the pathetic, hopeful tone of her voice. Hadn't she embarrassed herself enough tonight?

"Uh huh." His lips trailed across her cheek. His nose nudged aside her hair. He kissed the outer shell of her ear.

She shivered.

"As for these clothes." His whisper skimmed across her skin. "I guess I'm a little old fashioned. I like to leave certain things to the imagination." His hands spanned the exposed flesh at her waist.

She jerked against him. Her breath caught, even as her heart hammered into overtime.

His thumb stroked her navel. "At least at first." Warm lips slid down her throat.

She shivered. "But you don't want to—"

He cut her off by grasping her hips. Through the denim of his jeans, the hard ridge of his arousal pressed against her.

"Oh," she gasped on a quick intake of air.

"You were saying?" The amused tone of his voice couldn't hide the husky note of desire.

His mouth claimed hers. As he kissed her, he rotated his hips.

She tore her mouth from his. Her eyes rose to his. They smoldered with undisguised desire. When was the last time someone had looked at her that way?

He brought her hands to the bottom of his T-shirt.

Her pulse pounded. Her breath came in short gasps. At the same time her heart squeezed. He left the decision up to her. Let her take control.

Was she really ready for this?

She held his intense gaze for a moment longer.

Then she grabbed the hem of his shirt.

Her hands stroked over his bare flesh as she drew the cotton fabric up. His muscles were hard beneath her palms. He raised his arms, and she tugged the shirt over his head. It fell to the floor at their feet.

He wound his arms around her. His heartbeat raced beneath her cheek. His hands roamed over her back, slipping beneath the cut-off hem to stroke her bare skin. She trembled.

His hand was warm around hers as he led her out of the bathroom and up the stairs into the loft. Once inside the room, he paused next to her bed.

His gaze fell on the remains of her hasty work from earlier. The legs of her jeans and the bottom of her T-shirt were scattered on the quilt. His lips twitched.

"You know," the husky whisper feathered across her nerves, "you're still wearing too many clothes." His finger traced the skin of her belly. He sat on the edge of the bed and guided her between his legs. He drew the shirt over her head, then bestowed a kiss onto the swell of her breast above the satin of her bra. She shuddered beneath his hot mouth.

He undid the button of her shorts. They slithered down her legs. She stepped out of them.

Her whole body trembled as she stood before him clad only in her bra and panties. She wished she could read his mind. What was he thinking? Did he like what he saw?

His hands spanned her waist and drew her close. He undid the clasp of her bra and then tossed the skimpy garment aside. He sucked in a quick breath.

She fought the urge to cross her arms over her chest.

He kissed the tip of one breast, sucking the nipple into his mouth. It tightened into a hard bud as his tongue swirled around it.

Her breath escaped in a shuddering sigh as she fell against him. He lay back on the bed, and she sprawled on top of him. Her bare breasts pressed against the muscled wall of his chest. Her legs draped his hips. His denim covered arousal nestled in the apex of her thighs. Her spread thighs.

His heat and hardness penetrated the thin cotton of her panties. A rush of liquid heat washed through her, settling in her core. She cried out as he flexed his hips upward, pushing himself tighter against her.

His hand speared through her hair, guiding her mouth to his. The hungry kiss brought another wave of pleasure crashing over her. Somewhere in the back of her mind, she recognized she'd gone from being the seducer to the seduced.

But she didn't care. All she cared about was how hot it was where their bodies touched. How his heartbeat raced. How his breath hitched in an uneven rhythm. How his mouth slanted over hers with just the right amount of pressure.

Without breaking the kiss, he twisted their bodies so their positions were reversed. His mouth traveled from her lips, to her jaw, then down her throat.

She arched her neck.

He sucked the peak of one breast into his mouth, tugging on the tip. When she gasped, he shifted his attention to the other. A tremor whispered through her and settled between her thighs.

Would she shatter from just the touch of his mouth on her breast?

As if sensing her thoughts, he flexed his hips away from hers, sliding his hand beneath her panties to touch her.

She jerked.

He laved her nipple with his tongue while he stroked her slick flesh with his finger.

She shook.

Waves of pleasure rolled over her, centering at the spot where his finger danced, quicker now. Tiny spasms set her legs trembling. With a hoarse cry, she contracted around him, squeezing her thighs together, trapping his hand, to hold onto the shivery spikes of liquid heat pouring through her.

Zach stared down at her, a look of deep satisfaction on his face.

"Wow," she breathed. Aftershocks raced through her, leaving her whole body tingling.

He smiled, then leaned in to kiss her. The kiss was intense, but sweet. Gone was the passion from earlier.

A tiny niggle of dread snuck into the back of her mind.

He broke the contact all too soon and settled her against his side. He kissed the top of her head. "Get some sleep." He sounded tense, almost uneasy.

The euphoria of seconds before vanished.

He didn't want to make love to her.

Refusing to cry, she propped herself up on one elbow to look down at him. "What?"

"It's been a long day. Aren't you tired?"

"We're not done." Anger made her brave. "We didn't—"

"Tonight was for you," he interrupted.

She shook her head. It hadn't been her pleasure she'd needed to know about tonight. Not entirely. She needed to know about him. Could she please him?

Why had he stopped? Had she done something wrong?

"Y...you..." She stilled the trembling of her voice and tried again. "You don't want to...finish?" She bit her lip.

He groaned and threw his arm over his eyes.

Couldn't he even stand to look at her? Her stomach twisted.

He mumbled something beneath his breath.

"What?"

"I want to...finish...more than anything in the world. I want to make you feel like that again. I want to watch your face while you come apart. But this time, I want to be inside you."

Her breath caught and her pulse raced. "Then..."

"I don't have...anything...with me."

Relief flooded through her. Her breath escaped on a shuddery sigh. She kissed him and stroked her palm down his chest. Her fingers found the snap of his jeans. She flicked it open.

He grabbed her hand. "Jess, did you hear what I said?"

"Mmm, hmmm," she whispered. "But you don't have to worry."

He opened his eyes to look at her. "What?"

She blushed and looked away, suddenly embarrassed once again. "I told you I wanted to seduce you tonight."

"Yeah." His tone was puzzled.

"So, I got these." She reached across him to open the nightstand drawer. She pulled out a box of condoms and placed it on his chest.

His gaze captured hers. "I love a woman who plans ahead."

In one swift movement, he flipped her onto her back and loomed above her. His mouth captured hers in a deep, hungry kiss.

She trembled beneath him. Her hands clutched his shoulders, drawing him closer. She raised one leg and hooked it around the back of his thigh.

He broke the kiss, then laughed softly. "You're going to have to wait for me this time," he whispered in her ear.

He divested himself of his jeans and boxers. "Now, where'd that box go?"

In a moment he turned back. His fingers traced over her cheekbone. The light touch caused an answering flutter in her stomach. She shifted beneath him.

His sheathed arousal nudged her hip. She twisted toward him. Her thigh brushed against him.

He sucked in a quick breath. "I'm trying to take this slow, Jess, make it good for you. But you're killing me here."

The words sent a thrill straight to her heart. He wanted her.

"It's already been good for me," she whispered, stoking her hand across his whisker-roughened cheek, then down his chest. "Now it's your turn."

"No. Now it's our turn." He claimed her lips. His hand cupped one breast. The thumb brushed her nipple. It hardened to aching awareness.

She arched into him.

His fingers feathered over the tight nipple until she shuddered. His hand slid lower. He traced a path around her navel with the tip of his finger.

Her stomach clenched. She quivered. Heat pooled between her thighs.

His fingers dipped lower to grasp the waistband of her panties and drag them down her legs. He skimmed his palm over her calf, past her knee, and up her thigh.

She trembled when he brushed the curls between her legs.

"Are you ready for me?" He whispered as his finger dipped inside her.

She tightened around him.

"Ah." His voice held a husky note of satisfaction. His uneven breath skittered across her skin. "I'm ready for you, too."

Debra St. John

He rolled her beneath him, then braced his arms on either side of her shoulders. With slow deliberation, he thrust into her.

She gasped as he slid deeper. She shook. The liquid heat turned molten. The flames consumed her. She bit her lip.

Above her, he groaned, kissing her as he filled her completely. He pulsed, hard and hot, inside her.

He waited until she opened her eyes. "That's it. I want to watch you. I want to see the look in your eyes as you come apart again."

Eyes locked with hers, he withdrew. Slid back. She whimpered at the friction.

Setting a rhythm that matched the pounding of her heart, he moved, slowly at first, but then faster, as her trembling increased. She contracted around him, pulling him deeper as the tiny spasms spread from the point of their joining outward to her limbs.

With a hoarse cry, he shuddered above her. He threw his head back and clenched his teeth. The muscles in his arms tautened. He bucked his hips against hers one final time, before the tension left his body.

She wrapped her arms around him. Her fingers smoothed over his sweat slick skin. He buried his face in her shoulder, his breath harsh against her neck. His chest crushed hers. His heartbeat thundered next to hers.

A tear slid down her cheek.

When he looked down at her, his eyes widened. With the pad of his thumb, he wiped away the moisture. "Don't cry, Jess."

Dammit. She didn't want to be one of those women who cried after sex. But for the first time in a long time her body had responded the way it should. And she'd been able to please him.

She shook her head. "I'm sorry. I—"

"Shhhh." He turned, tucking her to his side. "It's

144

okay."

Her cheek pillowed on his chest. Her arm draped across his chest. She thought about his words before slipping into slumber. He was wrong. Things were more than okay.

She was healed.

Chapter Thirteen

Zach awoke a few hours later. Jessica slept on her stomach, her face turned toward him, one hand above her head, one beside her. The sheet covered her lower body, but rode low enough to reveal the butterfly decorating the small of her back. Above it her skin still bore the faint trace of a bruise.

He fought the urge to touch her. He didn't want to wake her.

He shifted onto his side, propping his head on his hand.

His body stirred. He wanted her again. Wanted to see the look in her eyes as she took her pleasure. Wanted to feel her body tighten around him as he found his.

But he also wanted to know what tonight had been all about. What had she wanted to know? Why had she wanted to seduce him?

He hadn't fought very hard. Despite his vow to stay away, he'd given in without much of a fight. He hadn't been able to help himself.

As if the thought gave rise to the need for action, he feathered his fingers over her tattoo.

She stirred and murmured. Her eyes blinked open.

He traced down the side of her face with the tip of his finger. "Hi."

A blush spread over her cheeks. "Hi."

He leaned in and kissed her. "Can I ask you something?"

Her eyes grew wary. "Sure." She turned onto her side and tucked the sheet under her arms. She rested her head on her hand, matching his pose.

Despite her agreement, her voice sounded hesitant.

Inwardly he winced. He didn't want to ruin what they'd shared. He paused, then blew out a breath. "What did you need to know?"

"What?"

"Before, downstairs in the bathroom, you said you just needed to know. What did you need to know?"

She looked away.

He cursed silently. Why couldn't he have kept his mouth shut?

As he was about to tell her to forget he'd asked, she spoke, but avoided looking at him. "Remember I told you I started having sex when I was sixteen?" She gave a self-deprecating laugh.

A cold knot of jealousy tightened his stomach. Did he really want to hear this?

"Well, the thrill wore off pretty quickly. I mean, having sex was okay. It was nice. But for me it wasn't the big deal all my friends made it out to be. It was always a part of the relationships I had, but it never was the mind-blowing experience I'd always heard about. I started to think maybe there was something wrong with me.

"And then with Philip, when he drank too much, he couldn't"—her eyes flicked to his, then away—"perform. After a while I lost interest completely. Most of the time I'd just lay there. I was numb to the whole thing. Hoping he'd be quick. He would blame me, for not being able to... He'd, uh, say I was cold and didn't know how to please a man."

"Son of a bitch." The words hissed from between clenched teeth.

She shrugged. "I...it wasn't hard to believe. After all, my past experiences didn't leave me much to go on." Her breath whooshed out in a rush. "I figured it was what I deserved. Maybe my dad had been right, and this was my punishment for the choices I'd made. I'd disappointed everyone. My parents. Philip."

The pain in her voice knifed through him. "Jess—"

Her gaze met his again. Her eyes shimmered with tears. "No, please, let me finish."

He nodded, ignoring his desire to pull her into his arms. There would be time for that later.

She took a deep breath. "But then you kissed me. And I felt something."

Zach's heart lurched at the whispered confession.

Now she locked her gaze on his. "For the first time in a long time, I *felt* something. And I thought you did too. At least I hoped you did. I wanted to know how much I could feel with you. How much *you* could feel. With me. I wanted to know if I could please you." Her voice trembled.

"Oh, Jess." The agony her words caused echoed in his voice. "It wasn't your fault. You didn't do anything wrong. You didn't disappoint anyone."

She shrugged. "If someone tells you something often enough, you start to believe it."

Anger simmered through him. His blood boiled. "I want to kill him, you know."

Her fingers smoothed down his jaw. "It doesn't matter now. That part of my life is over."

He took her hand in his and brought it to his mouth. He kissed her palm. She sucked in a quick breath.

He smiled, but his tone remained serious. "All the same, he better not ever show up around here."

His fingers stroked down her side. Her skin was smooth and silky. His body stirred again. The anger melted away as passion flared in its place.

"You did, you know."

Her brow furrowed. "Did what?"

"Please me."

She blushed again. A soft smile formed on her lips. "I know."

He leaned in to nuzzle her neck. "Jess?"

"Hmnn?"

"Do you want to see if you can do it again?"

Her gaze flew to his, then softened with teasing lights. "Where'd that box go?"

****

In the morning Jessica found Zach in the kitchen. At first she'd been unsure how to feel, waking up alone. Why hadn't he wanted to stay? But the clatter of pots and pans had nudged her out of bed and down the stairs.

She stood in the doorway, watching him work. He wore faded jeans, but his chest was bare. The sight of it caused a little flutter in her stomach. The memory of his muscles straining beneath her hands as he found his release made her blush.

Heat gathered between her legs. She swallowed. "Hi," she whispered to draw his attention.

He turned and smiled a slow, sexy smile. His glance swept over her. "You look good in my shirt."

She'd slipped into the first thing she'd grabbed, which happened to be his discarded T-shirt from the bathroom floor.

"Come here." The command was soft. Intimate.

He met her halfway. His arms wound around her, and his gaze searched hers before he lowered his head for a kiss. She closed her eyes and savored the tender pressure of his mouth against her own. Her fingers threaded through the damp strands of his hair.

She broke the kiss. "How long have you been up?"

"About an hour. I didn't want to wake you." He grinned. "So I avoided temptation with a cold shower."

Her heart raced at the implication. He wanted her again.

She didn't know whether to be disappointed or grateful he'd let her sleep. They hadn't gotten much last night.

"You hungry?" After one more kiss, he returned to the stove.

"Starved." And not just for food.

"Have a seat. You'll have a potato-and-egg skillet coming your way in a minute or two."

True to his word, in short order he slid the steaming dish in front of her. Jessica studied him from under her lashes while they ate.

What would happen now? Things had changed between them. But what did it all mean? She wasn't ready for another relationship.

"So, you have anything special planned for today?" His words jolted her from her thoughts.

"I have some work I need to get done."

"I thought maybe we could spend the day by the creek. It's supposed to be hot today. But if you have work to do..."

She weighed her options. Swimming in the creek all day with Zach wearing nothing but swim trunks or staring at her laptop screen? She bit her lip. No contest really, but...

"I really need to get some work done. Tell you what, give me a couple of hours, and then I'll join you at the swimming hole."

"A couple of hours?" He frowned. "Jess, you work too hard."

She shook her head and folded her arms across her chest. "Now don't be hypocritical."

"Hypocritical?" He raised an eyebrow.

"You work harder than anyone I know."

"What?" He sounded shocked.

She hid a smile. "You've been working your tail

off around here, and most nights you go to work, too. Face it, Zach, you're working two jobs. If that's not working hard, I don't know what is."

For a moment he looked nonplussed. Then he waved his hand in a dismissive gesture. "Not really. Taking care of Ben's place is fun."

Jessica laughed. "Yeah, well, for me, designing web pages is fun." She laid a hand on his arm. She hoped he hadn't taken her comments the wrong way. After the incredible night they'd shared, she didn't want anything to ruin it. "Look, we can continue to debate this, or I can get to work. The sooner I get started, the sooner I'll be done."

"Great. I'll clean up in here and you—"

"No, I'll clean up." She rose to gather the plates. "You're spoiling me. I won't know what to do with myself when Pops comes home and you leave." The words fell heavily on her heart. As much as she looked forward to seeing Pops again, when he returned, Zach would leave.

"Have you heard from him lately?" Zach's tone was casual. "Do you know when he's coming back?"

She looked over her shoulder at him. "I talked to my mom a couple weeks ago." Had it been only a few weeks ago she'd wanted to leave to avoid Zach? Now they were lovers. What would happen when Pops got home? What did she want to happen?

Zach's arms wrapped around her waist. "Well, I for one hope they decide to prolong their trip." He kissed her neck, then sighed. His breath tickled. "I guess while you work, I'll go play in the barn."

She hid a smile at the slight emphasis he put on the word 'play.'

"Let me know when you're done, and we'll head down to the water."

After finishing the dishes, she grabbed her laptop. Dispelling images of her and Zach tangled together in the sheets of her bed, she forced herself to concentrate.

Exactly two hours later, she stretched. Satisfied with the work she'd accomplished, she logged out of her program. She opened the front door and hollered out, "Zach? I'll be out in five minutes."

Upstairs she grabbed a one-piece swimsuit from the drawer. But then she reconsidered. Zach had already seen her completely naked. A blush crept into her cheeks. What difference would it make for him to see her in a bikini now?

She donned the suit, then wiggled into a pair of cut-off jeans. The strings dangling from the ragged ends tickled her legs as she walked.

Back in the kitchen she threw some fruit and cheese into a small cooler with several bottles of water. She met Zach out by the barn. He'd changed from jeans into a swimsuit and had a towel slung over his shoulders.

"Darn. I forgot a towel. I'll be right back."

He twirled the towel from his shoulders and wrapped it around hers. He used the ends to tug her near for a kiss. "No problem. We can share."

She handed him the food. "Here. I thought this would save us a trip back up if we got hungry."

He secured the cooler to one of the ATVs. "Like I said last night, I love a woman who's prepared."

Her heart skipped a beat at the words. He didn't mean he really loved her, but the idea got her excited and nervous all at once. Falling in love with Zach wasn't an option.

Although her body responded to him in ways she'd never experienced, she knew better than to confuse sex with love. She ignored the tiny niggle in the back of her mind telling her what they'd shared went way beyond sex.

"All set?"

She forced the disturbing thoughts from her head and nodded. "You bet."

Down at the creek, the hot sun beat down on them.

"Yikes, it's hot already. And it's only ten o'clock."

"That water's going to feel mighty good," Zach said. He walked to the edge of the rocks and made a shallow dive out into the deeper part of the swimming hole. He popped up, flinging the hair out of his face with a toss of his head. "Ah, that's better. Coming in?"

Jessica shimmied out of her shorts and let them fall to the rocks. She entered the creek a little more cautiously, sucking in a breath when the cool water hit her stomach. After a moment she became brave enough to slide beneath the surface. She stroked over to where Zach treaded water a couple yards away.

"There's snorkeling gear in the box on the ATV. Want to give it a try?" he asked.

"Sure. Why not?"

He swam to the rocky shore. She admired the play of muscles in his back as he hoisted himself up. He retrieved the gear and then slid back into the water.

He handed her a lime green face mask and tube. She dipped it into the water before sliding it over her head. She tightened the strap to ensure an airtight fit.

She turned. Zach peered out at her from the transparent window of his turquoise mask. He grinned. "All set?"

"You bet." She fitted the tube in her mouth and eased into the water. Small fish darted out of her path as she made her way through the crystal clear water.

They explored for an hour, then climbed out of the water to grab something to eat from the cooler.

Zach spread the towel on the rocks. He motioned for her to sit. The heat of the sun beat down on her shoulders, drying the drops of water dappling her skin.

He sat down across from her, setting the fruit on the makeshift picnic blanket. His damp hair fell across his forehead. It reminded her of the first time she'd seen him.

In the bathtub.

How eager she'd been to get rid of him at first.

And now, he'd be leaving soon. Once Pops returned, Zach wouldn't be staying at the cabin any longer.

What would happen then? Would they continue on like they were? As lovers. Or would they simply fade out of each other's lives?

"Jess?"

Her attention snapped to Zach. "Wh...what?"

"You zoned out on me. Are you okay?"

"Uh, fine...just thinking."

He nodded. "I think I'll take it easy for a while before heading back into the water." He cleared their lunch things away, then grabbed a bottle of sunblock.

She swallowed to ease the dryness in her throat as he spread the lotion across his chest and arms. She pictured her own hands making the same journey. Feeling the play of firm muscle beneath her palms.

She bit her lip and looked away. Damn. If it was too soon after eating to go back in the water, it probably was too soon for other strenuous activities as well. She sighed.

Zach stretched out on the towel, closed his eyes, and tilted his face toward the sun.

She studied him, her mind returning to her earlier musings. The thought of not seeing Zach anymore caused a little stabbing ache right in the center of her heart. Wasn't that even more reason to end this, whatever this was, before it went any further? She wasn't ready for a relationship, so wasn't going their separate ways the only thing that could happen?

She'd found out what she needed to know. She wasn't cold inside. She could feel. Remembering all of the delicious things Zach had made her feel made her shiver despite the heat of the sun beating down.

More importantly, she'd made him feel. Their lovemaking hadn't been one sided. She'd brought him as much pleasure as he'd brought her.

But she could also feel herself falling into old habits. Becoming too attached too soon. To the wrong kind of man. She didn't want to go down that path again.

In some ways Zach was the right man. He'd brought her alive, healed the hurt inside. Made her whole again.

But in doing so, he'd made her realize she couldn't ever settle for less than what she wanted in a relationship. Of course the physical part was important, but it couldn't be the only part. There had to be more. She needed a man she could depend on. Someone who knew what he wanted out of life.

Zach had no idea what he wanted out of life.

Her gaze slid over his naked chest, and she sighed. No matter how Zach made her feel physically, ending things with him when Pops got home was for the best. For both of them.

****

"Have you ever gone skinny dipping?"

Zach looked over to where Jessica dangled her toes in the clear water. An image of her naked body visible in the sparkling water formed in his mind.

He raised an eyebrow. "Here?"

She nodded. A mischievous smile played around her mouth.

He closed his eyes and leaned back on his elbows. He tilted his face up toward the warmth of

155

the sun. "Nope."

"Liar."

A sprinkle of water scattered over him. He opened one eye. Jessica's hand poised over the stream, ready to scoop another handful of water to send in his direction. Although the cool water brought a welcome distraction from his heated thoughts, he warned, "Don't do it."

Truth was, he loved it when Jessica played. When she let go of the shadows that still lurked in her eyes, and he could catch a glimpse of her carefree spirit.

"C'mon, truth or dare," she taunted as she sent another splash of water at him. The droplets splattered across his chest.

He kicked at the water, sending a spray in her direction. "Okay. Dare."

Jessica blinked, then smiled the lazy smile of a seductress. She slid gracefully into the water. She swam beneath the surface until she reached his feet.

Zach sat up as she rose out of the water like a nymph rising from the depths of the sea. Water cascaded down her body as she stood between his knees.

His heart raced at the sight of her wet, glistening skin. Drops of water beaded on her shoulders. He had the wild urge to lick them away. He hardened.

Jessica's eyes widened at the sight of his straining swimsuit. She shook her head. A rueful smile graced her face. "You're so easy."

He wrapped the long strands of her wet hair around his fist. With a gentle tug he tilted her head back. "Only for you, Jess, only for you." His lips took hers. He kissed her deeply, running the tip of his tongue over her lower lip.

She gasped. His tongue slipped inside her mouth. He stroked against hers.

An endless time later he broke the kiss. His breath escaped in a harsh rhythm. Never taking his gaze from hers, he untied the top of her bikini and drew it away to bare her breasts. He tossed the flimsy bit of fabric to the side. He cupped her, teasing the nipples into tight buds with gentle flicks of his thumbs.

Her head fell back. She bit her lip.

A groan rumbled from his chest. He slipped out of his swim trunks and into the water. It was icy against his heated skin, but did nothing to diminish his desire.

She wound her arms around his neck. The jut of his arousal brushed her belly.

"So, that cold water thing is just a myth, huh?" Her lips traced the underside of his jaw.

"When you're around, definitely." He claimed her mouth in a deep kiss. Beneath the water he slid the bottom of her suit down her legs, then tossed it onto the rocks.

With a teasing glint in her eyes, she swam away from him. Her naked body glided through the transparent water. The sunlight shimmered against her bare skin. Her butterfly floated just beneath the surface.

Despite the chill of the creek, the flames licking his body threatened to consume him.

A couple of powerful strokes brought him to her. He grabbed her ankle to stop her progress. She turned, her smile impish. He tugged her closer and scooped her into his arms. Once in shallower water, he loosened his grip. Her slick, wet body slid down his own.

His lips trailed down her throat, licking the water droplets there. She shuddered as his tongue swept over her collarbone.

Her arms banded around him. Her fingers trailed down his back. The nails lightly raked his flesh. Goose bumps that didn't have anything to do with the temperature of the water peppered his skin.

She grabbed his hips. He jerked against her.

"Enough skinny dipping." His voice was hoarse. He lifted her and placed her on the rocks on the edge of the creek. He spread her legs so he could stand between them. Her lips trembled beneath his when he kissed her. "The pocket of my suit," he managed to say.

She handed him the square packet.

When he was ready, he grasped one of her thighs in each hand. He nuzzled her neck, kissing the pulse that raced at the base of her throat. "Are you ready for me?" he whispered, then traced the shell of her ear with his tongue.

She shuddered. "Yes." Her voice escaped on a breathy sigh.

He slid forward into her moist heat.

Her body tightened around him, drawing him further in. She wrapped her arms around his neck and tilted her hips up.

He sank deeper.

Then pulled away.

He continued the steady rhythm until her body convulsed around him. Her head fell back, and he kissed her neck as he thrust into her one last time as molten fire raced through his body and he shuddered into her.

His hands found her waist, holding her to him as he strained inside of her. Her body trembled beneath his on the rocks.

After the tremors subsided, he released her. "It just keeps getting better." The words gritted out between harsh breaths. His heart thundered in his chest. "Are you still wondering if you please me?" His lips traced along her jaw, moving up so he could whisper in her ear. "'Cause, Jess, let me tell you, if you pleased me anymore, I'd be mindless."

He kissed her one last time, then fell backward with a splash.

The refreshing water closed over his head, cooling his sweat-slick body.

Chapter Fourteen

"Ever go to the rodeo in town?"

Jessica looked up from the breakfast quiche in front of her. "Sure. Pops used to take me all the time when I was a kid."

"Want to relive your youth?" Zach grinned at her.

"Um, sure. Why? What's up?"

"Jake's riding today, and I'm meeting Sharlie and Logan there. You should come."

"Jake's riding?"

"He's a bull rider." He answered the unspoken part of her question.

Her eyes widened. "Bulls? Isn't that dangerous?"

"It can be. Jake's really good at it though. He wins a lot."

"Wow."

"Yeah, so do you want to come with me? Make it a double date."

Jessica hesitated. She remembered how fun the rodeo could be, but going out with Zach would blur the lines of their relationship. Would having an actual date with him weaken her resolve about it only being about sex? And what would Sharlie and Logan think about them being together?

"Come on," Zach coaxed. "You haven't left this place in weeks."

Against her better judgment, she gave in. A day at the rodeo sounded like fun. "Okay, I'm in."

****

The strong smell of horse manure permeated Jessica's nostrils as she and Zach walked toward the grandstand. She wrinkled her nose. "Whew. I'm glad Pops doesn't keep horses at the cabin."

Zach laughed. "Yeah, I probably wouldn't have taken on the job of house-sitter if he did. I'm not one for mucking out stalls."

She looked over at him. She had to admit, the cowboy hat and boots were a damn good look on him. She tried to imagine arriving at the cabin and finding someone else as the house-sitter, but she couldn't quite picture it. Not after all she and Zach had been through.

They found Sharlie and Logan without too much trouble, even though the bleachers were jammed with spectators. Owen's stroller sat in the aisle next to Sharlie. She greeted Jessica with a hug and Zach with a kiss on the cheek.

"You guys are right on time. The opening ceremony is just about to start." Sharlie waved at the horses cantering into the arena. A cowgirl in a flashy, sequined outfit took the center. She gripped an American flag in her hand.

"Please rise and join in our National Anthem," the master of ceremonies instructed over the loudspeaker.

As one, the huge crowd surged to its feet. Zach and Logan, along with the other men present, doffed their hats, holding them over their hearts as music swelled throughout the open-air stadium.

After the last notes faded away, Logan turned to Sharlie. "That's my cue. I'll be back." He kissed her, then brushed his lips over Owen's forehead.

Jessica looked at Zach. "Where's he going?"

"Logan runs a rodeo camp for kids. He needs to get them ready for their part of the festivities."

She frowned. "I thought Logan owned The Corral."

"He does. The camp is more like a hobby, I guess. Although he works just as hard there." This time Zach frowned. "As if one job weren't enough."

Jessica rolled her eyes. What was with him and his hang ups about working? He worked harder than anyone she knew, yet he seemed so disgruntled when someone mentioned it.

The beginning of the saddle bronc riding competition caught her attention, so with an effort she shrugged off thoughts of Zach and his anti-working sentiments and focused on the pageantry before her.

The morning passed quickly. She'd forgotten how much she'd enjoyed the rodeo when Pops had taken her. After Logan's camp kids did their parts, he rejoined his family. Following a hair-raising ride that had her digging her nails into Zach's palm—he'd winced theatrically—Jake scored well enough to make it into the final round of the bull-riding competition, scheduled for later in the afternoon.

"Wow," she said when his ride was over and she could breathe again. "That was unbelievably scary. I never thought about how really dangerous it was until I knew the person riding."

Sharlie nodded. "Freaks me out every time. But Jake's really good. He's had his fair share of bumps, bruises, and breaks, but most of the time he finishes at or close to the top. As you can tell," she gestured out over the crowd, which still stood, applauding enthusiastically, "he's one of the favorites."

"And he does this just for fun?"

"Well, he does enjoy it. I think he wants to go bigger than this someday. Ride the professional circuit. He'll be great there, too," Sharlie said, pride evident in her voice. "But we'll really miss him when he goes."

They resumed their seats as the applause finally died down. The master of ceremonies thanked everyone for coming out and reminded them when the afternoon session would begin. "Hope to see y'all back here then," he concluded.

Zach looked at his watch. "How about we find a spot to sit and have some lunch?"

"Sounds good to me, I'm starving," Jessica agreed.

They made their way off the crowded bleachers. Zach nodded toward a large tree at the edge of the grounds. "Why don't you ladies head over and get the blankets set up. Logan and I will grab the food."

He turned to Jessica. "What do you have a taste for?"

She shrugged. "Anything is fine. You're the food expert. Just get me whatever you think looks good." She smiled up at him. "Although I'm sure whatever it is won't be as good as anything you make."

He laughed. "I don't know about that."

"It's true," she insisted. "You've spoiled me. I don't how I'm ever going to be able to eat my own cooking again after..." The words trailed off. She didn't want to finish the sentence. But the thought completed itself in her head. After he left.

Pops and her parents would be home soon. And then her time with Zach would be over.

She stared up into his eyes. Her heart warred with her common sense.

The logical part of her accepted it had to happen. From the beginning their time together had been limited. And the reason behind it had been straight-forward. She'd needed to know if she could feel real passion. And if someone could desire her.

She had her answers. A resounding *yes* on both accounts. Her experiment, for lack of a better word, had been a success. Time to move on.

So why was the thought of moving on so difficult? Painful almost.

Behind her, Logan discreetly cleared his throat. Only then did she realize she'd been staring at Zach for several long heartbeats. And he'd been staring back.

She blinked. A blush crept into her cheeks.

Zach smiled and touched his finger to the tip of her nose. "We won't be long."

The men walked off. Zach's easy swagger caused a little flip in the pit of her stomach. The way the faded denim of his jeans hugged his hips and thighs was downright sinful.

Sharlie's gaze lingered on Logan a moment before she turned to Jessica with a speculative look in her eye. "So..."

Uh-oh. Jessica braced herself for the question to come.

"Zach's never brought someone to the rodeo before."

"What?" The comment was unexpected.

Sharlie nodded. "Before Logan moved back, Zach and I came to the rodeo every year together. Now it's been the three of us. But he's never made it a foursome." She looked down at the stroller she pushed in front of her. "Well, a fivesome, I guess."

Jessica hid her shock. "I find that hard to believe."

Sharlie shrugged.

"Never?"

"Never."

"But, he's had women in his life, right? I mean girlfriends?"

"Some," Sharlie admitted. "But I've never seen him like this before."

Jessica swallowed. "What do you mean?"

"He's happy. Don't get me wrong," the other woman laughed, "I'm not saying he was miserable before. But now, it's different." She glanced over at Jessica. "It's good."

Jessica didn't comment. What could she say? She sipped her drink, hoping the cold beverage would dissolve the huge lump in her throat.

"I think he's falling in love with you."

Jessica choked. The soda burned as it went down the wrong way. "What?" Her heart sped.

Sharlie smiled. "I've known Zach a long time. He's never been like this with anyone else. I can tell by looking at him. By the way he looks at you."

Jessica forced down the panic rising in her throat. Zach couldn't be falling in love with her. Their relationship was about sex, not love.

She shook her head. "I think you're wrong. I mean, it's not like that between Zach and me." It couldn't be. "We're just friends. That's all."

Sharlie raised an eyebrow. "Just friends?" Her skepticism was apparent.

"Yes," Jessica said, her voice firm.

Sharlie's lips twitched. "Friends with benefits, maybe."

Jessica's mouth dropped open. "That's...what...how...I..." She snapped her lips together.

Sharlie grinned, a smug look on her face. "That's what I thought."

Jessica shook her head.

They walked in silence until they reached the shade of the tree. After spreading the blankets, Jessica sat, folding her legs beneath her.

She bit her lip. Debating. Since Sharlie had already figured out that something was going on between her and Zach, what would it hurt to ask a couple of questions?

"So," she said, striving for a nonchalant tone. "Has Zach always been a bouncer at The Corral?"

"For as long as I've known him."

"So he's not really interested in doing anything else?" Although Jessica already knew the answer, she asked the question anyway.

Sharlie frowned. "What do you mean?"

Unable to meet the other woman's gaze, Jessica

studied a group of ants scrambling around the base of the nearby tree. "I don't know, something in business or something like that," she faltered.

Sharlie shook her head. "When I cut down on my hours after we got Owen, we offered him the manager's job, but he wasn't interested."

Of course not.

Sharlie grinned, oblivious to the negative vibe of Jessica's thoughts. "Zach's one of those happy-go-lucky guys. I can't really picture him in a suit and tie working a nine-to-five desk job, you know? Although managing The Corral isn't really a nine-to-five job." She laughed.

Her expression turned wary. "Did Zach say something about wanting a different job? I'd really miss him if he left The Corral. He's a part of it. Part of my family really."

"No, definitely not," Jessica quickly assured her. "I didn't mean to imply that. I was just wondering."

Sharlie unbuckled Owen from the stroller, then fished a bottle out of his diaper bag. She gazed at him while he greedily sucked the milk, a thoughtful look on her face.

"Of course, if he had a good reason for leaving, like he got married and moved someplace else, I'd be okay with that." Her gaze met Jessica's for a brief moment before returning to the baby's face. "I'd still miss him like crazy, but as long as he was happy, that's all that would matter." She looked up at Jessica again. "Zach's a good man. He deserves to be happy."

Jessica couldn't respond. Her chest ached with a mixture of guilt and unease. Guilt because Sharlie had misconstrued the meaning behind her questions about Zach's job. And unease because putting *Zach* and *marriage* in the same sentence made her head spin. Not to mention what happened when she coupled them with Sharlie's earlier comment.

She breathed shallowly, hoping to dispel the lightheadedness. The underwater-without-oxygen sensation eventually subsided, but her thoughts continued to whirl. She went through the motions of enjoying the rest of the rodeo, but even the feats of the daring cowboys in front of her weren't enough to chase the unsettling thoughts away. They hovered in the back of her mind like clouds threatening to ruin the Fourth of July.

****

Later that night, without any distractions to keep them safely corralled in the back of her subconscious, the thoughts spun through her head in an endless litany. Zach had gone outside to check on something or other, which gave Jessica nothing to do but ponder Sharlie's words.

Zach was a good man, but he couldn't be falling in love with her. He'd only known her for a short while. Too short a while.

The fault, as usual, was hers, she supposed. She'd set the boundaries of their relationship, but had she ever told him? Told him it was only about sex?

He had to know, didn't he? Of course she hadn't come right out and said it in so many words. But she'd explained why she had wanted to seduce him. Had explained what she needed to know. Wouldn't he have figured it out?

He was confusing sex with love. Mixing the two together. Women did it all the time. No reason to think a man wouldn't make the same mistake.

Sharlie was wrong.

She had to be.

Jessica's cell phone rang, startling her from her troubled thoughts.

"Hello?"

"Jessica, it's Mom, how are you?"

"I'm fine." Now wasn't the time to share the

details of how she'd messed up her life. Again. Her mom didn't even know about Philip yet.

"That's good. Listen, honey, it's hard to hear you, this connection isn't the greatest, but I wanted to let you know we'll be home tomorrow."

The phone almost slid from Jessica's suddenly lifeless fingers. "T...tomorrow?"

"Yes, I wanted to call so you'll know to expect us."

Jessica forced herself to concentrate. The nervous buzz in her brain made it difficult. She shook her head to clear it. "Do you need me to pick you up at the airport?"

"No, we have a driver all set. We should get to the cabin sometime in the late afternoon."

Less than twenty-four hours. Something like panic flooded through her. Despite her earlier misgivings about Zach's feelings, she wasn't ready for things to end. She needed more time to prepare herself to say good-bye.

"Can't wait to see you."

Jessica wrenched her attention back to her mother. "Yeah, you, too."

"Bye, sweetie, see you tomorrow."

Jessica closed the phone. She sat and stared at nothing.

Eventually Zach returned to the house. He brushed a kiss on the top of her head as he walked past. She mustered a half-hearted smile.

He stopped and laid a hand on her shoulder. "Why so sad?"

She tilted her head to rest her cheek against his hand.

"My mom called while you were outside."

He hunkered down in front of her. His knuckles brushed her face. "And?"

Before answering she stared into his mocha irises. Now they reflected his concern, but they could also darken with passion. Passion, at least for the moment, for her. He'd made her whole again. She'd never forget the thrill of the want-to look in his eyes. No matter what happened now.

She sighed. "And she said they'll be home tomorrow."

The expression in his eyes changed, but she couldn't read it. "Ah, so my services won't be needed around here any longer, is that what you're trying to tell me?"

She didn't miss the double entendre in his words. She offered another half smile for his attempt at levity. "Very funny."

"Ben will be home tomorrow," he murmured, almost to himself. He wound one of Jessica's curls around his finger, then studied it intently as he asked, "So, what happens now?"

His gaze rose to meet hers when she didn't answer. His expression remained unreadable.

Had it been only a few weeks ago she'd been trying to figure out how to get rid of Zach? What would happen now that he'd be leaving? Would she ever see him again? Would they ever be lovers again? What did he want? What did she want?

She shook her head. "I...I don't know." She bit her lip.

He smoothed his thumb over the spot. She closed her eyes against the prick of tears the familiar touch brought.

He rose, and in a smooth motion, drew her up and into his arms. She nestled into him, savoring the feel of his arms wrapped around her. The steady thump of his heart beneath her ear. The rise and fall of his chest as he took a deep breath, then exhaled.

"Don't worry," he whispered into her hair. "We'll figure it out."

How? she wanted to ask, but remained silent. And was there really anything to work out? Her time with Zach had served its purpose. She'd found pleasure in his arms. He'd taken his in hers. That's what it had been about. Nothing more.

She pushed away the memory of Sharlie's words from the rodeo. Zach wasn't falling in love with her. Like she'd said before, love wasn't the same thing as sex.

And just because he was the only man who had ever made her feel so alive, so fulfilled, so satisfied, didn't mean anything beyond the fact she desired him. If anything else she was grateful. Relieved.

That was it.

She resolutely ignored the voice in her head telling her what she had with Zach went way beyond sex and seduction. She couldn't let it be anything more.

She stepped away from him and jammed her hands into her back pockets. "So, um, what will you do now? Since Pops won't need you to take care of this place, will you go back to being just a bouncer?" Or saving more lost women from the demons haunting their souls?

He frowned at her tone. "Just a bouncer?"

"Well, you know, you mentioned before you weren't really interested in doing anything else." She looked away. "So I guess it will be back to the easy life for you, huh?"

He folded his arms across his chest. "Why do you have such a problem with my career choice?"

"Career? Zach, working at a bar isn't a career, it's..." she waved her hand, but words escaped her, "...well, I don't know what it is, but it's not a career. I mean, being a chef or something, that would be a career."

His brow furrowed. "A chef? Jess, cooking is something I enjoy. I just do it for fun."

"Who says you can't have a job that's fun? I like what I do."

"I do like my job. At The Corral." The tone of his voice indicated the conversation was over.

But Jessica couldn't let it go. Whether she wanted to remind herself about his lack of goals or make him into a different person to justify the feelings she wouldn't admit she had for him, she couldn't tell. "But you—"

"Why are you bringing this up now? Are you trying to start a fight?" He stepped forward and tangled his fingers in her hair. He tilted her face up. "It's our last night together here. I don't want to spend it arguing with you." His lips brushed hers.

She sighed. She didn't want to argue either. She wanted to make love with Zach. Would it be the last time? Urgency flooded through her. She wound her arms around his neck and threaded her fingers through the strands of his hair as he deepened the kiss.

She tugged the shirt over his head. Her hands skimmed down his chest. The steady thud of his heartbeat accelerating beneath her palms never failed to thrill her. The taut muscles in his stomach clenched as her exploring fingers drifted lower.

His lips slid down her throat, trailing hot, moist kisses in their wake. He nudged the strap of her tank top to the side to gently bite the soft curve of her shoulder.

Her head fell back. "Let's go in your room," she whispered.

But he shook his head. "No. Upstairs." He took her hand.

On the way up she kicked off her flip flops. He stopped on the second floor landing to undo the tie at the top of her shorts. They slithered down her legs to pool at her feet. She stepped out of them, then tugged on his hand, leading him up the final flight of stairs.

In the loft, a single lamp on the dresser lit the

room with a soft, warm glow. Jessica unfastened the snap of his jeans, slid the zipper over his straining arousal, and dragged him down on the bed.

He sprawled over her. The hard length of him pressed between her thighs. A shivery tingle began. She flexed her hips, rubbing herself against him.

Her hands gripped his upper arms. The muscles tightened as he held himself above her. His mouth stroked over hers. His tongue mimicked the slow, circular movement of her hips against his.

When she gasped in a deep breath, his mouth left hers and found her breast. Through her shirt he sucked on the tip. The ribbed cotton added to the delicious friction. Her fingers dug into his shoulders.

He shifted slightly, and one hand slipped beneath the tank top to cup her other breast. His fingers feathered over the crest. With his teeth he grazed the nipple in his mouth.

She jerked against him. The tingle became more insistent. A fiery heat spread through her veins. The blood turned molten, making her limbs languid.

The tip of his index finger traced down her stomach, circled her navel. She squirmed. He caught the waist of her panties to drag them down her legs. His hand grasped her ankle, then slid over the curve of her calf to the back of her knee. He stroked the sensitive skin there.

She bit her lip to hold back a moan.

His groan escaped. He kissed her again, running his tongue over the fullness of her bottom lip. "You know that drives me crazy." His voice was low. Gritty. Unsteady.

Her heart thrilled to the words. They added to the heady feeling of him hard and hot against her core. Almost as if reading her thoughts, he shifted again. The denim of his jeans rubbed against her.

Almost as desperate as the first time they'd made love to feel him inside of her, her hands trembled as she hooked her fingers in his belt loops and dragged the pants down his legs. She freed him from his boxers. He jerked in her hand.

"Where's that box?" she whispered.

His lips curved against her throat. He rolled away, but turned back almost in the same movement.

"Ah," she managed to tease even though his mouth had returned to her breast. "I'll bet you were a good Boy Scout. Always prepared."

"Mmn, hmn," he murmured. "Gotta love a woman who appreciates a man in uniform."

A small lump of panic settled in her throat at his casual use of the word. But she refused to let it distract her. Instead she concentrated on the erotic tug of his mouth and the corresponding tug that pulsed between her thighs.

Again, as if reading her mind, his finger dipped inside of her. "You're ready for me." The deep note of satisfaction in his voice purled around her.

"I'm always. Ready. For you." The words slipped out as he stroked her.

She tightened around him as tiny shards of heat made her tremble beneath his gentle touch. "Z...Zach?" her voice shook.

"Mmn hmn?" He barely moved from her breast to answer. The sound vibrated over the sensitive tip.

"T...together," she managed to get out.

"Together," he agreed, his voice little more than a breath against her skin, then slid into her.

The moment couldn't last. She was way too close to the edge. Her arms wrapped around him, holding him close to the frantic beat of her heart. His own heartbeat thudded next to hers.

The steel length of him stroked deep inside of her. Her hips matched his rhythm, increasing the tempo of her movements as he did.

"Together," he repeated, his voice hoarse, as he

slid into her one final time. As he shuddered over her, she contracted around him, pulling him even deeper as tremors raced through her body. Their mingled release lingered, leaving her panting. Several long, delicious moments later he relaxed against her, his breathing harsh against the hollow of her throat.

Her arms tightened around his neck, and she hid her face in his shoulder as a lone tear trickled down her cheek. She'd cried the first time they'd made love. Her emotions had gotten the best of her then, too. But for an entirely different reason.

Then she'd cried because she'd found pleasure with Zach. Now she cried because she feared she'd never feel passion like theirs again. Their lovemaking tonight had been their good-bye.

Unable to say the words, she'd put everything she wanted to tell him into this one final time. Together.

When he turned away after a moment, she wiped at her tears with the back of her hand. She didn't want him to see her cry. He'd want to know why. And she didn't have the words to tell him.

He tucked her against his side. She snuggled into him. Memorizing the feel of his breath whispering through her hair. The now steady pulse of his heart beneath her ear. And the warm strength of his arm around her. She didn't ever want to forget.

She lay in his arms until sleep claimed him.

"Good-bye, Zach," she whispered.

His breathing hitched, and a moment of panic stabbed into her. Was he awake? Had he heard the soft words?

But the steady rhythm of his breath continued, and she sighed in relief. The smooth cadence soon lulled her to sleep.

Chapter Fifteen

The next morning Jessica awoke alone. That wasn't unusual. Zach often got up ahead of her to make breakfast. But she couldn't help but worry if his early rising this particular morning had a deeper meaning. Had he heard her whispered words last night? What was he thinking if he had? She'd been too afraid to say the words out loud, but had needed to say them. For her sake. And his.

She'd needed to verbally acknowledge what she'd admitted in her head already. She had to say good-bye to Zach. Let him go. So she could get on with her life. And he could get on with his.

Unease swirled in her stomach as she headed downstairs after getting dressed. A trail of discarded clothing led her down both flights of stairs and into the family room. Despite the acrobatics going on inside of her, she smiled wryly. Good thing Pops and her parents hadn't arrived early.

She picked up Zach's T-shirt. At the door to his bedroom she paused. Several boxes were piled around on the floor. He was packing a duffel bag. Her stomach did another funny flip.

"You've been busy this morning."

He looked up, his expression enigmatic. "Yeah, I wanted to clear this stuff out before Ben gets home."

"Oh. Right."

He opened a dresser drawer and transferred several more things to another bag.

"Um, here's your shirt. From last night." She blushed. He seemed so distant. Talking about the intimacies they'd shared seemed out of place.

Awkward. She held out the garment. Her hand trembled.

"Thanks." His fingers brushed hers as he took it. Despite her unease, the small, brief touch caused a spark of awareness.

Had Zach noticed? She studied him. He appeared to be absorbed in his task. Too absorbed. The knot in her stomach tightened.

"Is something wrong?"

He glanced at her briefly. "No, why?"

Her teeth worried her bottom lip. "It just seems like something's on your mind."

His hands stilled. He looked around the room, then exhaled a long, slow breath. "I was just thinking about Ben coming home today. Pretty soon I have to look him in the eye and pretend like I haven't betrayed his trust while we've been living here together."

"What are you talking about?"

He met her gaze before his slid back to the bag in front of him. "I feel like I've betrayed Ben by making love to you."

The words took her by surprise. Hadn't he gotten past his guilt?

She walked over to him to lay her hand on his arm. "You didn't betray anyone's trust. I told you before. I'm a big girl. I make my own decisions. What happened between us has nothing to do with my grandfather. You didn't betray anyone's trust," she repeated. "In fact, you taught me how to trust myself again."

His visage told her she hadn't swayed him. Sometimes he was too noble for his own good. She framed his face in her hands, forcing him to look at her. "Please don't think like that."

His eyes bored into hers before he looked away. "I need to finish this up and then check around outside. I want to make sure everything's in order for Ben when he gets here."

She sensed his emotional withdrawal, too, like a tiny stab of rejection in her heart. Her hands dropped to her sides.

But wasn't it better this way? Easier? Everything was ending. Why make it harder than it was?

Jessica sat with her laptop in the family room and attempted to work while Zach finished packing and hauled his things out to his truck. When he was done he headed out to the barn. An ATV rumbled to life. The sound faded as the vehicle traveled down the path toward the creek.

Was he really taking a last look around to make sure everything was in order, or was he avoiding her? She dashed away the tears that pricked her eyes. She couldn't have it both ways with Zach. What they had was over. Last night had been their good-bye. If that made today awkward, then that's the way it had to be.

Zach returned a couple hours later to start dinner for Pops and her parents when they arrived.

Unable to concentrate on her work, Jessica shut down her computer with a sigh. She hadn't accomplished anything in the hours she'd spent staring at the screen. Not sure what else to do with herself, she wandered out onto the deck. As she swayed with the gentle motion of the swing, the events of the last few weeks drifted through her mind. She'd come to the cabin to get away. To find the peace and healing her heart and soul so desperately craved. She'd found it. But not in the way she'd expected.

She hadn't expected someone else to play such a vital role in the healing process. She hadn't expected Zach.

Her time with him had been almost enough to ease the ache of past regrets. Almost.

But would her relationship with him be another one of those things she'd regret when she looked back on it? Would it haunt her? Would she ever be sorry for what she'd done?

Thinking about her time with him as something to look back on caused a little pang in her chest. But with Zach, there wasn't anything to look forward to, so back was the only way to look. He didn't want anything out of life. Sure, for now he was content working as a bouncer at a bar. But how long would that last? How long before he decided even that was too much and quit?

Somewhere in the back of her mind she knew her prejudices were unfair to Zach. He worked hard. He'd worked his tail off around the cabin for Pops. Maybe the past clouded her vision. But by his own admission he wasn't interested in anything else. Didn't want to worry about the future. What did that say about him?

With a sigh, she stood. The swing hit the side of the house with a dull thunk.

Inside, the delicious aroma of brown sugar wafted to her. Zach's meatloaf smelled scrumptious. She wandered around the family room. She ran her fingers over the shelves as she gazed at the pictures. It had been too long since she'd seen her family. What would she tell them about Philip? And would they say anything about her and Zach living together while Pops had been gone?

She glanced at the clock. When would everyone arrive? She gazed out the sliding door. For once the spectacular view couldn't sooth her.

"Hey."

She jumped when Zach touched her arm. She blew out a breath. "You startled me."

"Sorry, I thought you heard me come in."

She shook her head and crossed her arms over her chest.

"You're all tense. You need to relax." He put his hands on her shoulders, then smoothed them up and down her arms.

Her foolish heart soared at the contact. After the distance he'd kept today, she hadn't expected him to touch her again.

She exhaled softly. "I know." She looked around, then up at him. "I just haven't seen my family in so long and they're going to ask me about Philip and I don't know what to tell them and what will they say about us living here together this whole time and you're leaving tonight and I—"

Zach embraced her. "Shh. Jess, stop. You're making yourself crazy. Everything's going to be fine."

She took a moment to savor the feel of his arms around her. The beat of his heart beneath her ear. The gentle brush of his lips against her hair.

Then she lifted her gaze to his. "Easy for you to say. You don't have to tell your family you've made another horrendous mistake in your life."

"I sure hope you're talking about Philip and not me." His tone teased, but his mocha eyes were serious.

"Oh, Zach, of course I mean Philip. Our time together here has been...I mean I've never...it's not like..." Words failed her. She placed her hands on either side of his face. "Our time together has been wonderful." That was an understatement, but she wasn't about to get all weepy on him again. "I'll never, ever forget it as long as I live. And I'll never regret it. I've done some things in the past I wish I could take back. Do over, or not do as it were. But being with you isn't one of them."

"You sound like you're saying good-bye."

She flinched, hearing the word out loud, and bit her lip. They'd said their good-byes last night. Passionately. Silently. What more could be said in the light of day? "Aren't we? I mean, everyone will be here soon."

"That doesn't mean we have to say good-bye. I'm moving back into town, not to Mars."

"I know. It's just..." She didn't know what to say.

"You don't want your family to know about us." It wasn't a question.

"It's not that, I..." She couldn't explain. And he was right. She didn't want her family to know. Bad enough she'd have to explain Philip's absence. How in the world would she explain her relationship with Zach?

She could imagine the conversation. *"Mom, Dad, this is Zach. I've been using him for sex."*

Yeah, that would go over well. Of course, based on her track record, maybe they wouldn't be surprised.

She looked up at him. "Besides, do you want my family to know? This morning you were all worried about what Ben would think."

He winced, then sighed. "You're right." He hesitated. "Can I ask you something?"

The emotion in his eyes burned into her. She bit her lip and nodded.

"What do you think happened between the two of us?"

"Wha...what?"

"These last two weeks. What was it all about?"

She swallowed. "You know what it was all about." Unable to meet his eyes, her gaze slid past him. "I mean, I told you, I needed to know..."

"And that's it? After I leave here today, what if I called you and asked you to go out? Would you say yes?"

Tires crunching on the gravel outside saved her from answering. "They're here," Jessica whispered. Her voice shook the slightest bit.

Zach sighed again, then brushed one last kiss

across her forehead. "Everything's going to be okay."

She didn't agree, but nodded anyway. She sucked a deep breath into her lungs and then let it out one heartbeat at a time.

She stepped out onto the porch as everyone piled out of the car.

"Jessica, sweetheart, it's been too long." Pops embraced her.

She squeezed him back, inhaling the familiar scent of Old Spice.

"Let me look at you, girl." He surveyed her. "Yep, cabin livin' sure agrees with you. You look fabulous. Not that you ever don't."

"Thanks, Pops. You don't look too shabby yourself. European travel must agree with you."

"Jessica."

Jessica turned to her mother while Pops shook hands with Zach, who had followed her outside.

"Mom." Jessica hugged her mom, holding on for a little longer than usual.

Her mom studied her. "Dad's right. You do look great. Where's Phil—" Her gaze focused on something behind Jessica. "Who's that?"

Jessica turned. Her eyes met and held Zach's for one brief instant. "That's Pops' house-sitter, Zach." She kept her tone even, trying not to betray any emotion as she said his name.

Her mother raised an eyebrow. "*That's* Dad's house-sitter?"

"Yeah, why?" Keep it casual, she reminded herself.

"I guess I was picturing someone...older."

"How's my little girl?" Thankfully her dad interrupted, saving Jessica from needing to comment on her mother's statement.

"I'm good, Dad." She kissed his cheek.

After they'd unloaded the luggage from the car, her dad paid the driver, then they all piled into the house.

Jessica plopped down on the sofa. "So, did you guys have a good time?"

"The best," Pops replied. "Your mom and dad will tell you all about it. As for me, I've missed this place. Zach, how about taking me around and showing me what's been going on while I've been gone?"

"You bet."

Jessica's mom stepped forward. "I don't think we've met. I'm Kathleen Hart, Ben's daughter. Jessica's mother," she added as she held out her hand.

"Zach Rawlings. It's a pleasure to meet you, ma'am."

"Stephen Hart." Her dad offered his hand as well. "Nice to meet you, Zach."

Pops clapped a hand on Zach's shoulder. "Zach's been taking care of the place while I've been gone."

Her father laughed. "Well, you must be a hell of a guy, Zach. Ben wouldn't trust this place to just anybody."

Zach cast a brief look at Jessica before addressing the comment. "Well, sir, I think I love this place almost as much as Ben does."

Pops nodded. "Damn straight. Now, let's hop on some ATVs and take a look around. Stephen, want to join us?"

As they headed out the door, Zach paused. "Jess, would you put together the salad?"

"No problem." She rose and headed into the kitchen.

Her mother followed.

Jessica opened the refrigerator door. Taking her time, she transferred the salad makings from the fridge to the counter, hoping to delay the inevitable conversation. Finally, with nothing else to do, she closed the door. With a deep, but hopefully imperceptible breath, she turned to face her mom.

A stern expression Jessica knew well greeted her. "Jessica, what's going on?"

Jessica bit her lip. "What do you mean?"

Her mother let out an exasperated sigh. "You know what I mean. What's going on between you and Dad's house-sitter? And where's Philip?"

Jessica ignored the second question. "What makes you think there's something going on?" She busied herself with the salad and hoped her mother wouldn't see how her hands trembled.

"I'm not blind. I can see the way you two were looking at each other. And you never answered my other question. Where's Philip?"

"It's not what you think. I mean Zach and me." She continued to avoid her mom's gaze. Could she hear the lie in Jessica's voice? "And Philip and I aren't...together anymore."

"Oh, Jessica." Her mother's tone held equal measures of dismay and censure. "What happened this time?"

Jessica bristled at the implication. Not so long ago she would have agreed with her mother's assessment of the situation. She would have blamed herself. But not anymore. She raised her chin. "It just didn't work out. That's all." Now wasn't the time to share all the sordid details.

"Well, I can't say I'm surprised." She paused. "Or that I'm sorry." She laid a gentle hand on Jessica's shoulder. "I always thought you were too good for him."

Jessica's eyes snapped to those so similar to her own.

"But don't you think it's too soon to have...moved on?"

"I told you. It's not like that. Zach and I are friends. He helped me get through a rough time." That part was true. But no way would she share the nitty-gritty details with her mother. Not a chance in hell.

"So, what are you going to do?"

Jessica could tell her mother still didn't believe her, but for now wouldn't push the issue. She shrugged. "I'm not sure. I might hang out here with Pops for a while. And then I thought maybe I'd come up and spend some time with you and Dad."

"That would be wonderful."

"Yeah, it will be nice," Jessica agreed. She ignored the tiny ache in her heart that reminded her spending time with her parents meant leaving Zach.

She'd known, they'd both known, their time together had been temporary. A stolen moment. For her, he'd been a way to heal. Nothing more. Maybe if she told herself often enough, she'd start to believe it.

What had it been for him? He couldn't really be in love with her like Sharlie thought. But Jessica had been afraid to answer his question earlier. About what it had all meant.

Things were already different. He wouldn't be staying at the cabin anymore. Tonight he'd go back to his own apartment. She couldn't imagine not sleeping in his arms. Waking up with him beside her. Although it had been only a few nights, she already was used to his presence in her bed. In her life. Which wasn't good.

"Jessica?"

She forced her attention to her mother. "What? Did you say something?"

"I wondered if—"

"Hey, ladies." Zach sauntered into the room.

Jessica's heart tripped at the sight of him. Not good. Not good at all.

"That was a fast ride," she commented. Did her voice sound as breathy to everyone else as it did to her own ears?

"I need to check on the meatloaf."

"Oh, right," Jessica said. "The salad's done."

"Great." Zach opened the oven door. The heady aroma of rosemary permeated the kitchen.

"My that smells good," her mother said. "What are you making?"

"Brown sugar meatloaf, potatoes with rosemary and dill, and green beans with almonds and water chestnuts."

"That sounds absolutely delicious." She studied Zach as he tested the potatoes with a fork. "Do you cook often?"

"Every chance I get."

"Zach's a fabulous chef," Jessica put it. "You should taste his chicken parmesan." Zach's culinary skills were a nice, safe topic of conversation.

"Do you own a restaurant?"

"No, cooking's just a hobby." He tossed Jessica an enigmatic look. "Dinner will be ready in about half an hour. Would you like something to drink while we wait, Mrs. Hart? A glass of wine?"

"No, no, thank you. And, please, call me Kathleen."

During dinner, everyone attempted to catch up with one another. Pops and her parents regaled everyone with stories about their recent trip. Zach filled Pops in on what he'd done around the property. Jessica listened to the talk flowing around her, but didn't participate.

When Zach's leg brushed hers under the table, she cast a glance at him, but he appeared engrossed in conversation with Pops. The touch had been accidental. Would it be the last time she'd feel it?

After dessert, Zach pushed back his chair. "Well, I need to get these dishes cleaned up, and then I guess I should get going." His glance flicked to Jessica.

Her mom stood. "Don't be silly, Zach. You made

dinner, we'll clean up."

"Super," Pops said as he, too, rose. "I need to settle up with Zach what I owe him for taking care of things around here while I was away."

Zach's gaze found Jessica's for a brief moment again, before he followed Pops from the room.

Jessica and her mom worked in silence, clearing the dishes from the table and loading them into the dishwasher.

"Wait, Mom," Jessica said as her mom placed a pan in the machine. "That can't go in there."

"What?"

"The dishwasher will ruin the non-stick coating on that pan. You have to wash it by hand." She hid a smile at the memory the words evoked. She vividly recalled a similar conversation with Zach the morning after she'd arrived.

Her mother looked at her as if she'd grown two heads. "Since when do you know anything about non-stick coatings?"

"I don't. Those are Zach's pans. I just know what he told me."

"I see."

Before her mother could comment further, Jessica grabbed the pan and scrubbed it with the brush from the sink. Once dry, she placed it in the open box near the door. The only thing Zach hadn't taken out to his truck yet.

With nothing left to do in the kitchen, she walked out into the family room. Zach looked up.

"Are you sure you won't stick around for a beer?" Pops asked.

Zach turned back to the older man. "No, I should get going." His eyes flicked to Jessica again. "I'm sure you all have a lot of catching up to do."

"Well, again, Zach." Pops shook his hand. "I can't thank you enough. Knowing you were here taking care of things helped me enjoy my trip even more."

"No, problem. It was my pleasure." This time he avoided looking at her.

"Well, don't be a stranger."

"I won't," Zach promised, his hand on the door.

A stab of fear spiked into her. Was this it? When he walked out, would that be it? Would she ever see him again?

"Your box," she blurted.

Zach turned.

"Um, you have another box in the kitchen. Your pots and pans and things."

"Right. Thanks, I almost forgot about that one." He strode past her to the kitchen. The crisp scent of his aftershave washed over her. She inhaled, savoring the bittersweet reminder of his skin against hers.

With the box tucked under one arm, Zach returned to the family room. "Stephen, Kathleen, it was nice meeting you. Ben, I'm sure I'll see you around The Corral."

"Count on it."

"Jessica." Could everyone else hear the soft caress of his voice as he said her name? Or was it only her imagination?

She folded her arms across her chest to quell the urge to reach out to him. They'd said their good-byes. She hadn't expected to have another moment alone with him once her family got home.

"Bye, Zach." Her voice trembled. She bit her lip.

The door closed behind him.

An emptiness settled inside her.

Chapter Sixteen

The hollow ache lingered. Having to pretend she didn't miss Zach while her parents were still there made it more difficult. And of course, her mother wanted more details about what had happened with Philip.

One day while Pops and her dad were out on the ATVs, her mom brought it up again. "So, what really happened between you and Philip?" Her tone held no censure, but reflected her honest concern.

Jessica glanced up from the book she'd been pretending to read. She hadn't been able to concentrate. Truth was, concentrating on anything besides how much she missed Zach was difficult.

Her mom waited, a patient expression on her face. Jessica had avoided the topic of Philip longer than she'd thought possible. Her mom had been busy helping Pops settle back in. But Jessica had known it would come back up eventually. She took a deep breath. Might as well get it over with. "He started drinking way too much. All the time. He, uh, wouldn't get help. It got really bad." She looked away, unable to share the more humiliating details. "I couldn't take it anymore. So, I ended it."

Her breath huffed out as she waited for a response. Would her mother say she hadn't tried hard enough to make it work? Would she think it was Jessica's fault?

Not too long ago, she would have shouldered the blame. But not now. Not since Zach had come into her life and healed her. Her heart squeezed a little at the thought of him.

"Oh, Jessica." Tears clogged her mother's voice.

Jessica's head jerked up. Moisture swam in Kathleen Hart's eyes. "Mom? Are you crying?" Was she that disappointed in her? Jessica swallowed the lump in her throat.

"I am so sorry."

"Sorry?"

Her mom took Jessica's hand. "I didn't know," she whispered. "Why didn't you tell us? I thought you were happy."

Jessica tightened her fingers around her mom's. "That's what I wanted you to think. I didn't want you to know. I didn't want you to be disappointed in me."

The other woman's head snapped up. "Why would we be disappointed in *you*?"

Jessica looked away again. "I thought maybe you would think this was my fault." After all, *she'd* thought that. Up until Zach.

"Your fault?" Her mom sounded horrified. "Why in the world would I ever think something like that would be your fault?"

Jessica shrugged. "Well, I've made some decisions that haven't been the best when it comes to men. And I don't have the greatest track record when it comes to relationships. I've made so many mistakes." Which was why she wasn't going to make one again with Zach. She needed to learn from her mistakes, not keep repeating them.

Her mom's lips quirked. "I will admit you've made some, ah, interesting decisions in the past."

Jessica smiled, too. "You could say that."

"But, Jessica, ending things with Philip wasn't a mistake."

"I know. But getting involved with him in the first place was a big one."

Her mother sighed. "I can't say I'm sorry it's over. Don't get me wrong, I'm sorry, more sorry than you'll ever know, you had to go through all of that. And that you felt the need to keep it from your family. But there's no doubt you made the right decision in ending it. I'm sure it couldn't have been easy. I'm proud of you. And, to be honest, I never really cared for Philip. Like I said the other day, I always thought he wasn't anywhere near good enough for you." Her lips tightened. "I just wish I hadn't been quite so right."

Tears welled in Jessica's eyes. "Thanks, Mom."

"You just jumped into that whole relationship with Philip so fast. Maybe if you'd had time to get to know him better first, things wouldn't have turned out so badly in the end." Her mom's voice held an equal combination of motherly concern and loving censure.

"I know. And believe me, I won't ever make that mistake again." It had been a painful lesson to learn, but she'd learned it. Which was why her time with Zach could only be about sex. It was too soon for anything else.

What would have happened if she'd met him a year from now? Two years from now? Would it be different? Her time with Philip wouldn't have been so fresh in her mind.

Would someone else have healed her soul instead of Zach? Would that have been better? Finding him later, when she could trust him with her heart and her body?

No, she couldn't imagine that. Zach had come into her life at this time for a reason. She'd needed *him* to heal the demons haunting her. And she did trust him with her body. She just wasn't ready to trust anyone with her heart. Not when she couldn't trust it herself.

"So," her mom broke into her thoughts. "Are you, okay," she hesitated over the word, "with everything now?"

"I'm not sure," she admitted. She was definitely okay with certain things. Definitely not okay with others. "It wasn't easy, but I made it through." She smiled over at her mother. "That's why I came to the cabin in the first place. After everything, I needed to get away. To escape."

Her mother gazed at her as if contemplating something. Finally, she spoke. "Can I ask you something?"

"Sure."

"How does Zach fit into all of this?"

Jessica bit her lip. She averted her eyes. "I was surprised to find him here, that's for sure." That was also an understatement, but her mom didn't need, and wasn't going to get, all of the details. "I hadn't called first, so I didn't know Pops was gone. Zach explained he'd been hired to take care of the place, but I told him in no uncertain terms since I was here he could leave."

Her mother's lips twitched. "I'm sure you did."

"But he was stubborn." She smiled at those early memories. "Told me I wouldn't be able to take care of things around here." She shook her head. "Turns out he was right." She looked back at her mom. "I always think of this place as a quiet, restful getaway. Do you have any idea how much *work* there is to do around here?"

Kathleen Hart laughed. "I can only imagine."

"So, anyway, after several sad attempts at trying to do things around here," she grimaced at the memory, "I practically wound up begging Zach to help." She glanced away again. "Turns out it was nice having someone around."

"And that's it? It was *nice* having Zach around?" Her mother sounded skeptical.

"Yep," Jessica said firmly. "That's it. He really kept to himself for the most part." Well, that had been true at first. "He kept pretty busy around here during the day, and a lot of nights he had to work." Vivid memories of the recent nights they'd spent together when Zach hadn't worked flooded her mind.

She lowered her head, hoping her mom wouldn't see the incriminating flush staining her cheeks.

"So," she said to change the subject and the direction of her thoughts. "I know you and Dad are leaving in a couple of days. I thought I'd spend a little more time with Pops and then come up and stay with you guys for a while. That is, if you'll have me."

"Of course we'll have you. I can't think of anything I'd like better."

"Thanks. Although you might change your mind fairly soon. I'm homeless at the moment, remember?" Jessica chuckled.

Her mom laughed, too, but then grew serious. "It's been a while since we've spent time with you, Jessica. You can stay as long as you want."

****

In the whirlwind of her parents leaving and making plans to join them soon, Jessica rarely had time to think about Zach over the next couple of days. At least consciously. Thoughts, memories, and visions hovered in the back of her mind. During the day it was easier to not think about him. The nights were harder. She missed sleeping in his arms.

Once her parents had gone, though, Jessica found she had too much time alone with her thoughts.

He hadn't called. She'd half expected him to. And although not hearing from him was probably better all the way around, she couldn't help but wonder why he didn't call. Did he think about her as much as she thought about him? Did he think about her at all?

At least one thing was certain. Zach didn't have feelings for her. Sharlie had been wrong on that account. If he did, wouldn't he have called? This epiphany should have brought a sense of relief. She didn't want Zach to have feelings for her.

Because of course she didn't have feelings for him. She couldn't. It was too soon.

But she couldn't deny she missed him.

Jessica's phone chirped, interrupting her reverie. She flipped it open. "Hello?"

"Hi." The husky voice skittered over her.

Speak of the devil. "Zach." She breathed his name.

"So, is Ben settling back in?"

"Yeah, I think he's glad to be home."

He paused. "How have you been?"

"Fine," she lied. She couldn't tell him she hadn't slept in the last two nights since her parents had left, and she almost ached with weariness. Her small bed was much too big and lonely without Zach in it.

"Good." He hesitated again. "So, you never answered my question the other day."

She frowned. "What question?"

"About if I called and asked you to go out. About what your answer would be."

"Oh." She remembered the question. She also remembered her relief when the arrival of Pops and her parents had saved her from answering.

"So..."

"So?" her voice quavered.

"I'm calling you, Jess."

"Oh," she said again. Her stomach quivered.

"Will you go out with me tonight?"

Her heart stuttered. Every ounce of her being wanted to say *yes*, but her fear got in the way. They'd said good-bye. The time since, without him, hadn't been easy. Wouldn't seeing him again make it all the harder to leave?

You wanted him to call, she reminded herself. What did she expect? For him to say *hello* and leave it at that? But seeing him again was a bad idea.

"Jess? Are you still there?"

"I'm still here." Her voice was almost a whisper.

"So?"

"What...what did you want to do?" Dang it. Her fickle heart was winning out over her common sense. Never a good thing.

"I wondered if you wanted to meet me at The Corral."

She bit her lip. A bar? He wanted her to go to a bar? That alone should be enough incentive to refuse. She couldn't imagine setting foot in a bar.

But still, she wavered. Because she wanted to. For Zach. The chance to see him again tempted her enough to overcome her misgivings. About many things.

"A...at the bar? Why there?"

"Yes, at the bar." He paused. "I want you to see what it's like. I want you to see where I work."

Did she imagine the hint of a challenge in his voice?

"So, what do you say? I'm meeting Sharlie and Logan and Jake there. I want you to come."

"I don't know if that's a good idea."

"Hanging out with me or being in a bar?"

Both. She hesitated.

"I know you've had bad experiences with people who drink, but The Corral's not like that."

"It's a bar, Zach."

"I know. I didn't mean it like that. Of course people go there to drink. But it's mellow. Comfortable. I just wanted to share it with you."

Jessica bit her lip. How could she be this torn? Her answer should be an immediate *no*. She'd had enough bad experiences with people who drank to last a lifetime. Why court more trouble by purposely putting herself in a place where drinking was the main reason for being there? Of course she shouldn't go. So what compelled her to tell him she'd be there?

The temptation to see him one last time overwhelmed her. Another reason she should say no. She had to be strong. Not give in.

It's not like seeing him one more time would change anything. It wouldn't change who he was and what he believed. Or who she was and what she believed.

She opened her mouth to decline. "I...I'll think about it." The refusal wouldn't come.

Zach sighed. "I guess that's better than a *no*." Even through the phone she discerned the mix of amusement and chagrin in his voice.

"I'm sorry."

"No, I understand." The genuine empathy in his voice touched her. "I know I'm asking a lot. I was just hoping..." He cleared his throat. "I'll be there around seven, in case you decide to come."

"Okay."

"Bye, Jess."

"Bye, Zach." She closed the phone and stared out into space.

"Who were you talking to?"

She jumped at the sound of Pops' voice. "Oh. You startled me."

"Sorry, sweetheart." He nodded toward the phone in her hand. "Was that your mom? I needed to ask her something."

"No." She hesitated. "It was Zach."

"Oh?" Pops raised an eyebrow.

"He, uh, he wondered if I wanted to hang out at The Corral tonight with him and his friends."

"Well, that sounds nice." Now he hesitated. "Zach's a good man."

"I know."

"Yeah, well, right. I just wanted you to know I think so, too." He studied her intently for a long moment. "You should have fun tonight, then."

She gnawed her lip. "I'm not sure I'm going."

"Really? Why not?"

"I'm not really a bar kind of girl. And with you being in Ireland I feel like I haven't had a lot of time to spend with you. And I'll be heading up to Mom and Dad's soon." The thought made her heart hurt. Pops wasn't the only one she'd miss when she left.

"Well, honey, you know I love spending time with you, too, of course, but we still have lots of time to visit before you leave. I don't want to keep you from your friends. And besides, if you go out, I can walk around naked." He winked.

Jessica laughed, but realized Pops really might want to spend some time alone. He'd been with her parents for almost two months, and then she'd stayed when they'd left. For someone used to the solitude of the cabin, being around people for so long was probably driving him crazy.

"Well, Pops, I definitely don't want to see that, so going out might be in my best interest after all." She kissed him on the top of his head. "But I'm not going out until seven, so keep your pants on until then."

They laughed together, the enjoyment settling into her heart and making it feel lighter. Then she sighed. If she were honest with herself, she'd have to admit it wasn't sharing a joke with Pops that made her feel better, but the thought of seeing Zach again. And Pops' desire to be alone simply gave her a convenient excuse. No matter what excuse she gave, it all boiled down to the fact despite her misgivings, she really did want to see Zach again. One last time.

So at seven-fifteen that night, she sat in her car and contemplated the weathered wooden sign in front of her: *The Corral—Restaurant and Bar*. The word *bar* taunted her.

Did she have the courage to do this? To walk into a bar? The bar where Zach worked.

His name, as usual, brought a small ache to her chest. It had been ages since she'd seen him. The thought alone propelled her forward. She took a deep breath and shoved open the door. Her shoes crunched in the gravel as she made her way across the crowded parking lot. She pushed the revolving door, and it rotated to carry her into the building. Straight ahead was an area holding a few scattered tables, empty save for one. An arrow pointing down the stairs to her left indicated where she'd find the bar.

She took another deep breath and slowly descended, one cautious step at a time. Downstairs, loud country music filled the barroom. Hundreds of people crowded on the dance floor and gathered around several bars. She grimaced.

Maybe this hadn't been a good idea. She could still change her mind. Leave before Zach saw her. He'd never even know she'd been there. Would he be disappointed she hadn't shown up?

She'd have to hang out at a coffee shop or someplace for a while, just in case Pops hadn't been joking about the naked stuff. She turned back toward the stairs.

But before she could put her escape plan into action, she glimpsed Zach heading toward her from across the room. The tension left her body, replaced by a giddy sense of anticipation. And nerves of a whole different sort.

When he reached her, her gaze swept over him. The wide span of his shoulders strained the fabric of his western-cut, button-down shirt. Faded blue jeans, outlining and emphasizing his masculinity, fitted like a second skin and had her pulse racing. Snakeskin boots adorned his feet. Her glance slid to his face. A black cowboy hat pulled low over his forehead shaded his eyes, hiding his expression from her. He looked sexy as all hell. And like he belonged.

Right there in the bar.

Damn.

"You came." His tone reflected his pleasure. "I wasn't sure you would."

"I wasn't sure I would either," she admitted. She looked around. "Lots of people come here to drink, huh?"

Zach put his arm around her shoulders. "And to talk. And dance. And hang out with their friends." He steered her across the room. People they passed greeted him by name.

"So, why did you come?"

"I missed you." The words slipped out. She bit her lip.

Zach stopped. Right there in the middle of the barroom, he tugged her into his arms. His kiss was warm and soft.

"Me too," he whispered.

This close, the shadow from the brim of his hat couldn't hide his eyes. She let herself get lost in the deep intensity of his gaze.

"Hey, isn't there a policy about public displays of affection in this place?" Jake's cheerful voice cut into the moment.

"I certainly hope not," Logan said as he walked up beside Jake, his arm around Sharlie's shoulders. He leaned down and kissed his wife.

"Someone should really talk to the owner," Jake joked.

The group headed toward a corner of the bar where they grabbed a table. Zach held out a high chair for Jessica. She climbed on to it. Sharlie scooted onto a similar one across from her.

"So, where's your girl tonight?" Zach asked Jake.

Jake grinned and looked around the bar. "I haven't decided who the lucky lady will be for the night."

"You know, one of these days you need to settle

in and stick with one woman," Sharlie said.

An expression of mock horror crossed Jake's face. "Why would I want to do that and deny all these wonderful ladies," his hand swept out, "the chance to partake of my company?"

Sharlie rolled her eyes and turned her attention to Jessica. "How's Ben? Is he glad to be home?"

Jessica nodded. "I think he is. I know he had a really great time, but it's always nice to come home when you've been away for a while. And I think he was glad I went out tonight. He needed some alone time." She didn't mention the naked part. *Had* Pops been serious? "Where's Owen tonight?"

"One of the high school girls from Logan's camp is babysitting."

"I'm going to head to the bar. What does everyone want to drink?" Logan asked.

Sharlie and Jake stated their preferences. Logan turned to Jessica. "What can I get for you?"

"Just a soda, thanks."

"Zach?"

"Soda's fine."

Logan nodded and turned away.

Jessica turned to Zach. "You don't have to do that," she said softly so Jake and Sharlie wouldn't overhear.

"Do what?" Zach sounded puzzled.

"Have soda. I..." She paused. "I don't mind if you have a beer."

He shook his head. "I know you don't like it when I drink."

"No, really it's fine. I know...I know you're not like Philip. If you want a beer, please don't feel you can't have one on my account."

"I'm good. Maybe I'll have one later." He studied her, a peculiar expression in his eyes. "Was it really difficult? Coming here tonight?"

She bit her lip. "At first I wasn't sure I'd come,"

she admitted. "I couldn't quite image myself walking into a bar. I didn't know if I'd be able to do it."

"But you did." The warm tone of his voice melted through her. "What made you decide to come? How did you know you'd be able to do it?"

"Well, I was torn about coming. I wanted to see you again," she blushed, "but I wasn't so sure it was a good idea. But then"—she hurried on before he could comment—"Pops said he needed some naked alone time, so I figured I should get the hell out of the cabin before I found out firsthand if he'd been joking or not."

Zach's jaw dropped. "Naked alone time? Was he serious?"

She shrugged. "Like I said, I didn't stick around to find out." She met his gaze. "But really that was just an excuse. Deep down I'd made up my mind as soon as you called. I wanted to see you." She took a deep breath. "I almost changed my mind at the last minute. When I saw how many people were here," her gaze darted around the crowded room, "drinking, I didn't know if I'd be able to stay, but then I saw you. And it seemed like forever since you'd left Pops' place. So I decided to stay. For you."

For a moment Zach looked staggered. A stab of remorse pricked her. Was it cruel to be so honest? In the long run, admitting how much she'd missed him wasn't going to make leaving any easier. For either one of them.

"And besides," she added in an attempt to lighten the suddenly serious mood. "I didn't want to take any chances and go back to the cabin. God only knows if Pops was kidding."

Zach laughed. "Probably a good choice." He glanced over at the dance floor. "Want to dance?" His tone was lighter as well, as if he too wanted to shake off the intensity that still hung in the air around them.

Jessica shook her head. "No, thanks. I don't know how to do any of that stuff." She nodded toward the line dancers moving in complicated patterns across the parquet floor.

"This stuff's not really my style either, but they'll play something different soon."

Sure enough, a little while later the DJ switched to a ballad. The dancers paired off and swayed to the music. Zach grabbed her hand and led her out onto the floor. Logan and Sharlie joined them.

Zach swept his hat from his head, then drew Jessica into his embrace. His arms wrapped around her, meeting at her waist, where he held the hat in his hands.

She wound her arms around his neck and tucked her head beneath his chin. The crisp scent of his aftershave tickled her senses when she inhaled.

She sighed in contentment. It seemed like ages since she'd touched him. Since he'd touched her.

As if reading her mind, Zach nuzzled the hair away from her neck and kissed her throat. His lips trailed to her ear, where he touched his tongue to the shell.

She shivered.

"Did you really miss me?" he whispered.

"Yes," she breathed on a sigh.

"Good. I missed you so damn much it hurt."

Her heartbeat quickened at the admission. She ignored the tiny voice in the back of her mind telling her she was in too deep. Their relationship had gone far beyond what she'd intended.

But she didn't want to think about that. Instead she concentrated on the tiny ripples of pleasure radiating from the small of her back, where Zach lightly stoked her skin through the thin cotton of her shirt.

When the song ended, she stayed in his arms, not wanting the embrace to end. Zach remained still as well.

But when a group of line dancers flooded the dance floor, jostling around them, he sighed. He placed his hat back on his head, then led her from the floor.

Back at the table, instead of letting her climb back up on her chair, he pulled her against his chest and wrapped his arms around her from behind.

She didn't mind. She wasn't done being touched by him yet. Would she ever be? Apprehension gripped her heart and spread. She was in too deep with a man she couldn't see herself having a future with.

She ignored the tingle of fear. She wouldn't think about that right now. She'd concentrate on how...satisfying it was to be in his arms again. And the delicious shivers that slid over her body when he brushed his lips against her ear again.

"Will you come over to my place later? Before you go back to the cabin?" The meaning behind the words was clear.

The thrill of him wanting her coursed through her. "I—"

"Your grandfather said I would find you here." The familiar voice interrupted her.

Her head snapped up. Her heart stalled before starting again with a painful thud. A lump formed in her throat. "Philip," she managed.

Zach stiffened. His arms tightened around her.

Philip looked at Zach and scowled. "Get your hands off my wife."

Chapter Seventeen

A thundering silence met the words.

Behind her Zach stiffened.

"I said, get your hands of off her," Philip repeated. He took a step closer.

Zach shifted, moving beside her. He kept his arm draped around her shoulders. Logan and Jake stood on either side of her.

Philip's eyes darted between the men. "Look," he said. "I don't want any trouble. I just want to talk to my wife."

"Stop calling me that," Jessica ground out from between clenched teeth. She dared not look at Zach, too afraid to see the look on his face. "I'm not your wife anymore."

"I just want to talk to you." He reached for her arm.

She jerked away. "I don't have anything to say to you." Angry tears trembled in her voice.

"I—"

"You heard the lady," Zach broke in. The control in his voice sounded forced.

She bit her lip. What was he thinking?

"This doesn't have anything to do with you. Stay out of it," Philip snarled.

Zach's arm dropped from her shoulders. He took a half step forward and to the side, moving in front of her. "I think it does."

Philip's gaze jerked to Zach, then back to her. "I see you've made some new friends. Is this why you left me? For him? Does he know?" His eyes slid over her. A look of disgust crossed his face.

"Know what?" The words came out hoarse.

"That you're a tease. You look like a hot piece of ass, but there's nothing underneath but ice."

"Son of a—" Zach surged forward, clenching his fist.

"It's not worth it, Zach." Jake laid a restraining hand on his arm.

"I've been on the receiving end of one of Zach's punches. Believe me, you don't want to go there," Logan added. His attempt at humor did little to ease the tension in the air.

"Sharlie?" Zach didn't turn as he spoke. "Can you take Jessica to your office?"

"Sure."

Jessica jumped when Sharlie laid a hand on her arm. Her eyes hadn't strayed from Philip. She couldn't believe he stood there in front of her. Couldn't believe he'd called her his wife. She shuddered. In front of Zach.

"Come on, let's get out of here."

Jessica shook her head. "No, I..." She tore her gaze from Philip to stare at Zach. He wouldn't look at her. Her heart beat so fast a painful ache spread through her chest. She trembled. She hadn't meant for him to find out this way. Hadn't meant for him to find out at all. What would he think of her now?

"Jess, please. Go." His gaze touched hers for a brief moment. "I'll be right there."

With reluctance slowing every step, she allowed Sharlie to guide her up the stairs and into an office. The door closed with a soft click. She sank into a chair.

"Do you want something to drink?"

"No."

Sharlie sat in the chair next to hers, but didn't say anything.

"Do you ever get the feeling you can't escape from your past?" Jessica broke the silence.

Sharlie's smile was sad. "Oh, I'm very familiar with that feeling."

"I thought I was done with that part of my life. But now I think the mistakes I've made are going to haunt me forever."

Sharlie sighed. "The past is always a part of our lives. The trick is to not dwell on your mistakes. Overcome them, don't let them overcome you. And try not to make the same ones again."

"You sound like you speak from experience."

"A lot of it."

"So, how did you do it? You know, overcome your past."

"I had a lot of help from my friends. The people who cared about me. Especially Zach."

Jessica looked away. "He didn't know."

"Didn't know what?"

"That I'd been married."

"Ah."

"A hell of a way for him to find out, huh?"

Sharlie remained silent.

Finally Jessica whispered. "I'm sorry. I know how much he means to you. I...I didn't mean to hurt him."

Sharlie sighed again. "Like I said, we all make mistakes." She paused. "Don't worry. I'm sure the two of you will get through all of this. Everything will be okay. He really cares about you."

Now Jessica fell silent. Everything wouldn't be okay. He shouldn't care about her, and she shouldn't have come to The Corral tonight. She'd led Zach on. Not purposely. Not maliciously. But she'd done it all the same. She didn't want a relationship with him, but she'd used him to fight her own inner demons. It hadn't been fair.

And she hadn't told him everything. So now she needed to face Zach's anger, his disgust about her marriage to Philip. Then, she could put her time with him behind her. Maybe his anger would make it easier for her to leave. To forget the pain she'd caused him.

"I...I need to talk to him."

Sharlie nodded and rose. "I'll go get him."

****

"You okay?" Jake asked. He sat with Zach and Logan in Logan's office.

Zach nodded. "Yeah, I just need a minute."

"I didn't know Jessica was married before."

Jessica had been married. Jessica had been married. Jessica had been married. The refrain echoed through his head like a bass drum. Pounding. Relentless. He couldn't escape from it. The bastard who'd treated her so cruelly had been her husband. He clenched his fists as rage poured through him again.

Fast on the heels of the rage came the hurt. Why hadn't she told him?

"Neither did I." He dropped his face into his hands.

Jake laid a hand on his shoulder. "I'm sorry." He hesitated. "What are you going to do?"

"Do?"

"Well, I'm thinking the two of you had better talk."

Zach nodded again and sighed. "Yeah, we should."

"Does it matter? To you? That Jessica was married before." Jake asked.

Zach looked up and shook his head. "I don't know. I don't think so." He huffed out a breath. "I just can't wrap my head around this. I knew about her past, but it never crossed my mind she'd been married. To that bastard. I want to kill him." And he wanted to know why she'd lied to him. Well, not lied, exactly, but withheld the truth.

"I think we all do, but that won't help matters."

Zach ran his fingers through his hair. "I know. I know."

"You need to focus on Jessica. I bet she's freaking out right now."

Zach half rose from his chair. "Why? Is that scum-bag still here? I'll—"

Jake laid a hand on his shoulder. "He's gone. I meant she's probably freaking out wondering what you're thinking." He studied Zach. "Does this change things between you two?"

"To be honest, I don't know what's between us." He looked down at his hands. "She was married," he said the words almost to himself. Saying them out loud caused the hurt to stab a little deeper. For all her talk of trust, she hadn't trusted him with the whole truth.

His gaze found Jake's again. "What do I say to her?"

Jake shook his head.

"You love her, you'll figure it out," Logan cut in.

Zach's gaze snapped to his. "Love her?"

Jake chuckled. "It's pretty obvious, man." He jerked his thumb at Logan. "It's like watching him with Sharlie."

Staggered, Zach mused over Jake and Logan's words. Spending time with Logan and Sharlie left no doubt in anyone's mind how much they loved each other. When they were together their love was a tangible thing. Was it like that for him and Jessica? Was Logan right? Was Zach in love with her?

Something must have changed in his expression, because Jake laughed. "Ah, the light dawns," he ribbed. "So, I guess back to my original question. Does it matter to you she's divorced? Does it change the way you feel?"

Zach didn't even have to think about it. "No. Not one damn bit."

Jake grinned. "Then go talk to her."

Zach nodded. At the door he turned to look at Logan. "Would it have mattered to you? When you came back, if Sharlie had been divorced?"

Logan shook his head, although his expression tightened. "It would have been hard, knowing she'd been someone else's wife, but it wouldn't have changed the way I feel about her."

Understanding passed between the two men.

Sharlie poked her head into the room. "Hey." She smiled at Logan, then turned her attention to Zach. "Jessica's in my office."

Zach nodded.

She laid her hand on his arm. "Go easy on her. She's hurting, too." She moved to Logan and put her arms around his waist. He wrapped his arms around her and inclined his head to kiss her. She snuggled against his chest.

Zach looked over at Jake and raised an eyebrow. "Really?" he gestured toward Sharlie and Logan with his thumb. "Like that?"

Jake rolled his eyes. "Yeah. Like that. Sometimes worse."

Zach grinned.

"I just hope it's not contagious," Jake muttered beneath his breath.

Logan's laughter followed Zach down the hallway.

Zach paused at the door to the office. What would he say to Jessica? Would she admit she loved him, too, or would she be too afraid? She *did* love him, of that he was sure, although he couldn't say *why* he was so certain. But getting her to admit it...well that was a whole other issue.

The door stood slightly ajar. Jessica sat, her face in her hands. His heart squeezed at the dejected pose.

He could almost tell what she must be thinking. Blaming herself for everything that had happened earlier. The revelation. The fight that had nearly ensued.

His fingers clenched, the knuckles tightening. He still wanted to ram his fist into Philip's face. The mere thought of the man and what he'd done to Jessica formed a hollow ache in his stomach.

But he wouldn't think about that right now. He let the wondrous feel of loving Jessica flood his heart. His hand relaxed. Opened.

He pushed the door wider and stepped through. "I guess there was something you forgot to tell me."

****

Jessica's head snapped up.

Zach leaned against the doorframe, his arms folded across his chest.

She kept her gaze focused on his, although she wanted to bury her head in her hands again. "I'm sorry. I know you must be angry with me, and I—"

He shook his head. "I'm not angry. Well, not with you." He straightened. "Surprised. Caught off guard. Curious. Hurt."

She flinched at his honesty.

"But not angry."

She'd expected his anger. The calm tone of his voice confused her. "You should be."

"Why?"

"Well, because, I didn't tell you. About Philip. That we were married."

"I'm upset you didn't tell me. But not in an angry way." He studied her. "You say you trust me, but how can I trust you when you don't tell me everything?"

She looked away and bit her lip.

Zach sat down across from her. "Why didn't you tell me?"

"I was too ashamed," she whispered.

"Ashamed?" Zach's surprise was evident in his voice.

She nodded. "You already knew what my...relationship with him was like. I...I didn't want you to be any more disappointed in me."

His brow furrowed. "Why would I be disappointed in you?"

Why wouldn't he be disappointed in her? Why should he be any different than anyone else? She'd disappointed everyone she'd ever cared about. "Because I was stupid enough to marry someone like that."

Zach took her hand and stroked his fingers over the back of it. "Did you know what he was like when you married him?"

"No. He changed. I changed. We changed. Oh, I don't know." Unable to be still, she jumped up to pace the small office.

Zach remained quiet.

Finally she turned to face him again. "Maybe I never knew him at all. It all happened so fast. Too fast. Believe me, this isn't a decision I'm proud of."

"Are you going to tell me about it?"

He deserved to know. Before she left. She blew out a breath. "I don't know where to start."

"How about at the beginning?"

"Right." She inhaled a deep gulp of air, then slowly released it. She turned away, unable to look into Zach's compassionate eyes. She didn't deserve his sympathy.

"I met Philip at a party at a friend's house. He was a musician. Totally my type, or so I thought at the time. We hit it off right away. We got pretty serious. Fast. A couple of months after we started dating, he got a gig in Vegas. We decided to get married." She threw a glance over her shoulder. "Pretty stupid, huh?"

Before Zach could comment, she rushed on. "For a while everything was great. The rock star lifestyle thrilled me. But it got old. Fast. And then it got harder and harder for him to get gigs. The music business is a tough one. And he didn't really make an effort. He expected everyone to come to him. He wanted people to come knock on *his* door.

"I started taking classes at a local college. Computer graphics and web design stuff. At first it got me out of the house, so I wasn't around Philip while he moped. But then I really started to enjoy it. As I got more interested in my career, Philip got less interested in his. He didn't even try to get gigs anymore. The guys in the band argued constantly. Everything fell apart."

"That's when the trouble really started. He lost interest in doing anything. He laid around the house all day. Didn't work. And then he started drinking. A lot. All the time instead of just at the bars at night." Her eyes darted to Zach's, then away. "Well, you know what happened next. Finally I couldn't stand it anymore. I moved out and filed for divorce. He wasn't happy about that either. He made it difficult."

"Difficult?" Tension leaked back into Zach's tone.

"He didn't return paperwork or show up for appointments with our lawyers. Eventually everything was finalized, but it took forever. Luckily a couple of friends let me stay with them."

"While it was all going on, I finished my degree and started my own web design business. But I was so wiped out from everything, I had to get away. Escape. So I came here." Her eyes met his. "And found you. And you were kind and caring and wonderful, and..." She paused. "I do trust you," she whispered.

His eyes were sad. He shook his head. "Do you really?"

How could he ask that? After all she'd confided in him. After she'd slept with him.

Almost as if reading her mind, he smiled, but it was rueful. "You trust me with your body. But what about your heart?"

Her head jerked up. "Wh...what?"

"What do you think is happening between us, Jessica?"

Nothing, she wanted to say, but the word wouldn't come. "I...I don't know," she said instead.

"You don't know?" The sad smile was back.

"We're having fun. We have a good time together."

"That's it?"

She lowered her gaze, unable to bear the emotion in his any longer. "Yes," she whispered.

"What are you afraid of?"

Her chin jutted up. "Nothing."

"I think you are. I think you're afraid of how you feel when I kiss you. Touch you." His voice dropped. "Make love to you."

"Wh...why would I be afraid of that?" Her voice trembled.

"I don't know. You tell me."

She shook her head. She couldn't tell him. He wasn't anything like Philip, but a deep, dark place inside of her couldn't help comparing them. Seeing how they *were* alike.

Zach had no goals for the future. He worked at a bar. And was content doing it. As much as she cared—and she refused to use any other word to describe her feelings—about him, he wasn't right for her.

She ignored the ache in her heart.

He wasn't good for her. She'd learned a lot about herself over the past few years, and one of those things was she needed someone who knew what *he* wanted out of life.

"I always fall for the wrong guy," she said, almost to herself. "It's the same, don't you see?" she whispered.

"The same as what?"

"Y...your job," she stuttered, but couldn't go on. The excuse sounded lame. But how could she put it into words? How could she explain?

His eyes narrowed. "My job?"

"You don't have a real job."

"We're not talking about my job." Now a touch of anger slipped into his voice. He took a deep breath before continuing, his voice calm once again. "We're talking about us."

"There is no us." Her voice trembled. "I...I can't get involved with you."

"It's a little too late, don't you think?" He rose. His knuckles grazed her cheek, leaving her skin tingling in their wake. "We're already involved."

She shook her head.

His gaze probed hers. A deep emotion swam in the depths of his dark irises. Her heartbeat stuttered. Even before he opened his mouth, she knew what he was going to say. She could read it in his eyes. And it scared her.

"Jessica, I lo—"

She put her fingers over his lips to stop the words. "Please. Don't say it." Zach couldn't love her. And she couldn't be falling in love with him. She'd only known him for a short while. It was too soon.

She wouldn't repeat her mistakes. She'd been reckless in the past. She couldn't do it ever again. Not with her heart. Not when her scars were so fresh.

He sighed. The intense emotion in his eyes dimmed, tempered by the pain of her rejection. "So what happens now?"

"I...I don't know."

"Right." He ran his fingers through his hair.

"I'm sorry. I..." But she didn't know what to say.

He stared at her until she couldn't bear it any longer. She looked away. The confession she hadn't allowed him to make weighed upon her heart.

He exhaled. "I guess we should get you home. I'll follow you in my truck."

"You don't need to do that. I'll be fine."

"Humor me. I'd feel better knowing you'd gotten home safely."

She nodded without a word. There was nothing left to say.

****

Jake caught up with Zach before work a few nights later.

"What happened with Jessica the other night? Did you get past the whole ex-husband thing?"

Zach laughed, but the sound held no humor. "Oh, yeah. That part was fine. Turns out that's the least of our problems." He ran his fingers through his hair, then readjusted his hat on his head. "She's so damn stubborn," he muttered.

"Stubborn?"

"She's got it in her head we can't be together because I don't have a real job?"

"A real job?"

"Apparently being a bouncer isn't good enough for her. She thinks I need to have some kind of grand plan for the future."

Jake didn't respond right away. When he spoke, the words were quiet, thoughtful. "Maybe you're the one being stubborn."

Zach whipped his head around. "What?"

"*Are* you going to be a bouncer your whole life?"

"Great. Not you, too. I like what I do," Zach said from between gritted teeth.

"I know you do, but you're what? Thirty-two? Are you really going to do this for the rest of your life? I mean, bouncing isn't necessarily looked upon as a career. A side gig to earn a little extra cash, maybe."

"Maybe I'm not looking for a career. You have to work too hard at a career. It doesn't leave you any

214

time for fun."

Jake shook his head. A smile played on his mouth. "Zach, you're the hardest working guy I know. You worked your ass off at the cabin while Ben was gone, and you enjoyed every minute of it."

"That's different."

"How?"

He waved his hand. "That was a temporary thing. Just for fun."

"Plenty of people have careers they think are fun."

Zach frowned. Was Jake taking pages out of Jessica's book? "Yeah, well, like I said, I'm not looking for a career."

"Maybe you're not. If you're satisfied with this," Jake swept his hand out, "then great. But if what Jessica is saying gets to you so much, maybe she's got a point. Maybe it's time to take a closer look at what you want out of life."

****

Jake's words rolled through Zach's head later that night as he tried to fall asleep. Endless questions tumbled through his mind.

Did Jessica's opinion bother him so much because it was so close to the mark? Was he really the one being stubborn? Was he letting his feelings about his parents' careers get in the way of having one of his own?

Did he want something more out of life?

He truly did enjoy his job. But if he were honest with himself, bouncing itself wasn't anything to write home about. The people at The Corral made it special. Jake and Sharlie and Logan. Much of his life was tied to theirs and memories of them together. Meeting Sharlie for the first time. Logan coming back to town and taking over. Even Jake always complaining about how bad the food sucked.

A comment Jessica had made in passing sprang

into his mind. An idea occurred out of the blue. Why hadn't he ever thought of it before?

He wouldn't ever want to leave The Corral. But could he take the place he loved and combine it with something else he enjoyed?

He sat up, turned on the light, and grabbed a notepad from the table next to his bed. His fingers could barely keep up with the ideas pouring through his mind. Soon, he had several pages covered with notes.

The next morning he awoke with the air of excitement still humming through him. He looked through his notes again, a small smile playing on his lips. What would Logan think?

Needing some reassurance, he called Jake and explained his idea. "So, what do you think?"

"I think you should talk to Logan."

"I'm on my way there right now."

Zach grabbed his truck keys. A glance at his watch showed it was too early to find Logan at The Corral. He'd have to head out to the ranch.

Once there, he bounded up the stairs. His hand shook as he knocked on the door.

Sharlie, with Owen in her arms, smiled through the screen. She opened it to greet Zach with a kiss on the cheek. "You're out and about early today. What brings you here?"

"I need to talk to Logan about something. Is he around?"

"Yeah, he's right inside. Come on in."

Zach walked into the spacious family room, his boots echoing on the hardwood floor.

Logan set his paper aside and rose. "Hey, Zach, what's up?"

Zach took a deep breath. "Can I talk to you about something?"

Chapter Eighteen

"Howdy there, Zach. Logan said I'd find you in here."

"Ben." Zach rose from his crouch on the dusty floor of the storage closet and wiped his hands on the back of his jeans, then held one out.

The other man's grip was firm, despite his advancing years.

"What brings you here?"

Ben looked Zach in the eye. "I wanted to apologize."

Zach raised an eyebrow. "Apologize? For what?"

"For sending that no good ex-husband of my granddaughter's here the other night."

"Oh." Zach didn't know what else to say.

Ben continued. "If I would have known..." He glanced at Zach again. "Jessica never told us she and Philip," Ben's tone revealed his disgust for the man, "had gotten a divorce.

"Of course I was curious as to why she'd come to the cabin alone, but figured she'd tell me in her own time. She's always been an independent little thing."

Despite himself, Zach's lips quirked at the description.

"Then while she was over here the other night with you, Philip showed up at my place. Said they'd had a big fight, and he needed to find her so they could talk. I sent him here." Ben huffed out a sigh. "It wasn't until Jessica got home that I found out what had happened between the two of them."

Zach kept his expression neutral. Had Jessica told Ben everything, or an edited version?

"Anyway, like I said, I wanted to apologize. I didn't mean to mess things up between you and Jessica by sending him here."

Zach couldn't contain his surprise. What else had Jessica told her grandfather? Surely not the nature of her relationship with Zach.

"You didn't mess anything up." He hesitated. "There's nothing to mess up." It wasn't really a lie. Jessica had made her feelings about being with him perfectly clear.

Ben raised an eyebrow. "Oh?" He looked like he wanted to add something, but changed his mind. "Well, then I guess I'm sorry I interrupted."

"You didn't. I needed a break."

Ben headed for the door.

"Ben?"

The other man turned.

"Thanks for coming down here. I appreciate it."

Ben nodded. "Can I ask you something?"

"Sure."

"Jessica's been talking about heading up to stay with her parents for a while."

Zach frowned. "Yeah?"

"And I was wondering how you felt about that."

Zach had guessed she wouldn't stick around, but the thought of her leaving made him feel like a piece of himself was being torn away. He hoped his feelings weren't visible as he looked into Ben's too perceptive eyes and sighed. He couldn't lie. "I wish she wouldn't go," he admitted. "But," he hurried on before Ben could say anything, "if there's nothing holding her here, and that's what she really wants to do, then it's her decision."

"Are you sure there's nothing holding her here?"

"Positive." His feelings didn't matter. Especially to Jessica. She didn't even want to hear about them.

Ben sighed. "She's still recovering right now. Scared of getting hurt again."

Zach nodded. "I know."

"You know you're welcome at the cabin any time."

Zach smiled. "Thanks, I appreciate that."

"Well, then I hope I see you soon." He paused again. "She's not leaving for a week or so. Just in case you were wondering."

Zach stared at the door after Ben had left. Even if Jessica stayed for another week. Or two. What did it really matter?

He looked around the storeroom he'd been sorting through, then down at the inventory list in his hand.

Had he done all of this for Jessica? No, not for her. But because of her, he had to admit. Because of an idea she'd put into his head. Would it make a difference if he told her? And did he want that to be the reason she stayed? Would she stay if she knew?

"You've been in here all day. Whatcha doin'?" Jake's voice interrupted his reverie.

Zach shook his head to clear it. "Just sorting through some stuff."

"So did you talk to Logan?" Trust Jake to cut right to the chase.

Zach smiled. "Yep."

"And?"

"And we're going to work something out."

Jake grinned and clapped Zach on the back. "Excellent. Congratulations, man."

"Thanks."

"So when are you going to tell Jessica?"

Zach picked up a box and stacked it in the corner before answering. "I'm not sure I'm going to tell her."

Jake's eyebrows rose. "Really? Why not?"

"She's made up her mind to leave." Zach released a breath. "And I don't want this to be the reason she stays."

****

"Hey, Ben."

Jessica's head snapped up from her computer at the sound of Zach's voice. What was he doing here?

"Hey there, Zach."

"I hope you don't mind me stopping by."

Pops stepped back from the door. "Of course not. Come on in. I said you were welcome any time." He turned. "Jessica, look who's here."

"Hello, Zach." She kept her voice even, despite the trembling in her limbs. He looked so damn...good...standing there.

"Jess." The familiar way he said her name fell over her like a lover's caress.

Pops looked from one to the other. "You know, I just remembered I forgot to water those flowers outside." He scurried from the room.

Jessica gave a self-conscious laugh at his flimsy excuse and hasty departure. She rose to face Zach, but unable to meet his eyes, her gaze darted around the room before finally settling on her toes. "So, uh, what are you doing here?" She shoved her hands in the back pockets of her jeans.

"I heard you were leaving."

Her head jerked up. When he didn't say anything else, she swallowed. "Yeah, I'm, uh, going to spend some time with my mom and dad."

"Were you going to tell me?"

Her mouth opened. Then closed again. She had no answer. Truth be told she'd planned on taking the coward's way out. Not seeing Zach again might have made leaving easier. Less painful. The way it should have been in the first place. Maybe they could have avoided the whole fiasco at The Corral. Philip. Zach almost telling her how he felt. Not letting him.

But instead the ache was worse. Because a small, secret part deep down inside of herself questioned her decision. If leaving hurt so much, why was she so determined to go?

The answer was obvious. Fear. The inability to trust.

Not Zach. But herself.

Zach sighed. "That's what I thought," he said quietly. He studied her. This time she forced herself not to look away from the bittersweet intensity of his gaze.

"What are you going to do after that?"

She shook her head. "I don't really know."

"You keep telling me I need to figure out what to do with my life. Maybe you need to do the same."

Her chin rose a notch. "I have a career."

"I'm not talking about your career, Jess. I'm talking about your life."

"I know what I want out of life." And he couldn't be a part of it. She'd learned her lesson. The hard way.

"And that doesn't include me."

She looked away and folded her arms across her chest. "I'm sorry," she whispered.

"Because of my job."

"I..." Her gaze flicked back to his. The mocha irises bored into her.

"So that's it? You're really going to give up on us because you think I don't have a real job?" An edge of anger, mingled with something else, tinged his voice.

"Zach, I... Please. I just can't do this."

"*Don't* do this. We have something good here. Don't throw it away."

She couldn't meet his gaze. Couldn't stand to see the pain in his eyes. "It's always good at first. It started out great with the other guys, too, but I wound up divorced from an alcoholic."

A muscle jumped in his jaw. "Don't compare me to that bastard." The words hissed out.

She stepped closer and laid her palm on his

chest, unable to stop herself from touching him one last time. "I'm not."

"So you're going to walk away because other relationships have gone bad? You know, if those other relationships *hadn't* gone bad, you wouldn't be in this one." He brushed his knuckles down the side of her face. "It only takes one time for it to be right. Can't you feel how right this is?"

His touch threatened to undo her resolve. Although she hadn't let him say the words, she could almost *feel* his love in the gentle contact of his skin against hers.

As if reading her thoughts, he whispered. "You won't let me tell you how I feel, but how do you feel? About me?" His hand slid down her throat to rest against her chest. "What is your heart telling you?"

A tear rolled down her cheek. She shook her head, forcibly denying the feelings coursing through her. A part of her desperately wanted to admit he was right. But she was afraid. "Please, don't make this any harder than it already is."

His hand dropped to his side. The soft lights in his eyes hardened. "Right. No problem. I'm going to make this really easy for you." He headed toward the door.

A piece of her heart chipped away.

At the door he turned. "I'll be the one to walk away. Good-bye, Jessica."

The soft sound of the latch reverberated in the sudden silence.

"Good-bye, Zach," she whispered through her tears.

****

Outside Zach sucked a deep breath into his lungs, then slowly exhaled. He'd figured it wouldn't make a difference. Coming to see Jessica. But he'd had to try.

And now he knew. She wasn't willing to take a

chance on him. Was still too afraid. No matter what excuse she used. His lack of a career. Her past. It all came down to the same thing. After all they'd been through, she was afraid to trust him.

"Zach?"

He turned toward Ben's voice.

The older man eyed the keys in Zach's hand. "Leaving so soon?"

"Yeah."

"Oh." Disappointment laced Ben's voice. "I thought maybe you and Jessica would have more to talk about."

What could he say to that? What the hell, might as well be honest. "Me too."

"So, if you don't mind me asking, what happened?"

"I thought I could talk her into staying."

"No luck, huh?"

Zach huffed out a breath. "None."

"You want her to stay, then?"

Zach looked Ben in the eye. "Ben, I," he hesitated, "care about your granddaughter very much. But I'm not who or what she wants."

Ben offered a half smile. "Well, I'll be the first one to tell you my granddaughter can be stubborn. But like I said before, she's still hurting. Give her time. She'll come around."

Zach raised his gaze to the sky, then looked over at Ben. "With all due respect, sir, I don't think that's going to happen."

****

"Well, honey, you look like you're all packed."

Jessica turned with a start at the sound of Pops' voice. She sniffed and looked around the loft. While her face was turned away, she surreptitiously brushed her fingers across her cheek. She didn't want him to see her cry. "Yeah, I guess I am." No sense putting it off any longer. She'd made her decision. The right one. Now she had to stick with it.

"Can I carry something for you?"

"I just have these two bags. I didn't bring much with me." Except a broken heart. Which ironically enough she left with too. A different break, though. One that put all her past hurts to shame. Nothing compared to this.

Downstairs, Pops asked. "Do you want something to eat before you go?"

She shook her head. "No, I want to get on the road before it gets too late." Before she changed her mind. "I don't want to drive in the dark."

He nodded. "Makes sense." He took one of the bags from her shoulder. "I'll walk you to your car."

When her things were stowed in the trunk, she turned to him. He gathered her close in a tight hug. She squeezed her eyes against the tears that threatened.

She opened the car door.

"Wait."

She frowned. "What's the matter?"

Pops took her hand in his. "Jessica, why are you doing this?"

"What?"

"Why are you running away?"

His deliberate choice of words made her feel guilty. Which was crazy. She hadn't done anything to feel guilty about. "I...I'm not running away," she denied. "I don't have any place to live, so I'm going to spend some time with Mom and Dad."

"You could stay here."

"No."

He raised an eyebrow at her vehement tone. "Why not? There's plenty of room. We wouldn't get in each other's way. And you love it here."

She lowered her gaze. "Yes, I do." She bit her lip to stem the tears once again.

"Then why are you leaving?"

"I have to."

"Because of Zach?"

Her eyes snapped to his. "W...why would you say that?" How could Pops know?

"He loves you, you know."

Her eyes welled up and spilled over. One tear, followed by another and another, coursed down her face. "I. Know." Her voice broke. "Th...that's why I have to leave. He can't love me."

"Why not?"

She shook her head. She couldn't explain.

"How do you feel about him?"

Again, she shook her head, but the motion was more denial than uncertainty. "I...I can't," she stopped. A sob tore from her throat.

He put his arm around her shoulders. "Come on, honey. Let's go back inside."

Unable to do anything else, she let him lead her back into the house. He settled her on the couch, then disappeared. He returned a moment later and pressed a glass into her hand. "Here, drink this."

The icy water brought cool relief to her raw throat. She looked up at Pops and tried a smile. "Thanks. I'm sorry. I don't know what's wrong with me."

"You don't?" Pops asked with a gentle smile. "I do."

"Wh...what?"

"You don't want to leave."

"Oh." She looked away. "But I have to."

"Why?"

She took a deep breath. "Because I think I'm in love with Zach," she whispered. Relief flooded through her to admit it at last. But she also ached with the admission. What did it matter?

Pops sat down next to her. "Why is that a bad thing?"

"Because it's too soon. And he doesn't have a

real job," she mumbled.

Pops looked puzzled. "Zach has a job."

"Not really. I mean, he just works at a bar. As a bouncer."

He shook his head. "I'm not following you. He goes to work. Gets paid. Sounds like a real job to me."

"But it's not a *real* job. And how long is he going to work there? I mean, what happens when he gets tired of it?"

Confusion still clouded Pops' features. "Well, then I guess he'd find another job. But Zach seems to really enjoy working at The Corral. I can't imagine he'd ever want to leave. Has he ever told you he thought about leaving?"

"Well, no, but, don't you see? That's the problem. He's a grown man. And he works as a bouncer."

"So?"

"It's not a real job," she repeated, although even to herself she didn't sound as sure as she had before. Did it really matter what Zach did for a living? Or had that simply been a convenient excuse all along? A way to avoid the real reason she was afraid to have a relationship with him.

"Honey, that doesn't make one lick of sense. So, let's forget about his job for the time being and focus on the real issue here. He loves you. You love him. Sounds pretty simple to me. Why are you making it so complicated?"

She pinched her nose between her forefinger and her thumb. Could it really be as simple as Pops said? She shook her head. No, it wasn't that simple. There were other things to consider. The most important being love wasn't new to her. She'd been in love before. "Don't you understand?" She struggled to explain. "I thought I was in love before. More than once. And look what happened. With Philip."

Pops' lips compressed into a thin line.

"I can't make the same mistake again." Her voice hitched.

"Well, I can't argue with you Philip was a mistake, but can I ask you something?"

"Of course."

"How did you feel when things ended with Philip? When you left?"

"How did I feel?"

"Were you sad?"

She hesitated. "No, not sad. Relieved."

"And how about the others? The ones you thought you loved."

She shrugged. "Pretty much the same. I mean, I guess I realized I didn't love them anymore. Maybe I'd never loved them." Maybe she didn't know what love was.

"And how do you feel about leaving here?" Pops continued. "Leaving Zach?"

Tears welled again. "I..." She couldn't go on. Although she'd been ready to go earlier, or at least had managed to convince herself she was ready to go, thinking about leaving Zach again now caused a stabbing pain in the middle of her chest.

"That's what I thought." He squeezed her hand. "This isn't anything like those other relationships."

"How can you be so sure?"

"Well, I can't make you any guarantees. Would you buy 'grandfather's intuition'?"

She managed a smile.

"Can I tell you something? Something you probably never knew. Because it didn't really matter."

"Sure."

"How long do you think your grandmother and I knew each other before we got married?"

Jessica shrugged. "I don't know. A couple of years?"

Pops looked smug. "Nope. Try a couple of weeks."

Her mouth dropped open. "A couple of weeks? And you got married?" She couldn't keep the shock from her voice.

"Yep. And we had more than forty years together. I loved her until the day she died. I still love her."

"I never knew that."

"Like I said, why would you have ever needed to?"

She slowly shook her head, trying to process what Pops had told her. Her grandparents had had one of the most loving relationships she'd ever seen. And they'd known each other for less than a month before they'd gotten married. She'd already known Zach for almost that long. But she couldn't even imagine getting married again so soon.

"I'm not ready to get married again." She voiced her thoughts aloud. "I'm afraid," she admitted.

"I'm not saying you have to run out and get married tomorrow. But the way I see it, you have two choices. You can tell Zach how you feel, fears and all, and see what happens. Or, you can leave and second-guess yourself for the rest of your life, always wondering what might have been."

"You're right," she whispered. "I would always wonder." She leaned her head on his shoulder. "Why have I been so stupid?"

Pops put his arm around her. "Oh, honey, not stupid. Just scared." He kissed the top of her head. "So what are you going to do?"

She smiled up at him, sure of herself for the first time in a long time. "I'm going to talk to Zach."

Chapter Nineteen

For the second time in her life, but hopefully not the last, Jessica pulled her car into the parking lot of The Corral. Once again, a shiver of nerves trembled through her. But this time for a whole different reason. What would Zach say? Would he even want to talk to her? Would he listen to what she had to say? Would he want to hear it?

Only one way to get the answers to the questions tumbling through her head. With a fortifying breath, she pushed open the door. Zach's truck was parked nearby, next to another, newer truck she recognized as Logan's. A few other vehicles were scattered around, but the parking lot was empty for the most part. The bar wasn't open yet.

Inside, she looked around. Where would Zach be? Down in the barroom? In one of the offices? Before she could think about it further, Sharlie walked around the corner.

"Sharlie."

"Jessica. Hi."

The other woman didn't seem surprised to see her. Had Zach said anything to his friends about her leaving? "Hi. Um, is Zach working tonight?"

Sharlie rolled her eyes. "Are you kidding? He and Logan have been closed up in Logan's office for days now. He's always working these days. But I'm sure he won't mind the interruption."

Zach worked all the time with Logan in his office? That seemed odd, but before she could ask, Sharlie turned and led the way down the hall.

"This is so great. I can't even imagine how

fabulous this is going to be." She looked over her shoulder at Jessica. "Aren't you excited?"

Excited? About what? Seeing how she'd left things with Zach, Jessica couldn't imagine applying the word to anything at the moment. But Sharlie embodied the word. She almost sparkled with it.

Before Jessica could answer, Sharlie rushed on. "They have most of the menu decided already. The main dishes anyway. Hey, Zach said you do web design and stuff. Maybe you could help us out with that. It would be a good way to get the word out."

More lost than ever, Jessica could only nod. What in the world did Sharlie mean?

"When Zach came to Logan with this idea, we were so thrilled. It's exactly what this place needs. When I started as manager, long before Logan bought this place, my goal was to clean this place up. It had become a real dive," Sharlie chattered on, oblivious to Jessica's confusion. "It's come a long way, and this will be the icing on the cake."

At the door to Logan's office, Jessica laid a hand on Sharlie's arm. "Okay, I'm lost. I have no idea what you're talking about."

Sharlie looked at her, a frown marring her features. "What? Zach didn't tell you?"

Jessica looked away. "We, um, we haven't really talked. Recently."

Sharlie's face fell. "Oh. I thought—I mean, that is, I thought you guys were..."

"We were, but then I told him I had to leave. And, now, I just really need to talk to him."

"Oh." Sharlie put her hand on the doorknob, then stopped. She studied Jessica. "Look, this may be none of my business, but if you're going to hurt him, maybe you shouldn't go in."

Jessica hung her head. She'd already hurt him. Would he even be willing to listen? Then she raised her eyes to Sharlie's. "I'm not planning on it."

Sharlie studied her before nodding. She walked into the office. "Hey, you two, how about a little break?"

Two pairs of eyes turned toward her voice. Logan focused on Sharlie, but Zach's gaze captured Jessica's. He frowned.

Her heart thumped in her chest.

"Hi, Logan." She swallowed. "Sorry to interrupt, but I need to talk to Zach." Even though she addressed the raven-haired man, her eyes never strayed from Zach.

Logan rose from behind the desk. "No problem, we could use a break." He placed his arm around Sharlie, then guided her out the door.

Zach stood as well, coming around to perch on the edge of the desk. He continued to regard her, an unreadable expression on his face. His eyes looked...blank. Her hollow heart contracted. She'd caused the carefully veiled pain in his eyes.

"So," he said at last, breaking the oppressive silence. "What are you doing here? I thought you left."

She wrung her hands and bit her lip. He looked away. Her pulse raced. "I couldn't leave."

His gaze returned to her.

"I was all set. Packed. Said good-bye to Pops. But I couldn't go."

"Oh? Why not?" His voice still held a forced note of calm.

"Because of you."

"Because of me?" His tone was lighter now.

Her gaze found his again. She took a deep breath. "I love you."

Until the words made it past the lump in her throat, she hadn't been sure she'd be able to say them. But hearing them out loud made her realize more than ever how true they were. For better or worse, too soon or not soon enough, she'd fallen in love with Zach.

His eyes widened. "What?"

She couldn't tell if her admission pleased him or not. "I didn't plan on it. Didn't see it coming. You see, I thought I'd been in love before. But what I feel for you isn't like anything else I've ever experienced. I've made a lot of mistakes in the past, but this is different. I trust this."

Her heart pounded more furiously than before. Would he accept her declaration? Believe her? When she'd never let him make his own. Did he still feel the same way? Or had her callous rejection driven any feelings of love for her from his heart? Was she too late?

He crossed his arms over his chest. "What about my job? Or lack thereof?" The words held a hint of a challenge, but his expression had softened.

She shrugged. "It's not up to me to decide what you should do with your life. I...I just want to be a part of it. That is if you'll let me. If you still want me to, I'm going to stick around." She held her breath. What would he say? *Did* he want her to stay?

He closed his eyes, then let out a long breath. When he opened them, he smiled.

Her heart began to hope. He stood and raised his hand to her face. His knuckles brushed across her cheek. "I love you, Jess."

Her breath escaped at the whispered confession. And suddenly she was whole, complete, in a way she never had been before.

"And hell, yes, I want you to stay." His lips captured hers.

Her mouth opened beneath his. The familiar heat of his kiss coursed through her. His lips stroked hers tenderly, before he gathered her to his chest.

His heart raced beneath her ear, as if echoing the words he'd spoken out loud. She reveled in the sound.

After a moment she spoke. "I..." she hesitated. She didn't want to ruin the moment, but there was something he needed to know. Would he be angry when she told him? But she had to be honest with him. He deserved to know where she was at with everything. As much as she loved him, there were some things she wasn't ready for. Not yet. She took a deep breath. "I'm not ready to get married again."

His lips quirked. "I didn't ask."

She looked down and bit her lip. "I know, I—" A blush crept into her cheeks. Maybe he had no intention of marrying her. She wasn't ready now, but in the future...

He lifted her chin with a finger. "But, Jess, someday I will."

Relief flooded through her. She nodded and offered a shaky smile. "You'd better."

He grinned and lowered his mouth to hers. The pressure of his lips stroking against her own brought a familiar weakness to her knees. But this kiss was different as well. As if by admitting her feelings for him, and letting him admit his for her, the kiss spoke not only of his passion, but his love as well.

When breathing became a necessity, he broke the kiss, but cradled her to his chest. She laid her head against his chest. The thundering beat of his heart pounded beneath her ear. The thrust of his arousal sent heat to places deep and secret. Even now, the proof of his desire for her thrilled her. Would that feeling ever go away?

The way her body sang with anticipation, she doubted it. She smiled and looked up at him. "So, do you think Logan would be upset if we messed up the papers on his desk?" She rotated her hips against his.

He groaned. "I'm sure Logan and Sharlie have messed up the papers on his desk lots of times, but maybe you and I should find someplace a bit more, ah, discreet? After all, Logan does have a key." He nuzzled her ear. "But I do like the way you think."

She shivered. "When will you be finished here?"

"Right now."

He tugged her toward the door, but suddenly curiosity warred with her desire. Knowing she'd spend the rest of her life being loved by Zach allowed the curiosity to win.

She pulled on his hand to stop him. "Wait. What have you and Logan been doing in here that's got Sharlie all excited?"

He raised an eyebrow. "You really want to talk about this now? How about if we talk about what's got *me* all excited?"

She laughed. "I'm curious. And besides, we have all night, and the next night and the next and the next...well, you get picture."

"Well, when you put it like that, I guess another five minutes won't kill me. But that's it. Any more and it might," he warned.

"Okay, five minutes. But seriously, Sharlie's bubbling over. What's going on?"

He glanced away and cleared his throat. He almost looked embarrassed. "Well, I kind of had this idea. You started me to thinking, and I've been talking to Jake." He blew out a breath. "So I ran it by Logan to see what he thought."

More puzzled than ever, Jessica frowned. "What idea?"

Zach shuffled his feet. "See, Jake's always going on about how the food here sucks, and I thought, maybe we could change that. Attract a new type of clientele. Expand the bar. So, um, I asked Logan if he'd be interested in opening a steakhouse on the first floor. Convert the restaurant space. It hardly gets used. No one really eats here."

"Zach, that's a great idea."

He nodded. "Logan got on board right away. So,

that's what we're going to do. This place is going to be 'The Corral: Steakhouse and Saloon.'" He cleared his throat. "I'm going to take some classes at a culinary school and be the head chef." His eyes met hers.

Jessica gaped at him. She glanced down at the papers scattered over the desk. "How long have you been planning this?"

"A couple of weeks now."

Her gaze flew to his. "A couple of weeks?" she repeated. She sank into the chair. "Why didn't you tell me?"

He hunkered down in front of her, then took her hand in his. He traced idle circles over the back of it. "I wanted you to want me for *who* I am. Not *what* I am." He looked up. "I wanted you to trust me."

"So, the other day, when I told you I was leaving, you had already started working on this?"

He nodded.

"And you let me say all those terrible things to you?" She ached for the pain she'd caused him. "Why didn't you say something?"

"Remember that first night we made love?" His eyes darkened, as if aroused by the memory.

"Yes." She'd never forget if she lived to be a hundred.

"You told me you wanted to make love because you needed to know. Well, this was something *I* needed to know. I needed to know you wanted to be with me, no matter what."

"Oh, Zach. I've been so foolish."

"No, you've been hurt and afraid to trust. Jess," his grip on her hand tightened, "I'll never hurt you. You can always trust me. I'll always love you."

She smiled through a blur of tears. "I know," she whispered before touching her lips to his. She traced a finger over his jaw. "I was so sure I couldn't be in love with you. I'd jumped the gun so many times.

But the way I feel about you makes me realize I never even knew what real love was before. Thanks for being patient with me."

His familiar smile turned her insides to mush. "No problem." He stood. "But on that note, I'm done being patient. We're leaving. Now."

She grinned up at him. "No argument from me."

On their way out the door, Zach grabbed a box sitting off to the side.

Jessica raised an eyebrow.

Zach grinned. He tucked the box under one arm and slung the other over her shoulders. "Just taking home some work, love."

The endearment caused a little flutter in her heart, but his other words caused her eyes to widen. "Well, that's quite a change," she teased.

"Something like that." His expression made her feel like she'd missed something.

In Zach's truck—they'd come back to The Corral for her car later—Jessica sat close beside him on the bench seat spanning the interior. They rode in companionable silence. She'd ridden in his truck before, but this was different. Declaring her feelings for him and letting him declare his for her had changed her. Irrevocably and forever. Nothing would ever be the same again. A sense of rightness settled over her. She sighed in contentment.

Zach's hand caressed her knee. Goose bumps blossomed. She shivered with the anticipation of more intimate touches to come.

"What are you thinking?" Zach's low voice broke the quiet.

She glanced up at him, taking a moment to appreciate the strong line of his jaw. "You," she said at last in answer to his question. "And me. Us." She smiled.

"I like the sound of that."

"Me too."

At his apartment, he ushered her inside.

She glanced at him over her shoulder. "I've never seen your apartment before."

"There's not much to see. This is the living room." He swept his hand out in front of him. "The kitchen is to the left." He pointed. "But most importantly, the bedroom is down the hall on the right." He gave her a gentle nudge in that direction. "That's the only room you need to worry about right now."

"Impatient, aren't we?" she teased.

"You have no idea." He kissed her hungrily. "Now go," he said with a nod down the hallway.

"Aren't you coming?" Confusion tinged her voice.

He grinned. "I'll be there in a minute. I need to, ah, take care of this first." He indicated the box he'd brought from The Corral.

Her eyebrows rose. "Aren't you taking this 'working at home' thing a little too seriously? I mean, don't get me wrong, I'm thrilled you're so excited about this chef thing, but...now? Really?" Her lower lip jutted out in a mock pout. Inside she laughed at the irony. How many times had she wanted him to be more serious about his job?

He chuckled at her disgruntled expression. The pad of his thumb brushed over the sensitive skin of her inner lip. "I just need one minute." His eyes twinkled. "I swear."

A secret danced in his mocha irises. One that sent a shiver of anticipation through her. "One minute," she relented. "That's all you get."

"That's all I need." He turned toward the kitchen.

She headed down the hall to his bedroom. The room wasn't large. A double bed took up most of the space in the middle. The bedside table next to it was cluttered with culinary magazines and a course book from the local community college. Other paraphernalia littered the small surface as well: loose change, the picture from Sharlie's wedding, a watch. Zach's cowboy hats, one black, one straw, perched on top of a tall dresser which stood against the far wall. The overall color scheme was a pleasing blend of deep blues and warm browns.

A series of electronic beeps came from the direction of the kitchen, followed by the whir of the microwave. She frowned. What was Zach doing in there?

Then she laughed at her own impatience. And at how things had changed in the course of the last two months. If someone had told her then her body would be humming with sexual tension while she waited for the man she loved to come relieve it, she would have said they were certifiably insane. Ready to be committed.

Yet here she stood. Restless. Impatient.

She sat down on the foot of the bed and kicked off her shoes. Down the hall, the microwave emitted three long, drawn out beeps. A drawer scraped open. Silverware clinked together. The drawer closed with a soft thud.

Zach appeared in the doorway a moment later. He held one hand behind his back. His eyes literally danced with mischief.

"What are you hiding?"

"Oh, you'll see." His voice held a throaty promise. "Scoot up against the headboard."

More puzzled than ever, she complied. Mostly because the look on his face had her pulse racing.

He set whatever he held next to the bed. She leaned over to see what it was.

"Nuh, uh," he said. "No peeking."

He yanked his T-shirt over his head, letting it fall to the floor at his feet. As always, the sight of his bare chest set her heart tripping. He crawled onto the bed, supporting his weight on his hands and

238

knees as he leaned over her. His kiss left her breathless. Wanting. Aching.

Her teeth bit into her bottom lip. He bit back a groan and grasped the hem of her shirt. He drew it over her head, then tossed it aside. The front clasp of her bra easily came undone with a flick of his fingers. His gazed roved appreciatively over her.

She reached for him.

"Not yet," he whispered.

She raised an eyebrow. His body hummed with the same tension as hers. It emanated from him. What was he waiting for?

He shifted to sit next to her against the headboard. Then he pulled her onto his lap. She straddled him, his denim-covered arousal nestled in the juncture of her thighs.

"This is nice," she murmured as she wrapped her arms around his neck.

His hands ran up and down her back. She shivered.

"Do you trust me, Jess?" His eyes twinkled at her again. The look sent a quiver of anticipation to settle in her tummy.

"Yes." Her answer was immediate. Sure.

"Good." He smiled again and her insides turned to mush. "Then close your eyes."

At first, surprised by the request, they opened wider. But after staring into the fathomless depths of his for endless seconds, her lids lowered.

"That's my girl." She heard the smile in his voice.

He shifted slightly, reaching down next to the bed. Metal clinked against glass. A trail of thick, warm liquid spread over the top of her breast.

Unable to stop them, her eyes popped open. Zach wore an expression of utter satisfaction as he used his finger to spread the chocolate over her nipple. It hardened into a tight bud.

"Wha—" she began, but stopped when his mouth replaced his finger.

He licked the chocolate from the tip of her breast with a series of rapid flicks of his tongue. She shuddered. Her nails dug into his shoulders.

"Mmmnn," he murmured in appreciation. "I knew this would be the best way to decide."

"Wh...wha...what?" It took several tries, but finally the word made it out.

"You see." Zach dipped the spoon into the jar once again. "The food vendors have been sending a lot of samples to The Corral." He drizzled the hot fudge sauce over her other breast. His face was serious, intent, as he watched the liquid spread over her nipple, this time of its own accord. "I hadn't had a chance to try the chocolate sauce yet." His gaze found hers. His eyes shone with a mixture of amusement and desire. "And I'm nothing if not thorough. So I figured I'd bring my work home with me." His tongue darted out to capture a dab of thick chocolate as it rolled down the underside of her breast. He followed it up, then sucked the nipple into his mouth.

"Ahhh," she moaned. "And for so long I worried you'd never take your work seriously." Her voice hitched. "I never dreamed you'd be willing to work at home after hours."

He chuckled and then grabbed the spoon again. "How stupid was I?"

"Wait." She stilled the movement with trembling fingers. "You'll get it all over the bedspread."

He raised a disbelieving eyebrow. "Jess, I have you naked and covered in chocolate. Do you really think I care about the damn bedspread?" He tilted the spoon. The sauce ran down her stomach. He bent his head to lap it from her navel.

She squirmed on his lap. His arousal pressed more insistently against her.

"Okay," she said breathlessly when she could speak again. "Two can play at this game." She snatched the spoon to drizzle the chocolate on his shoulder. It ran in a dark rivulet down his bicep and onto his forearm.

The warm syrup tasted sweet as she licked it from his skin. She followed the trail it made down his arm, lingering in the crease of his elbow to lave the sensitive skin there with slow strokes of her tongue.

A shudder wracked him, but other than that he lay still beneath her ministrations. She looked up at him. He watched her, his eyes so dark they almost matched the chocolate on his skin.

When she finished with his arm, she spread more sauce on his upturned hand and onto his fingers. With the tip of her tongue, she licked across the lines of his palm. When she sucked each of his fingers into her mouth in turn, his breath grew shallow. She drew deeply on his index finger, her gaze meeting his once again.

His eyes smoldered. He swallowed convulsively. "Enough taste testing," he croaked. "Find that box."

****

Later, after their passion and the chocolate sauce had cooled, and they'd showered away the sticky remnants, Jessica snuggled up to Zach in his bed.

"I love you," he said, his voice soft in the encroaching darkness.

A shiver of contentment flowed through her. A marked contrast to the knot of unease that would have settled in her stomach not too long ago.

"I love you, too." She smiled against his chest. "But you know that." Her laugh was rueful. "I think you knew before I did."

"Well, I hoped." He kissed the top of her head. "What made *you* finally realize it?"

241

"I was ready to leave," she whispered, because even now, secure in his sheltering arms, the memory stabbed into her. "And I started to cry. Really cry. Pops wouldn't let me get in the car. We sat and talked, and it just hit me. All of a sudden I realized I was afraid, but not of what I thought I was afraid of." She laughed at her convoluted sentence.

She propped herself up on one elbow to look at him. "Did you know at the rodeo Sharlie told me she thought you were falling in love with me?"

His eyes widened. "No." The words were soft. Filled with an almost awed curiosity.

"She scared the hell out of me."

He raised an eyebrow.

Jessica traced an idle pattern across his chest. "I didn't want you to be in love with me." She looked up at him and offered an apology with her eyes. "And I certainly didn't want to admit I was falling in love with you. It was too soon." She grimaced and her glance slid from his. "Or that's what I thought.

"So, I convinced myself what we had was only about sex. Because that's the way I'd intended it to be all along. I had this instinctive feeling you'd be able to," she fumbled for the word, "heal me." Her gaze found his. "I was right. My body responded to you in ways I never imagined it could. And my heart wanted to follow. But I wouldn't let it. I'd been hurt too many times before. I couldn't let go of my past so I could embrace my future." Her voice dropped to a whisper. "I was afraid.

"But when I tried to leave, I understood that's what I really couldn't do. Leave you. It turned out leaving you scared me more than loving you. And I realized my whole hang up about your job was simply an excuse to help me deny my feelings for you."

He chuckled.

"So anyway, Pops said I should tell you

everything. How I felt. What I was afraid of. The whole deal."

"Ben is a smart man."

She nodded in agreement. "Can I ask you something?"

"Of course."

"You were so worried about what Pops would think if he ever found out about the two of us together. What changed your mind?"

"Ah, I did fight with my conscience about that for a long time." His eyes reflected his chagrin. "Can't say I'm too disappointed I lost that battle." He kissed her. "As for Ben, he came to talk to me at The Corral one day. He didn't say it in so many words, but in a round about way it seemed like he was giving us his blessing. And then later, after you'd decided to leave for sure, he told me to give you some time. That you'd come around. I figured if he was opposed to the idea of us being together he wouldn't be giving me advice as to how to win you over."

"You said it, Pops is one smart cookie." She kissed the underside of Zach's jaw. "And I for one am grateful you surrendered that particular battle."

"Me, too. Jess, these past two months have been the best of my life."

"Two months? Don't you mean two weeks? You know, since we've been...together?"

"No, I mean the last six. I've had the time of my life ever since you walked into the bathroom and told me to get the hell out of your grandfather's cabin."

She blushed and looked away. "It wasn't really like that, was it?"

He chuckled. "It was exactly like that. You were very adamant about where I should go."

She swatted him playfully on the arm. "I wasn't that bad."

He raised an eyebrow.

She laughed. "Okay, maybe at first. I'd come

there to be alone with Pops and there you were, acting like you owned the place and Pops nowhere in sight. I had to make sure you hadn't offed him or anything. But then I got to know you, and I realized Pops couldn't have entrusted his place to a better man."

Her gaze found his again. "And I couldn't have entrusted my heart to a better man. I'm yours," she whispered. "Heart. Body. And soul."

***This Can't Be Love* begins where *This Time for Always* ended.** Reconnect with all your favorite characters: Sharlie, Logan, and most of all, Zach, who stars as the hero of Debra St. John's newest novel. Zach deserves a love of his own, but will he find it with Jessica, who's running from love?

****

Don't miss Sharlie and Logan's story in *This Time for Always*, Debra St. John's debut novel from The Wild Rose Press.

As manager of a local bar, The Corral, Sharlie Montgomery has put the past behind her. That is until Logan Reed walks back into her life, turning her world upside down. His presence brings back painful reminders of the past: the love they once shared, the money he took from her father, and the baby she gave up for adoption. Logan wants to buy The Corral, and he's come back to town to prove he's made it on his own without the Montgomery money. Sparks fly whenever Sharlie and Logan are together. Anger, fear, and jealousy aren't enough to erase the love they once felt for each other. But is love enough? Logan wants a family—the one thing Sharlie can't give him.

A word about the author...

Debra St. John has been reading and writing romance since high school. She always dreamed about publishing a romance novel some day. *This Can't Be Love* is her third title with The Wild Rose Press. She lives in a suburb of Chicago with her husband, who is her real-life hero. Debra is past president of her local RWA chapter and has also served in the capacity of advisor, manuscript chair, and secretary.

Readers are invited to visit her at her website, www.debrastjohnromance.com. Or check out her posts on Sundays at the Acme Author's Link, http://acmeauthorslink.blogspot.com. She also posts blogs on Thursdays at Heroines with Hearts, http://heroineswithhearts.blogspot.com

Thank you for purchasing
this Wild Rose Press publication.
For other wonderful stories of romance,
please visit our on-line bookstore at
www.thewildrosepress.com.

For questions or more information
contact us at
info@thewildrosepress.com.

The Wild Rose Press
www.TheWildRosePress.com

www.ingramcontent.com/pod-product-compliance
Lightning Source LLC
Chambersburg PA
CBHW070913180626
46817CB00003B/1038